The Blood of the Warlord

Book 12 in the Border Knight Series

By

Griff Hosker

Published by Sword Books Ltd 2022

Copyright ©Griff Hosker First Edition

The author has asserted their moral right under the Copyright, Designs and Patents Act, 1988, to be identified as the author of this work.
All Rights reserved. No part of this publication may be reproduced, copied, stored in a retrieval system, or transmitted, in any form or by any means, without the prior written consent of the copyright holder, nor be otherwise circulated in any form of binding or cover other than that in which it is published and without a similar condition being imposed on the subsequent purchaser.
A CIP catalogue record for this title is available from the British Library.

Contents

The Blood of the Warlord i
The Land of the Warlord 2
Prologue 3
Chapter 1 13
Chapter 2 34
Chapter 3 46
Chapter 4 59
Chapter 5 77
Chapter 6 92
Chapter 7 104
Chapter 8 115
Chapter 9 125
Chapter 10 135
Chapter 11 146
Chapter 12 156
Chapter 13 168
Chapter 14 181
Chapter 15 196
Chapter 16 206
Chapter 17 218
Chapter 18 231
Epilogue 244
Historical Note 248
Other books by Griff Hosker 250

Dedicated to five grandchildren all of my blood but all wonderfully unique. I love you all and look forward to watching you grow.

Historical figures

King Henry III of England son of King John
Richard of Cornwall- 1st Earl of Cornwall second son of King John
Prince Edward- heir to the throne and known as The Lord Edward
Henry of Almain- the son of Richard of Cornwall
Simon de Montfort-the Earl of Leicester and Lord Lieutenant of Aquitaine and Gascony
William de Valance- King Henry's half-brother through his mother, Isabella of Angoulême
Guy de Lusignan-King Henry's half-brother through his mother, Isabella of Angoulême
Aymer de Lusignan- King Henry's half-brother through his mother, Isabella of Angoulême
King Louis IX of France-also known as St. Louis
Hispanus de Massanc- Archbishop of Auch
Alfonso X- King of Castile
Leonor of Castile- Later Eleanor and the great-great-granddaughter of Henry II of England

The Land of the Warlord

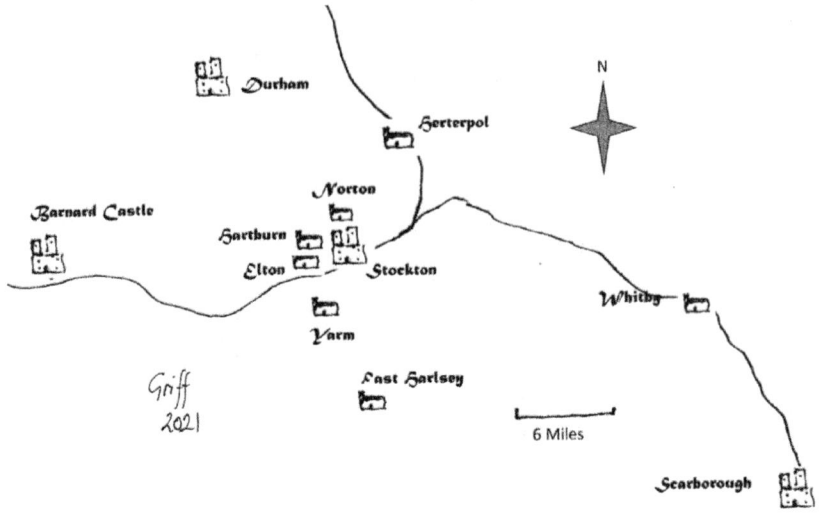

Prologue

Sir Guy de La Réole reined in his horse and held his right hand up to halt the column of men behind him. He stretched his back for he had ridden too far on this long chevauchée. They had ridden since dawn using a circuitous route to avoid being seen and although they now had only a few miles to go they had used all the cover that they could to avoid detection. It had made the short journey of a few miles seem much longer as they wished to arrive unseen and unheralded. In surprise lay their best chance of success. Behind him his men took the opportunity to drink from their wineskins. These were Gascons and not English. They were rarely far from a vineyard and wine was preferable to water in this land. They were professional soldiers and even when they drank their eyes ranged around them as they sought danger. They were the mesne of Sir Guy but as he was a landless knight, he was not yet rich. The result was that but three had mail hauberks while the others wore a variety of padded jackets covered by a tunic. That the tunic bore no design was deliberate. Sir Guy liked the anonymity of his work in the pay of the Lieutenant of Aquitaine, Simon de Montfort, the Earl of Leicester. The helmets were also as individual as the owners. Some still wore the helmet with the nasal while some had adopted the round helmet with a visor. Two of them just wore a coif over an arming cap. Their opposition often did not necessitate more. They carried lances which were long wooden weapons with a steel head. Their shields were flat-topped kite shields and hung over their left legs. They would not be needing them. The scuffed leather covers might have once displayed a design but no longer. It was their swords, clubs and maces that showed them for what they were, raiders. This would be their last raid. There was not an ounce of nobility between them and that included Sir Guy. The Seneschal of Gascony, Simon de Montfort, chose men like Sir Guy because they were discreet. He allowed them to punish the seigneurs, the lords of Gascony for that served his own ends. Sir Guy did not know what those ends were but he enjoyed the freedom to raid and pillage knowing that no one would seek retribution. The other villages and hamlets had been small but they had secured both food and coin for Sir Guy and his men. This would be their biggest payday. Saint Severin was a rich manor. It was rich because the people were peaceable, grew crops, raised animals and made fine wine. It also had a castle. Admittedly it was a simple keep and there was no wall around it but if the Gascons had warning of their approach then the taking of it would be harder. Sir Guy intended to surprise them.

 Sir Guy and his squire, Laurence, in contrast to their men, did wear a design. Their tunics and shields bore the three red chevrons on a blue background with three gold stars. As the third son of the seigneur of La Réole, he was entitled to wear it and he had hopes that one day, his elder brothers would die and he would inherit the lands for which he yearned. There was no love lost between Sir Guy and his brothers and he and his father hated each other. Until that day arrived he could continue to serve the Lord Lieutenant of Gascony and punish the seigneurs who defied his authority. Sir Guy was a clever young knight and he knew that King Henry of England, who had given the land of Aquitaine to his son, Prince Edward, would not be happy with the policy de Montfort had adopted. It was making a land ripe for revolt. Sir Guy did not care. He raided villages in the lands of seigneurs who did not do as de Montfort wished and his reward was the loot he took. He did not care that his men looked like vagabonds for what he did was not honourable but it was profitable. The bulk of the coins taken was kept by Sir Guy himself. His men were allowed to enjoy themselves when they took a village or small town and they did not complain. When he had a big enough war chest then he would turn his attention to La Réole.

 "My lord?"

 Sir Guy had almost forgotten Laurence, his squire. Dressed like his men, Laurence did not look like a courtly squire. He was a killer like the rest of the men. The difference was that he was of noble birth and the third son like his master. He stayed with Sir Guy in the hopes of a knighthood. "Yes, Laurence?"

"Saint Severin will be the last village before we return to our home?"

Sir Guy nodded, "Aye, it will show Phillippe, the Seigneur of Château de Barbezieux, that he should obey the commands of the Lord Lieutenant."

Laurence shook his head and laughed grimly, "If the Seneschal was trying to foster a revolt, he could not have chosen a better way."

"And does that concern us? In discord there is profit and we have the legitimacy of the Lord Lieutenant so let us use it. I have left Saint Severin until the last because it is the richest village. There is a small castle and a church. We ride in and take all and then head back to winter quarters." He turned in his saddle and shouted, "Alain, here!"

A rider detached himself from the thirty riders who followed Sir Guy. Alain of Auxerre was his sergeant at arms and was a tough veteran of the Poitevin wars. In the past, he had served good masters but they had died and he had been left without an income. There comes a time in a man's life when he has to think of himself. He did not like the work they did but he was now saving coins so that soon he could leave the service of the ruthless man he followed. He did not like Sir Guy but he had been given his orders by the man who paid him twice as much as Sir Guy did to ensure that his orders were carried out. Alain of Auxerre was a professional soldier while Sir Guy was a young noble out to make a profit and a name for himself. He was also the man who had hired the brigands. He was a true mercenary and a good one at that.

"Yes, my lord?"

"Send two good men to ride to the far side of the village. When we attack they stop any from leaving. Have the two wounded men stay with the horses. Saint Severin is just a mile away."

"Yes, my lord. I will send Jean and Jacques. They are the best mounted."

Sir Guy nodded. He did not care about the men's horses. They would take Saint Severin, stay the night and head back to the safety of the land along the Garonne. He would report his success to the Earl of Leicester and then spend the winter enjoying himself. As the two men detached themselves Sir Guy donned his helmet. He kept his visor open for he doubted that he would have to fight anyone of quality this day. He raised his lance, and the men began to move down the road. The lance was a good weapon to hunt farmers and peasants. They wore no mail and he would be able to strike them with impunity. Four men overtook him and they would lead the way. On the off chance that the villagers were not surprised they would be the casualties and not him.

The lord of the manor, Guillaume de Saint Severin was the direct opposite of Sir Guy de La Réole. His mail hauberk was old as were his sword and shield. He still used the long kite shield his father had. He had three sons and the eldest, Pierre, who would in a year or two be knighted, was his squire. He was also different in that he cared about his people. He had joined his villagers to dig a ditch around the village, but he knew that they needed a wooden palisade to withstand a determined attack. However, until the reign of Simon de Montfort, they had not needed one and he and his villagers had, instead, worked to improve their land and their livestock. The wine they produced was much sought after. They had been successful, and the manor was one of the most prosperous in the region. That was why when, two days since, the rider from Vigeois had ridden in to tell him of the attack by the mercenaries he did not bemoan his own procrastination but, instead, had decided to make the best of a bad job. He had his men stop work on their fields and plant lillia, stakes in the ditch. He had used the shepherd boys as scouts to watch from their lofty hills for the signs of the enemy. He had ensured that the priest kept a servant by the bell to toll for danger so that all could make the relative safety of the village and he had told every man and boy to keep his weapons close to hand. There were no non-belligerents. Even the smallest of boys had a sling and improvised pole weapons along with swords and bows made up their defences.

The shepherd boy had spotted the column far in the distance the previous evening as their scouts had descended upon the farm of Henri whose farm lay at Lusignac some miles away. The high ground was a favourite spot for the shepherd boy and his sheep. It gave him a good view far to the south and he had seen the glint of light on mail and swords. He knew what it meant. It was not in his manor but Guillaume regretted not being able to warn the old man and his wife. He hoped the raiders would spare them and when this was over, he would help them, if they were still alive, to rebuild. The shepherd boy had good eyes and he had observed all and yet remained hidden in the copse of trees while his dog watched the small flock. The warning, however, had allowed Guillaume to send to the seigneur for help. He was not hopeful, but it was his duty. He sent his youngest son, Louis.

As they prepared their defences, long before dawn, knowing that the raiders would attack swiftly, Guillaume strode around the village exuding confidence. His people needed his confidence for they were not warriors. They practised each Sunday after church but Guillaume knew that the men who came were professionals. It was some years since he had been a real warrior. He had been a crusader but a man never forgot how to fight. Pierre, his eldest son and squire, wearing his helmet and short hauberk for the first time and with a short sword strapped to his baldric was like a chattering magpie. Guillaume knew that it was just the excitement. Once the fighting began then his son would have that excitement replaced by fear, perhaps even terror. His son had seen fifteen summers, and he could use a sword but his blade had yet to bite into flesh and Guillaume knew that was a world away from striking at the pel.

"Good, Bertrand, those caltrops will cause them some dismay."

The village smith nodded as he spread the deadly three-pronged pieces of metal on the bridge over the ditch. The bridge was not removable but Bertrand's suggestion to use the deadly metal had been a good one. The village was in good heart. They would not be taken by surprise and whilst some might die then they knew that the attackers would not be unscathed.

"Won't they see them, father?"

Guillaume and his son picked their way through the caltrops so that he could see what the attackers would. It would soon be dawn and he wanted the village to appear at peace when the attackers came. "I hope that they will not but if they do then they will have to do as we just did and go slowly to negotiate them. Then the archers and those with slings who hide behind the walls of Gaston and Stephen's homes will have an easier target. A man who is stopped is easier to hit."

His son nodded, "And if they do not see them then their horses will be hurt."

"And if they try the ditch, thinking we have neglected it then they will also come to grief." He turned to look, as the first light of the new dawn illuminated the prosperous little village. "Good, now we prepare our own defence."

The two of them strode back through the village to the church and the castle. They lived cheek by jowl with the church and both were integral to the village. The knight waved over his second son, Caspar, "Go and fetch the women and the children. Bring them to the castle and the church." He would send the boys to the top of the tower to use their slings. The only access to the castle was up the stair to the door that was eight paces above the ground. Once inside it could be barred. He had contemplated using it for defence but with full barns and animals in the field, while they might save lives they would become poor and he and his people had worked too hard to be impoverished. He was risking all and trusting his people.

The men were already gathered. Bertrand was to command, along with Gaston, the archers and the older slingers. Bertrand was a veteran warrior, and he would not risk the lives of any he led. If they were in danger of being overrun, he would give the order to fall back to the main column. The other twenty men of the village were the ones who had a variety of weapons. Some of them had helmets and shields although the quality varied from leather helmets to round bucklers. They would all be used.

Waving his arm Guillaume said, "Hide yourselves next to the houses and when the bell tolls, and not before, then form up behind me as we practised yesterday." Caspar had returned and the women shepherded the children into the castle. Guillaume's wife, Eleanor, smiled at them all. She had with her their two daughters: Mary the eldest who was seventeen and Eleanor who was but ten. They were calm like their mother for they trusted their father who was like a rock. The whole family had the utmost trust in their father and the men of the village. She was the matriarch of this village and as much a weapon as Guillaume's sword.

He turned to his second son, "Caspar, you go with Charles and Paul. The three of you watch for an attack from the other end of the village. You have your horn?" His son held up the cow's horn. "Good. You are there to warn us and that is all. No heroics." As the three youths ran off Guillaume knew that they would not obey that last order."

He looked around to check that all looked normal. Most of the men were hiding but he and Pierre, along with Bertrand stood close to the bridge as though they were speaking of the harvest. It allowed him to keep watch on the woods from whence he knew that they had to come. He caught the sound of jingling metal and the clopping of horses as the raiders tried to use the woods to disguise their approach. He nodded to Bertrand and Pierre who wandered off to warn the men of the imminent attack.

It was Guillaume himself who gave the priest the order to ring the bell. He did so when the raiders were just twenty paces from the woods. He feigned surprise and ran but it was a measured run. The riders had more than a hundred paces to ride and that was more than enough time for Guillaume to reach the church. The fact that all the villagers were safely in the castle was no matter. The ringing bell would tell the raiders that they had taken the village by surprise. That they should have realised something was amiss, by the lack of people, was clear to the Gascon knight but perhaps these raiders were overconfident. If so they were going to pay the price. As the bell rang so the men of the village stepped out from the houses and formed a column five men wide behind Guillaume and Pierre. The ones with shields, helmets and better weapons were at the fore. The rest might be eager but they would be at the back.

Guillaume observed all with a critical eye. The men who came were the sweepings of the warrior hall. He saw that by the horses they rode, the variety of armour and helmets and the ragged way they approached. He recognised the livery of the knight and was not surprised at the occupation. Sir Guy was known as a man with venal appetites. It was no surprise that he had taken to brigandry, even though the course of action had been legitimised by the Earl of Leicester, it was what it was.

He turned to his son, "Stand behind me to my right. Do not move from there without my command."

The eagerness before the battle had now been replaced by nerves as the youth heard the hooves thundering towards them, "Yes, my lord." The youth saw the men with lances and that the ones at the fore were mailed and had visored helmets. This was no longer an adventure.

Guillaume shouted, "Now Bertrand!" when the horsemen were almost on the bridge. His smith would order the arrows, bolts and stones to be sent at the charging horsemen. They would be seen soon enough anyway, and he wanted their eyes distracted from the caltrops. That Guillaume could see them did not worry the knight. He knew where they were.

The horsemen would not be looking for the caltrops. The arrows sent at the horsemen were war arrows and hunting arrows. The first four raiders wore mail and it would be a lucky arrow that found flesh. Horses, however, were another matter and Bertrand had ordered the archers and their two crossbowmen to aim at those. The slingers, in contrast, enjoyed the freedom of sending their river pebbles at the heads and arms of the horsemen. Even with a helmet and arming cap, a horseman could still be rendered unconscious by such a blow. It could even break a limb. It was, however, the caltrops that did for the first four. The horses either screamed in pain and reared or hurled themselves to the side as they stepped on the sharpened spikes. One horse was impaled by the lillia while a second horse hurled its rider from its back to be speared by the stakes. The wily Sir Guy had the wit to negotiate the spikes. Sir Guillaume saw the desperate knight lead the rest of his men towards what he thought was just a knight and his son, backed by ill-armed villagers. Sir Guillaume and his men practised each Sunday. They were hardly a retinue, but they were trained.

Sir Guy lowered his lance and drove his horse directly at Sir Guillaume. The excitement before the battle had now given way to absolute terror for Pierre, who felt the need to empty his bowels. Sir Guillaume had been a crusader and he said, quietly, "The horse will not ride into us for it is not a warhorse and I will deal with the lance. You just watch that his squire does not strike me with his spear."

"Aye, father!"

Raising and angling his shield he prepared his sword. He held it above his right shoulder ready to sweep. He had fought enough times to know that an enemy can switch direction at the last minute. Sir Guillaume was ready for such a move. Sir Guy's movement betrayed his intent. He stood in the stirrups and pulled back with the lance. He intended to drive it at the throat of Sir Guillaume. Even if the strike was blocked by the shield the knight would still be forced back. Sir Guillaume began his swing even as the lance struck the slightly angled shield. The long, old fashioned kite shield was heavier and clumsier than the new ones but one advantage was that it was big and the metal head was turned to the side. Tha lance tore through the leather covering and even made a split in the wood but a shield could be repaired. The Gascon knight kept his feet and the horse, as Guillaume had expected, went to the right. The sword hacked down and across Sir Guy's leg. He wore chaussee but his shield was too short to afford better protection and the sword smashed into the leg of the knight. It was a powerful blow and it broke flesh. The real wound was caused by the weight of the sword. One of the bones was cracked. Sir Guy began to slip from the horse.

At that moment Sir Guy's squire saw his chance and he lunged with his spear at Guillaume's unprotected right side. Pierre recklessly stepped forward and blocked the strike with his own shield and lunged with his sword. He found flesh but it was the horse's and the horse screamed and bucked in pain. Pierre was shocked at the wound he had inflicted and in his panic twisted the sword which made the wound worse and the horse and rider crashed to the ground. Its body fell atop Sir Guy who screamed as every bone in his body was broken by the horseflesh.

As Bertrand along with his archers and slingers fell upon the rest of the warband and the villagers raced to finish off men unhorsed by caltrops and arrows, Alain of Auxerre, who had wisely ridden at the rear of the column, reined in. He knew when a cause was lost and this one clearly was. Their paymaster was dead. He shouted orders to the others. He had hired them and he knew they would obey, "Fall back and follow me!"

One of the men turned and said, "But they are just villagers!"

As an arrow slammed into the man's leg, Alain shook his head, "All is lost. Follow me and live!" He was not a coward but he had to tell his master what had happened. It was not a disaster but a setback and Alain of Auxerre knew that there would need to be a modification in his master's plans. He was a clever man and this would not stop his ultimate aim of becoming the most powerful man in Aquitaine. The eight men who rode after him were the only ones without a wound. The two men sent to cut off the village joined them an hour later having realised that their cause was lost. Simon de Montfort's plans had been partly thwarted by a lowly knight who stood firm with his villagers. Across Aquitaine, however, other bands, imposing the will of the Earl of Leicester on the seigneurs, were more successful. Letters were sent to London imploring the king to do something about his Lord Lieutenant who was behaving like a tyrant. The stones that begin an avalanche trickled down the slope.

Chapter 1

William

The Royal Hunt

I am Sir William of Stockton, the Earl of Cleveland, and I had not heard from the king since the aftermath of the battle of Jed Water. That suited me for I preferred when London kept its nose out of the north. Intervention from the king rarely benefitted us. Like my dead father, the legendary Sir Thomas, hero of Arsuf, I did not like this king. I was honour bound to defend him but that did not mean I had to like him. When I saw the royal coat of arms my heart sank for it meant the king was sending me a message. That usually meant work for my family. Since the days of the first Earl of Cleveland, Sir Alfred, the Warlord who had saved England for Empress Matilda and her son Henry, we had been used to get the royal family out of one trouble or another. The liveried messenger had two men at arms as guardians and as soon as he had delivered it, personally to me, he left.

I read the letter and then summoned my squire, Thomas, my nephew, "Ride to your cousins and ask them to join me here. The king requests our company. Just the men mind. We need not inflict an unnecessary journey on their ladies."

"War, uncle?"

I smiled, "No and that, in itself, is a surprise. We are invited to join him in the hunt."

"Hunt?"

I waved an irritated hand. I liked my nephew but my former squire, Geoffrey, knew how to obey orders and just do things. Thomas liked explanations and I had little time for such nonsense. "Just go. I will explain it once and that is all!"

He left and I wondered if I would ever manage to train him as a knight. His father had not done so but Thomas had begged for the chance to be thus trained. The rest all had the martial qualities of the warlord. My nephew, Henry Samuel, was the best of knights. Men had called our grandfather, the perfect knight. Already Henry Samuel was accorded that title by knights who knew whereof they spoke: Sir Petr, Sir Folki and the other knights of the valley. Some knights have an innate ability. My nephew was one such. I am not without skill but I know that Henry Samuel is better. His brother Alfred was also good but he was a bachelor knight. His mind was on the maidens of the valley. It was to be expected for he, like his brother, was handsome and would be a good catch. Henry Samuel had been lucky and rescued Eirwen in Wales. They were truly a match made in heaven. Sir Geoffrey was the youngest knight and was my squire before Thomas. I know that I gave him his spurs because he was ready, but he was a thoughtful knight and I was interested to see how he would turn out. The rest of the family were either squires or pages and I was just pleased that Henry Samuel had undertaken the training of Dick, my eldest son. I knew that he would prove to be a good knight for he had fought, even though young, at Jed Water. His mother knew not the extent of his involvement and would never hear it from my lips. Women were best protected from the horrors of war.

At that moment she entered. I suspect that Thomas had made a dramatic gesture whilst leaving. She gave me an inquisitive smile and I nodded, "Aye, we shall have company this evening. The king has invited us to hunt and I must inform them of the request."

"If it is from the king it is not a request, husband and we both know that." I nodded. "You travel south?"

"Aye but only as far as Pickering Castle and Pickering Forest."

She frowned and took a seat opposite me, "That is a long way to travel just for a hunt."

"It is a royal lodge and the hunting is supposed to be good," I sighed, "However, I think there is more to it than just a hunt. Our King Henry likes plots and subterfuge. Still, it is but a day away and I doubt we shall be absent for more than a week."

She was also a very astute woman, "Just the family or the knights of the valley?"

She had struck at the heart of it, "Just the men in the family and all are named. He wishes to see those with the blood of the warlord coursing through their veins."

My wife sighed, "Must it be ever thus?" I nodded. "At least we get to see the family this night." She stood and then stopped suddenly, "When do you leave?"

I had been dreading the question, "By the morrow."

Shaking her head she scurried off to find the steward and his wife, the housekeeper. My wife now ran the hall and after the smaller manor at Herterpol, the change had been dramatic. Stockton was an important castle and along with Barnard Castle guarded the Tees. Our larders were ever full. I went to the stables. Alan the horse master would choose the best horses. We did not need warhorses; indeed they were far too valuable to risk in a hunt besides which they were not suited to it. He and his grooms were schooling some hackneys. These were quite literally our workhorses. They were good for riding and, unless it was to be a charge in a battle, then they were useful beasts for war.

He knuckled his forehead and waved his grooms and their charges away to the far side of the outer bailey, "Yes, my lord?"

"The king wishes us to go on a hunt. We shall need at least eight horses. Do you have them?"

"Aye, my lord. Will you be hawking too?"

It was a good question, and the truth was I did not know. I suspected it made little difference. The king was using the hunt as an excuse, "I shall not be taking the hawks so we shall not need a horse for cadge and the cadger. The squires and pages can use their rouncys."

"Crow is the best of them and will suit you, my lord. As black as his name suggests he has a quick mind." He rubbed his chin, "Will you need the hounds and alaunts, my lord?"

"No, for we travel south for a day and they will only slow us. Tell the master of the pack that he need not stir."

"Alf will be pleased, my lord. He has a couple of new hounds he is training. I will let him know."

The two men were good friends and it made life easier for me for it to be so. The three men, horse master, master of the hounds and old codger might banter with each other but they were as loyal three men as you could wish to meet. They were loyal to the manor and to each other and that was how it should be. "Good. We will not bother with sumpters, and our supplies can be carried on rouncys. I wish a speedy journey and not one at the pace of a sumpter."

He smiled, "No place like home, eh my lord?"

I nodded, "My father's death has shown me that life is too short to spend travelling the length and breadth of a country which is a mere shadow of the valley in which we are gifted to live."

I then sought out the weaponsmith. We already had the weapons we would need but he would have to put edges on the boar spears. "And have some deer spears ready. I take it the fletcher has enough hunting arrows?"

I felt foolish the moment the words were out of my mouth for our archers were the best in the north of England and they would have plenty of arrows for us to take. A local hunt was one thing and we would all enjoy the spectacle and the hunt but riding to a king's hunting lodge with pampered and posturing nobles each trying to gain favour with the king was not my idea of enjoyment.

He nodded and kept a straight face, "Aye, Sir William."

By the time all was done the first of the family were arriving. Henry Samuel had a relatively short journey from Elton. The others arrived not long after. Thomas had, of course, speculated on the reason for the hunt and while many of the others were swept up in the speculation, I saw that Henry Samuel was not. "Thomas, we have been invited to a hunt. That is all we need to know. We may not wish to attend but we must. I for one would be happier being at my wife's side now that she is with child for the third time, I think I understand grandfather a little better now. He hated to be dragged off by the needs of the land." Henry Samuel had been the one closest to my father and they had spent longer together than any others in the family.

Thomas would not let the matter go, "But it may bring great honour. The king does not often travel to the north yet he comes here. Perhaps this family's recent service will be rewarded by him."

Even Alfred joined in Henry Samuel's laughter while Geoffrey just studied the man who had replaced him as my squire. Alfred, for all his attempts to get a lady, was a realist and he understood both the king and politics of the land, "Our kings have ever been parsimonious when it comes to rewarding this family, cousin. Why our grandfather had to fight to get back his land and serve in the Baltic to earn a crust. For my part, I shall be glad to ride to hunt with the men of this family. Whilst still dangerous, it is less likely that we will leave our blood far from this valley."

Henry Samuel said, "Amen to that, brother." The two were close and that was partly because their father, my elder brother, also Alfred, had died when they were still young.

I leaned forward and placed my hands on the table, "Now, all of you, heed my words. My father returned to this land an outlaw because he upset the father of the king who has invited us to hunt. This family suffered because of the vindictive nature of King John. Whilst his son is not cut from the same cloth we heed our tongues when we are amongst courtiers. It is one thing to speak openly here in the haven that is Stockton but to do so where every ear and eye may belong to King Henry's spies is quite another. We bow, we scrape, we laugh dutifully, we let the king show us how skilled he is at the hunt, and, with luck, we shall return to the valley with our lands intact."

Thomas was like a dog with a bone and while I saw Alfred, Geoffrey and Henry Samuel nod agreement he asked, "And is the king skilled at the hunt?"

I shook my head, "Thomas, it matters not if he does not know one end of a boar spear from the other whatever he does we applaud." The other squires and pages, along with my two knighted nephews and former squire all nodded but I could see that Thomas still had much I needed to teach him. What had I taken on?

We had less than forty miles to travel to reach Pickering and we knew the first part of the road well. We took neither men at arms nor archers. To have done so would have represented a threat to the king but the four men we took to lead the spare horses and act as servants had all once been warriors. They had swords and could handle themselves.

As we headed out of Stokesley, having watered our horses, I turned in my saddle to view my nephews. Poor Thomas had only been made my squire when he was already older than Geoffrey whom I had knighted. The last campaign on the borders had been his first and whilst he had acquitted himself passably well he was still learning how to be a knight. My son Dick was already easier in the role of squire than was Thomas and even little Matthew, riding his large pony, was happy to be a page. Edward and Edgar were both of an age with my son, Richard and poor Thomas stood out like a sore thumb. James, an old soldier who had served my father, led the servants and their mounts.

The land through which we travelled was the most peaceful I had ever seen. Perhaps it was because Scots when they came, poured through the rich vale of York. This land was also fertile but it was upland and had more sheep than people. The Scots ever wanted cattle and gold. There were churches and abbeys, but they tended to lie to the south of the hills. I enjoyed the ride which passed through Malton, with its Roman ruins and small wooden castle before passing through Kirkbymoorside and the fortified manor there. As earl, I was senior to all the nobles and lords. We were fed and watered well.

It was late afternoon when the castle that had first been built by William the Conqueror hove into view. Geoffrey asked, "A magnificent position, my lord, but why is the outside wall just herisson?"

Thomas had been ill-educated in warfare and that was his father's fault. "What is a herisson? I have never heard the word before."

Henry Samuel, in contrast, had spent so long with my grandfather that he could have written a book about castles and their defences. He gave a patient explanation, "It is a wooden wall and each villager is responsible for one perch of the wall." I was relieved that Thomas knew that a perch was a measurement of about five paces and he nodded.

"Every three years each villager has to replace his section of the wall around the outer ward. That is why it is uneven and hence its name which is from the French for a hedgehog."

"But this is a royal castle, surely it should be like Stockton's and made of stone."

Alfred sighed, "The town wall is made of wood and that is our equivalent of the outer wall of the castle."

Henry Samuel's words prompted me to issue a warning, "When we are here it will be like the court. They will speak French and mistakes will be frowned upon. I do not think it matters but the king and his courtiers will. There will be French nobles here at the castle and we will be judged. We owe it to our grandfather to uphold the family name. Thomas, keep all such questions for the journey home."

"Yes, uncle." I saw Thomas' shoulders slump and once again I cursed my brother-in-law for his lack of training. It was inexcusable for a man owed it to his sons to make them the best knights that they could be.

"Come, let us not keep the king waiting."

We passed through the town that owed its existence and employment to the castle. Foreheads were knuckled as our livery was recognised. The Warlord had saved the north at the Battle of the Standards and the folk who lived here had long memories. The bridge over the deep ditch was a narrow one and we rode in single file. Recognised by the sentries we were waved through to the outer ward. A sergeant at arms pointed to some stables to our left, "My lord, those are your stables, and your quarters are there." He pointed to some wooden buildings to our right."

Weary after the ride I dismounted, and the others followed suit. I handed my reins to Thomas. My knights did the same to their squires. "Thomas, see to the horses and when you have done so then come with James, the servants and other squires to our home for the next days will be busy ones. Matthew, you stay close to me."

My young son looked grateful while Thomas shook his head. He had my page's pony to deal with too. As we headed to the wooden hall which we would have called a warrior hall I studied the huge motte and imposing round donjon.

The three castles of Scarborough, York and Pickering were a triangle that guarded the passes through this exposed part of England. I had never heard of any attack on this castle, and I could see why. The ditch around the motte was as deep as the one around the outer wall and I saw that it was hewn from solid rock. The castle could not be undermined.

The steward who answered to the Sherriff of York was called Roger and he looked harassed. A royal visit was to be expected but the work he had to do was out of proportion to his normal efforts. I felt no sympathy for him as, for most of the year, he had an easy and comfortable job with royal lodgings.

"I have your beds, my lord. I have put you all together here."

I saw that the hall was not divided into chambers but all shared the same roof and fire. The knights at least had beds although the squires and my page would have to sleep on the floor. This would be another harsh lesson for Thomas. A good squire learned to improvise.

"Thank you. Matthew, if I might suggest? Find as much straw as you can and put it next to my bed," I pointed, "that one. Use your cloak to cover it, eh? It will be more comfortable." I hoped that Thomas would see what my son had done and emulate him.

The steward was obviously trying to impress us as he had ensured there was soap, water and towels but, after we had all washed and changed and he led us through the inner gatehouse to the king's hall I saw that we were far from the most important guests at the hunt. The king's hall was stone-built and close to the new chapel. King Henry had been busy but obviously, the Earl of Cleveland was not important enough for the new hall. I contented myself with the knowledge that there would be less bowing and scraping in the wooden hall and I would be with real warriors.

As soon as we entered, I spied the king in close conference with three nobles I did not recognise. From their dress they were French, and I detected a family resemblance that led me to believe they were brothers. I worked out who they were. When I had last visited with the Archbishop of

York to report more fully on the Battle of Jed Water and its ramifications, he had told me of three brothers who had come to England at the king's request. They were the sons of Isabella of Angoulême, King John's former wife. Unpopular in France, thanks to the king's disastrous attempt to retake lands lost by his father, he had given them huge estates in Wales. There was William de Valence who had changed his name from Guillaume de Lusignan. I think it was an attempt to make himself sound less French. His brothers were Guy de Lusignan and Aymer de Lusignan and from the archbishop's description, I was looking at the three. Also with them was Prince Edward and hovering close by the man I took to be his tutor, Bartholomew Pecche. A pair of liveried servants brought over goblets of wine for us. Thomas and the other squires and pages had wisely pressed themselves against the ornate tapestries hanging from the walls for it was better to be invisible in such company. Even Thomas knew that he was in an elevated company where he should make himself as inconspicuous as possible.

After thanking the servants I said, very quietly, "Do not drink too much and do not offer an opinion about anything. Watch and listen. Let us hope to get to the hunt without a disaster." The three were nervous and they all nodded.

There were others in the hall that I did recognise. They were the lords of Helmsley, Scarborough and Thirsk. The knights to whom they were chatting were strangers too but I recognised the liveries as manors further south in Yorkshire. This was not just a hunt but a conclave and I had been right to be suspicious about our invitation.

The man I took to be Sir William de Valance drew the king's attention to me and turning, the king clapped his hands together. The chatter ceased and King Henry said, in a somewhat reedy voice, "And now we can begin to feast for our chief guest is here. Earl William and his family, the Warlord's heirs!" The three Frenchmen began to applaud, a little half-heartedly and it was taken up by the rest of the hall. I liked not the attention, but I did as I had urged my family to do, I bowed and took it. As he came over, I saw that the table had been laid at the far end of the room and the clap of the king's hands had been the signal to bring the food to the table.

The king came over and gestured, first to his son and then the three Frenchmen, "This is Prince Edward, my son and these are my brothers, Sir William de Valence, Sir Guy de Lusignan and Sir Aymer de Lusignan. I think he used the term brothers rather than half-brothers to elevate them somewhat. They were related and therefore of importance. I bowed and scraped.

"And these are my two nephews, Sir Henry Samuel and Sir Alfred. Sir Geoffrey was my former squire."

The king frowned as though something was out of place but the frown quickly disappeared for he was the consummate politician. "Tonight you shall be our guest of honour and sit betwixt my son and me. I would have Sir Henry Samuel sit on the other side of my son while Sir Alfred can sit between Sir William and Sir Guy."

Sir Geoffrey was forgotten and I wondered at the omission. There was a plan here and if this was a battle then I would have worked out what it was but the murky waters of the court were something my father and I had assiduously avoided. We were babes in the wood compared with the others at the head of the table. I determined to drink as little as I could and keep my wits about me. This was not an ambush where a twitching nose might save my life this was a court, and I would not see the arrow sent at me for it would be words that would strike and not a bodkin.

This was the work that Thomas hated. He and the other squires would have to fetch and carry for every lord, no matter how lowly they were. He would have to be on hand to help me cut meat and he would need, along with Matthew, to keep my goblet filled. Matthew's face showed me that he was enjoying every moment of this elevated company. My son, Dick, was also astute enough to know that this evening would stand him in good stead for the future. Thomas, however, frowned and glowered and I took a sort of perverse pleasure in his discomfort.

I had a good eating knife that had been given to me by my mother. Inlaid with jet and silver it was a beautiful object in its own right, I used it to slice some meat after the king had finished with the venison fillet. I cut it into chunks before spearing a piece and eating it. The king had brought his own cooks from London and, as I had expected, they knew their business. The venison was perfectly cooked. I was just thinking that I might enjoy this feast when the king said, "Sir William, I would have you tell my son and my brothers about the fight against our treacherous neighbours."

As much as I might not wish to I had no choice and I laid down my knife and drank from my goblet. Wiping my mouth I began the tale. I did not mind telling such tales to my family but in this company, there was always the danger of making my part too great and having other nobles assume that I was embellishing. I told it as modestly as I could and I saw the silky smiles on the three French brothers as they murmured together during my telling. I saw Alfred colour and knew that the comments were disparaging. When I had finished, Prince Edward clapped his hands excitedly. I knew that he had been a sickly child and his father had kept him far from danger. He looked to me, to be a youth who was healthy. Perhaps he had changed. "I would that I had been there. Father, next time that Sir William and his knights ride to face the Scots I would be with them."

Before the king could answer Sir Guy de Lusignan snorted, "It seems to me that these Scots are like the Welsh that my brother faces. They have neither honour nor courage and scurry back into their holes rather than facing knights. I do not doubt that the men of the north did well but it is like the ridding of rats from the barn. It is necessary but we all know that until the rats' nest is gone, they will return."

I picked up my knife and gripped the hilt tightly. Good men had died in the battle and they were courageous men on both sides. While it was true that the Scots lacked the weaponry and mail of our men one could not doubt their courage and our victory had been paid for by the blood of men who were close to all my family. They were irreplaceable men. I sliced a piece of wild boar and filled my mouth so that I would not have to speak. The conversation noise rose as the knights around the table discussed the battle and the comments of Sir Guy. If this had been Stockton, then the ladies would have steered the conversation to matters less martial but this was a hunting lodge and there was not a woman in sight.

While Sir Henry Samuel chatted to an inquisitive Prince Edward the king said, "I thought you had three nephews, Sir William. I asked for them all to be brought. Why was my command ignored?"

I regretted taking such a large piece of meat and struggled to swallow it, "But I did, sire. Henry Samuel, Alfred and Thomas." I gestured to Thomas who was refilling my goblet.

The king smiled, "Ah, now I understand." He glanced down at Sir Geoffrey and then at Thomas. He frowned, "Why is it that you have knighted your squire but not your nephew who, it seems to me is older?"

I saw that Thomas was uncomfortable to have what he saw as his deficiencies highlighted by the king. "Thomas has only been a squire for a short time and he has much to learn. When he is ready then I shall dub him."

"He has the blood of the warlord in his veins and he should be knighted." The king banged a hand upon the table. "Before you quit this hall to return to Stockton, he shall be given his spurs." I opened my mouth to object and the king's eyes narrowed as he said, "It is not a request, Cleveland, it is a command and it shall be done as I said. I will have spurs made here in the castle for the smith is a good fellow with great skill."

Prince Edward and the others had heard the command but appeared not to notice the tone and they all clapped and cheered. Was this why I had been brought here? Was the king buying Thomas to be his man? My father had told me that King John had often done so. If that was the extent of the plotting then I would live with it but something told me that there was more to come. I endured the rest of the feast and, thankfully, the king chose to retire earlier than was expected. As he left closeted by his son and half-brothers, I knew that the sconces in the donjon on the mound would be burning late.

My nephews and sons, Matthew excepted, all knew that something troubled me and they respected my silence. The wooden hall was filled with other lords and was not the place for debate. We would have to wait until we left for the hunt. As he helped me to undress Thomas said, quietly, "I am not yet ready to be a knight, uncle and yet we cannot refuse the king can we?"

I was pleased that he recognised the truth and I nodded, "You are right but the king has his own plots and plans. No matter what happens, Thomas, I will ensure that your training continues apace. I shall not risk you in battle until I am convinced that you are ready."

He looked relieved and that pleased me for it marked a change in him.

Roger came in just as dawn was breaking. Many knights had already risen to make water and the hall was disturbed. The steward coughed and said, "My lords, the king has deemed that we hunt deer today with dogs. The forest is just two miles from here and food is ready in the hall."

The king had decided we would eat and hunt early. We dressed in our hunting clothes. A leather brigandine and hide breeches was my chosen garb. I would wear a hunting cap upon my head but that was merely to control unruly hair freed from an arming cap. When I held my spear, I would don my leather gauntlets. A short sword and rondel dagger completed my preparations.

Matthew had never hunted before and I gave him his lessons as we headed for the king's hall. "We hunt with dogs, alaunts. They will drive the deer towards us and you will be with Thomas and the other squires behind the knights. Whilst Thomas will hold my spare spears your sole task is to watch for the stag as it comes towards us. Your voice will help to warn our men that we are in danger. It is expected that the king will be the one to bring down the stag but it may well be that one of us has to help the king."

"We do not use bows, father?"

I smiled, and spoke quietly, "Bows require more skill and I suspect that King Henry cannot draw a bow well enough. A spear is a safer weapon but it brings the stag closer to us. A stag can kill a man. There will be a huntsman close to the king with a couple of alaunts and they will be released if the king fails to make a kill. Once he has made his kill then it will be easier, and it may prove to be a proper hunt."

Dick, my son, was close enough to speak to his brother, "When next our father hunts at home we shall show you how we hunt in the woods of Hartburn, eh father?"

I nodded but inside I wondered if the king had made plans that might mean we would not be at home. Either the king had breakfasted earlier, or he was eating in the keep for he was not there. The squires and pages went for the horses and that left the four of us to speak in the outer ward where we could not be overheard.

Sir Geoffrey shook his head, "So I was not invited, Sir William."

I heard the hurt in his voice, and I shook my head, "Take it as a compliment. The king thought that you were one of my nephews. There was no insult intended."

Sir Henry Samuel said, "But Thomas is not ready yet to be knighted, uncle. If the king has some task for us then he might endanger all of us through no fault of his own."

"He has improved." I knew my answer sounded weak and when Henry Samuel cocked an eyebrow I nodded, "Then the four of us will have to train him while we do whatever it is that the king wishes us to do."

We heard the sound of hooves as our squires led the horses across the wooden bridge. We had barely put our feet in the stirrups when the king and his party clattered out of the inner ward. I smiled for some of the lords who had slept in our hall had tarried over their breakfast too long and they had still to mount. They would have the embarrassment of having to chase after us.

The king was in good humour and shouted, "A gold piece to any knight who brings down a stag!" The barking of the dogs drowned out any further comment as the master of the hunt with a horn around his neck fetched out the wolfhounds also called alaunts, they would be there to protect the king. I knew that the other pack of dogs would already be in the forest ready to drive the animals towards us. The word hunt was a misnomer. When a king hunted, the animals were brought to him. A real hunt often resulted in a failure for animals can be cunning. I preferred the hunts of home where a knight's real skill was tested.

Thomas had been silent since the king's announcement and, as we headed north to the chosen hunting ground I reined in to ride next to him. "Today, Thomas, you shall need all your wits about you so put the spurs from your mind. You have been promised them by the king and you will be knighted."

He looked around to see if we were observed or could be overheard but the hooves and chatter masked all noise, "I wanted to be a knight and that was why I asked to be a squire but I feel as though I have yet to do enough to justify spurs."

"Your grandfather was knighted by a king after Arsuf. He was not sure that he was ready, and he was your namesake. Perhaps this is meant to be."

Thomas laughed, "And yet I have not only done no great deeds as he did, but I also have not even done any deed."

"Then it may be that one is just awaiting you."

We found the servants waiting for us at the small village of Lockton. Tables were there ready to be laden with food. Grooms stood by to take our horses into their care. This was a well-organised hunt. Thomas had no time for doubt and self-reflection for he had much to do and even more to carry. He would be a human sumpter and carry all that I might need in the hunt. We drank wine and then when we heard the distant horn we followed the huntsmen into the forest. This was a hunt but unlike home, where we chose our own places, we were with the king and we were allocated specific stands. The king's half-brothers were next to him and Prince Edward was behind. To his left were the local knights and we were to the right. Two local huntsmen marked the end of our line. The king was preceded by two huntsmen each with four alaunts on leashes. The beasts snapped, snarled and tugged as they smelled the prey. We could not smell it yet but with the breeze in our faces, we would soon enough.

The four of us from Cleveland had hunted before. The last time had been the hunt after my father had died. Then we had enjoyed the company of the other knights like Sir Richard, Sir Geoffroy, Sir Folki and Sir Petr but we four had kept together and that was because of the battle of Jed Water. Even now, as we walked purposefully towards the heart of the forest, we each held our spears identically and I noticed that we were in step. There was no order and I had not given a command yet we walked as one.

In the distance, we heard the baying of dogs as the deer were pursued. I did not envy the hunt master. It was one thing to find a stag suitable to be killed by a king and quite another to isolate him to make the kill an easy one. The dogs before the king also began to tug even harder on their leashes as the scent of the deer grew even stronger. The two men with the dogs began to move away from the king so that he should have a clearer throw for his spear. The ones close to us moved far enough to the right so that the hounds did not obscure our chances of hitting a deer but were still close enough to loose the dogs should the king be in any danger.

The cry from ahead told us that the hunt was not going well, "Rogue stags!" The strident horns also sounded the alarm. The huntsman had not managed to isolate a single stag and we had more than one coming at us. I said, "Cleveland, stand firm and act as one on my command."

I did not need acknowledgement to know that they had heard me. The stag, when it came through the forest, its flanks bloody from where the hounds had struck, was magnificent. The huntmaster would have been looking for a stag with at least twelve points on its antlers, a royal stag, but this beast had at least sixteen and was huge, it was a monarch. The blood on its antlers told me that not all dogs would be returning to their kennels. Had there just been the one stag then all might have been well but I heard the crash across our whole front. It was a herd that was heading for us. The huntsmen had not managed to cut out just one.

The two dog handlers close to us saw the stag as it ran directly at the king. He was not frozen with fear but he was also not quite ready to throw his spear. I saw the Lusignan brothers raise their spears. When they threw it would be an act of self-preservation. A heartbeat before the king finally threw, when the stag was thirty feet from him, the alaunts were released. The king's spear hit the stag but it was not a mortal blow. The three Frenchmen's spears were better throws and they made the stag slow. The four alaunts, however, ensured that the king was safe for they leapt on the wounded animal and went directly for the throat. It was a savage end to a fine animal.

Just at that moment, the huntsmen to our right shouted, "Ware, my lord!"

From the forest, a young stag, unwounded and panicked, led a small herd of six does and while the two huntsmen managed to shift the females away from the king their efforts directed the stag directly at the king and his party as it sought an escape. The four of them were too busy enjoying the spectacle of the stag in its death throes to have the wit to grab another spear. They turned in horror as the stag came across our front. It could not help but plough into them and such a beast would cause savage wounds. There was only one course of action and I took it. Shouting, "Cleveland, as one!" I stepped forward, pulling back my spear as I did so. I was taking us towards the path of the stag and hoping to stop it from killing our king and his heir. The stag was focussed on the path ahead and, as we thrust as one, was almost unaware of the danger we represented. The four spears individually might not have stopped the beast but the four of them, rammed as they were, together struck head, chest, stomach and rump and our strength was such that the stag was lifted from the ground and pushed away from the king. It fell just three paces from us and was dying. Unlike the magnificent monarch, the four wounds left the carcass largely intact. As the huntsmen pulled the alaunts from the monarch I knew that the cooks would have a hard job to make the meat from the animal killed by the king presentable.

The master of the hunt dropped to his knees before the king, "Sire, I am sorry that you were placed in such danger. The dogs must have started the smaller herd and we did not see it until we were too late."

I saw that the king was shaken as were his half-brothers. His son, in contrast, looked flushed with excitement. The king shook his head, "But for the intervention of the Earl of Cleveland and his family you might have lost your head for such incompetence!" I saw the man shaking with fear. It was not just his job that hung on the success of the hunt. "Tomorrow's hunt had better go more smoothly. Understand?"

"Yes, King Henry!"

The king turned to me, "That was bravely done. The stag could have turned and gored you."

"It was instinct, my lord. I could not allow the stag to hurt our king. Besides, it was not as large as the one you killed."

He had not killed the beast and all knew it, but one flattered a king. He shook his head ruefully, "Let us hope the beasts have not ruined the head."

There was just one alaunt that was unwounded. One had been gored and the others so hurt that I suspected they would have to be put down.

He went to the stag and taking his knife cut into the animal's guts to pull out the heart. He held it aloft and we all cheered. Two servants rushed up, one to take the heart and wrap it in cloth, to be stuffed and cooked for the feast while the other had water and a cloth to wipe the blood from the king's hands.

He turned to his half-brothers, "I would talk with my son and the earl, we shall see you back at Lockton."

"Will you be safe, King Henry?" I think Sir William de Valence was insulting me but I cared not. His opinion and words meant nothing to me.

"Earl, have your people watch our back but keep out of hearing."

"Yes, sire. Henry Samuel, make it so." I knew that I could rely on my nephew.

We headed back along the path to the village. The rest of the lords would be busy helping to fetch the two dead animals back to the village. The butchery would begin in the forest. Prince Edward and I flanked the king. I saw that

Prince Edward was growing. He was almost as tall as his father but he was thin and gangly with a drooping eyelid.

"Cleveland, I brought you and your nephews here for a purpose. Today has shown me that I was right to do so." I said nothing for the king was not inviting conversation. "You know that I appointed my son as Duke of Aquitaine?"

"Yes, sire."

"He is too young yet to take charge of the affairs of such a great county and so I have appointed a Lord Lieutenant, a Seneschal. The Earl of Leicester is a sound general, and I thought he would be a firm administrator. He handled well the expulsion of Jews from Leicester and I hoped his hand would steer Aquitaine and Gascony along a peaceful route."

My father and I had not approved of the expulsion of the Jews. Although de Montfort had said it was for his soul it was, quite simply, a way to increase his fortunes. I said nothing and waited for the next pronouncement.

His words surprised me, "Henry Samuel, is that a Jewish name?"

I sighed. Bishop Puiset had resented the fact that my grandmother had been born of Jewish blood and his desecration of her tomb had resulted in my father taking the drastic action of avenging that act. "He is named after the great knight Sir Samuel whose sacrifice saved the life of your uncle, the Lionheart."

He nodded, "Just so. He is a good leader is he not?"

I was on more comfortable ground now, "There is none better. My father spent longer training him than with any of the rest of the family. It is said he is the one who is the closest to the Warlord and we are all proud of him. All the knights of the valley are noble and honourable bur Sir Henry Samuel is the best and the others, even older knights like Sir Petr and Sir Folki respect and admire him."

The king shook his head, "Such names in England. You know that I have named my son after that great Saxon king, Edward the Confessor?" I nodded. "I would such names became more common than these foreign names." He was not inviting comment and merely censuring me for not making my men anglicise their names. He soon came to the meat of the meeting and as we approached the village where, in our absence, servants had erected a wall-less tent. The king waved me to a seat. I was honoured. "I know that you are loyal but I would have you swear that what I now say to you will remain with you."

I dropped to one knee and kissing the hem of his tunic said, "I so swear." Had it not been the king I might have kissed the hilt of my dagger but to draw a weapon in the company of a king was treasonous.

He looked relieved, "Good. I would have Sir Henry," I noticed he did not give him his full name, "lead a conroi of knights to Aquitaine. They will carry a message from me but they are there to help curb the excesses of de Montfort who has antagonised the locals to the point of insurrection."

"Sire, that is not a task for a banneret. That should be my task. I am an earl and can speak with the Earl of Leicester as an equal."

He shook his head, "No, for I need you and your other knights to keep a watch on the north. I do not trust the Scots and it may well be that if I sent the Earl of Cleveland to Aquitaine then they might cause mischief. Then the gains made at Jed Water would be as naught. Besides, I do not wish to antagonise de Montfort. Sending you and your knights might do so. No, Sir Henry will have my authority and that should be enough. He will take a small conroi that will not threaten the Earl of Leicester. He will be my eyes and ears in Aquitaine. The others, Alfred, Thomas, whom I shall dub this week and that fellow, Geoffrey?" I nodded. "Shall be his mesne. They will need a small escort of men at arms and archers and I will send with them a pursuivant to offer advice on the diplomatic side of his task."

He waved over a servant who brought us wine and then dismissed him. I saw Henry Samuel, my knights and squires, as they stood on guard twenty paces from us. Their faces told me that they were curious about the conversation.

Prince Edward said, "And I would go with Sir Henry to Aquitaine."

His father gave him a serious look, "My son, you have been ill and it is too dangerous for you."

He smiled, "I believe that the childhood ailments that have almost cost me my life were a test, a preparation and besides the clime of Aquitaine is healthier than that of England. My tutor has taught me all that he can about the world of books and my ancestry. It is time I learned how to be a warrior. Today showed me that these knights are the best and I feel safe with them." His father appeared not to be convinced but I knew that he was a cunning man and this could all be an act. "I now have a brother, Edmund and, thus far, he has not suffered the ailments that plagued my early life. If I am doomed to die you have an heir, father."

The young prince was a remarkably mature young man. His father nodded, a little too quickly to my mind, and Prince Edward beamed. I was riddled with doubts. I was saddling my nephew with more responsibility than I had ever had to shoulder and yet I could not refuse my monarch. I now saw the reason for our invitation.

Chapter 2

Henry Samuel

The Seeds of Discord

As we watched the king speaking with my uncle and the prince, I saw that my uncle was not happy and that was in direct contrast to the faces of the king and his son. I did not know what had been said but the fact that it had clearly annoyed my uncle made me uncomfortable, to say the least.

Sir Geoffrey said, "I hear the others coming."

I nodded, "We do as we were ordered and keep them from the king."

"Even his brothers?"

I turned to Thomas, "His half-brothers and, aye, we do. A command is a command and we obey it to the letter."

The danger passed, the hunters were now laughing and joking as they approached us. Sir William de Valence saw us and said, "Why do you bar our progress?"

"The king has commanded that he and my uncle have a private conference and we obey his orders."

He made to push past me, "We are his family and we do not take orders from a banneret."

I was stronger than he was, and he could not move me, "You do not take orders from a banneret, my lord, but from our king. I would happily let you pass but I obey orders. Do not make this unpleasant, eh?"

The three brothers' hands were going to their swords. Alfred smiled as he said, "We do not need swords to put three Frenchmen on their backs and, when we do, think how foolish you will look."

The easy words of my younger brother made them remove their hands from their weapons, but Sir Guy hissed, "This will be remembered."

I nodded, "Good for that way you will not be foolish enough to repeat it will you?"

The raised voices must have alerted the king for he rose and said, "Ah, you are here. We are done and all is settled. Come there is food and wine and I have an appetite. A brush with death will do that to a man."

I stepped aside and made an elaborate and mocking sweep of my hand to allow the Lusignan brothers through. As they joined the king Thomas said, "Was that wisely done, cuz?"

"When you have your spurs, you will learn that being a knight often involves doing things that are not wise." I put my arms around Alfred and Thomas, "Come, for I could eat a horse, with its skin on!"

Alfred laughed, "For my part, I would rather have a well-fried piece of ham at this hour of the day."

Despite the confrontation, the mood was lightened with the wine and the food although my uncle seemed worried about something. It was in the middle of the afternoon when we headed back to the castle. It had been a successful hunt for we had a sixteen-point stag and a twelve-point stag but we had been lucky. The other local knights were now looking forward to the next day's hunt where they hoped to show their skills.

Matthew was the most excited of us. He had been close enough to be sprayed by the blood of the stag we had speared, and he chattered like a magpie all the way back to our lodgings. My uncle could not help but answer him and by the time we passed into the outer ward he was smiling.

Before he left us, the king said, "And before we feast, we shall ennoble Thomas Fitzurse."

I saw my uncle's face darken and wondered why. He said, "Your last act as a squire, Thomas, shall be to see to the horses."

My cousin bowed and took my uncle's mount. I handed mine to Dick and as we headed towards the wooden hall asked, "Uncle, what is amiss?"

He shook his head, "I swore an oath and your curiosity will have to wait for the journey home to be satisfied. Here the walls have ears. Enjoy our time here for I do not think we shall be invited to a royal hunt again."

The spurs that were intended for Thomas were too well made to have been produced in a day. I suspect that the king had already ordered them for some other. It mattered not to Thomas who was dubbed and received his spurs from a king, a true honour. The ceremony was marred somewhat for me by two things: my uncle's distraction and the obvious enmity of the Lusignan brothers. It did not spoil it for Thomas who seemed caught up in the unexpected ceremony. I felt sorry for Richard, my cousin for he had been my squire for longer than Thomas and he deserved the knighthood more. He said nothing and I saw no resentment, but I knew that if I were him, I would wish it was me being knighted. When we returned north then I would press my uncle to knight him and I would seek another squire. That in itself would be a mighty task for the moulding of the raw clay of an eager page into a squire whose instincts could save a knight on a battlefield was not one to be taken on lightly.

Thomas was in good humour and drank too much, we had to put him to bed. We were family and we looked after our own. I had told the others that my uncle wished no discussion until we were on the road home and even then I suspected we would not be told all. We had servants with us.

The next day of hunting proved to be fruitless. The master of the hunt had told the king of an old boar that roamed the forest and the king was keen to hunt. Hunting boars was done from horseback and we wearied our horses as we trailed the almost mythical beast. The master of the hunt was berated in public when we returned empty handed to the castle and it seemed to send the king into a depressed mood that was not helped by the Lusignan brothers boasting of the wild boar that teemed in their lands in France. It seemed to me that their argument was a weak one as they had been forced to flee their homeland and chosen, instead, King Henry's realm. He declared the hunt over and said he would ride the next day to York and thence back to London. Much to the chagrin of the Lusignan brothers my uncle, the king and Prince Edward spent most of the late afternoon closeted in the solar in the donjon.

We left the next morning with the head and antlers of the stag we had killed. We were offered venison too but we had no shortage of that in the valley. We did my uncle the courtesy of holding our questions until we were halfway home.

"So uncle, why were you and the king so closely closeted and why has it put you in such low spirits?"

He smiled sadly, "I did not know that my mood had affected you all and for that, I apologise. If I took any of the shine from your knighthood, Thomas, then I am sorry."

Thomas shook his head, "Nothing can take the shine from being a bachelor knight. I am content uncle but sad that I shall no longer be your squire."

"I fear that you and I shall have the same problem and that is finding a squire to serve us but your task, Thomas… Sir Thomas, will be more urgent."

Enigmatically he would say no more and we were left pondering his words all the way to the ferry across the Tees. Once we reached the other side my uncle said, "Thomas, you had better ride to your parents. They should be the first to hear the news. Return on the morrow for I have news of my own that I must dispense."

Alfred could not contain himself, "Why not tonight, my lord? We have waited for days to hear what it was the king said to you."

"And as the matter concerns you all then all of you shall hear at the same time. Do not question me further, Alfred. I must speak with my wife and my mother first before I tell the pups what is in my mind."

We all rode to our own homes and Eirwen was pleased to see me. My son and daughter also made my welcome a warm one and my son Alfred, in particular, demanded my attention. So it was that it was not until late that we were alone. I put my hand on my wife's womb to feel the bairn inside, "How long do you think, my sweet?"

Eirwen was a clever woman and she read hidden meanings into my questions, "Why, do you leave again?"

I laughed, "I have just returned and having been away for some days wonder when I shall have another son or daughter."

Mollified she snuggled closer to me, "The midwives think within the month, and I think it is a boy."

"How?"

"The heartbeat."

Such things were a mystery to me and I honestly believed that a major difference between men and women was that women had a little of the witch in them. Not in the evil sense of the word but just being more connected to nature. My wife was a Celt and Welsh and seemed to be even more prescient than most.

It was good to be home but I could not wait to ride to Stockton Castle the next day. The only manor closer was Hartburn and I knew that I was lucky to have such an easily managed manor so close to my uncle. It meant that my family were always safe whenever I was sent to defend the king's borders. I wondered, as Dick and I rode the couple of miles to Stockton, if that was what the meeting would be about. Were we being sent to the north again? Sir Richard of Hartburn and my uncle, along with me, had defended Elsdon and Otterburn to make them safe. Was there now a need for us to return? I hoped not. The valley of the Tees was where my heart lay.

When we reached the castle, we were directed, not to the keep and the Great Hall but the chapel that had been recently enlarged and where the masons had just finished the effigy of my grandfather on his tomb. When we reached the chapel, I found my uncle kneeling in prayer before the tombs of his father and his great grandfather, the Warlord. The two tombs touched for they had been the greatest knights of our family. The other who should have resided there, Sir Samuel, lay in the Holy Land. It had always been a regret of my grandfather that he had not brought back the bones of the knight they called perfect. As he often told me, he had been too busy trying to avoid death, but he regretted it to his dying day. I knelt next to my uncle and I prayed to God. I knew that my grandsires were in heaven and I prayed to God to allow me to join them there. I heard footsteps behind me and Alfred dropped to his knees. A few moments later Geoffrey and Thomas joined us.

My uncle allowed them to pray for a few moments and then stood. Our squires and Matthew, his page stood watching. "Rise."

We did so and Geoffrey said, "I feel, Sir William, that I should not be here for this is a family chapel."

"This is the chapel of Stockton and none of the illustrious knights who sleep here would resent your presence. Dick, close the door for we need privacy."

His son closed the door and I saw that he stood with his back to it. My squire was in tune with the moment.

"I chose this place because of the knights who lie here. They each served a king. Sometimes, as with the second King Henry, they were good kings. Others, like King John, were less so. King Henry, the son of John Lackland has given you all a task. There is no way we can refuse it; the king made it quite clear to me and it is not a task that will be easy. It will take you all to Aquitaine and specifically the southern part that they call Gascony."

That it came as a shock to us all was clear from the intake of breath and the looks we gave each other. Thomas was about to say something but my uncle held up his hand. "Only Matthew from this company and myself will remain in England. The rest of you, under the banner of Sir Henry Samuel, will take chosen men at arms and archers to Aquitaine." He paused, "If that was all you had to contend with it might not be so bad but you are charged with protecting and training Prince Edward." He paused to allow that to sink in, "And it must be done in secret. Prince Edward will be with just his cousin Henry Almain and will not wear royal livery. He will be addressed merely as Lord Edward. I know that it is likely he will be recognised but we do all that we can to disguise his identity. The Lord Edward wishes us to make him a warrior."

I felt my heart sink. We were to be the bodyguards of a youth of little more than thirteen or fourteen years of age.

My uncle saw my face and nodded, "Aye, it is a task fit for Hercules, Henry Samuel. None shall know that he has crossed to Aquitaine although his identity may well be discovered."

"And what is it that we do, uncle?" I could not help but keep the edge from my voice.

He was patient and that told me that he did not agree with my orders, "I fear it is a hard task. The Earl of Leicester is Seneschal and rules Aquitaine for Prince Edward but he has angered the populace. You will ride to London where the Lord Lieutenant of Aquitaine has been summoned to account for his actions. You are to be the king's eyes and ears in Aquitaine when the earl returns there."

Alfred said, "Why not simply remove de Montfort from his post and put someone better suited to the task?"

"De Montfort has powerful allies both amongst the Poitevins and here in England. He is one of the richest men in this land. King Henry dares not challenge him…yet."

"And what powers do we have?"

My uncle proffered a parchment, "This is the letter that tells all you work for King Henry, it is a royal warrant. I fear this parchment will be your only protection apart from your mail. More, Prince Edward is keen to learn about his lands. He is too young yet to rule but he is clever and knows the value of a good scouting expedition. You will be travelling alone in Gascony and there will be more than enough enemies there."

I nodded and took the parchment. I read it and saw that it was quite clear that we had the protection of the crown but as the crown feared the man that we were supposed to tame that, in itself, made it almost a worthless document.

"And how long will this take?"

I saw from his face that this was the worst part of the news, "I know not. It could be weeks, but I fear years."

"So my unborn child may be toddling before I get to hold him?"

"Why do you think we are here? This is the burden the knights of this family have ever borne. The king trusts our blood and that is an honour."

I smiled at Geoffrey, "Perhaps you should ask to stay here with my uncle."

My uncle's former squire gave me a sad smile, "And where is the honour in that, Sir Henry?"

I rolled the parchment, "Then let us make a start for we have much to do. When are we due in London, uncle?"

"Ten days hence!"

My heart sank as even riding hard we would struggle to make London in a week. We had but three days to gather our men, equipment and say our goodbyes.

My uncle nodded, sagely and said, "It goes without saying that whatever I can do for you I shall."

My grandfather had taught me to deal with each problem as it arose. If you looked at the forest of problems there would be no way through. You studied each tree, I nodded to Thomas, "Thomas needs a squire."

Thomas gave me a sad smile, "My father is letting me have Ralph."

Ralph was his father's squire but as my aunt's husband had foregone war then he had no need of one. Ralph was as stout a warrior as you could wish and whilst no longer in the first flush of youth, he was a father who had an eighteen-year-old son, he would be able to guide Thomas and that was a relief.

"And how many men do we take?"

Alfred must have been thinking of this issue since we had been given the task, "We need to be mounted and that will limit us. I believe we have twenty archers who can ride well and," he added, "have no family commitments."

My uncle nodded, "Aye and that is a good point."

"And there are fourteen spearmen who are good riders. They may lack mail but that may prove useful."

My uncle looked at Geoffrey, his former squire, "You would not take men at arms?"

Geoffrey looked at me and I replied, "Geoffrey is right. We may well need speed and I cannot see us taking part in charges with heavy horse. Spearmen who can ride will suit. That will leave you with men at arms should the Scots become belligerent."

"I think that is highly unlikely. Our King Henry has a hidden plan and I cannot see it yet but he chose you for a reason, Henry Samuel, and I cannot yet fathom it." He stood and took out his sword. "Let us kneel here and swear an oath." We all did as he said, took out our swords and knelt, holding the crosspieces close to our mouths. "We are the blood of the warlord and as brothers in blood and brothers in arms swear to fight as one and to bring all home safely if it is possible."

We all swore and then my uncle said, "And may the spirits of the warriors past watch over the warriors present. Amen!"

That my aunt and grandmother were unhappy was made quite clear as we ate a final meal on the night before we left. Grandmother was tearful while Lady Mary scowled each time the king's name was mentioned. All the family was invited, including Sir Geoffrey Fitzurse, Thomas' father. Sir Richard of Hartburn was also present as were Sir Petr and Sir Folki. My uncle wished them to give us their advice. Sir Folki was the oldest knight and had fought in the Baltic. He knew better than any the problems of fighting far from home. All their advice was sage. Thomas' father said the least and that reflected his character. I confess that I was distracted and should not have been. Grandfather had often told me to make the most of such evenings but my mind was a maelstrom. It was filled with all the problems that might occur whilst on the king's service. Prince Edward was a major factor as was his cousin, Henry Almain. When they became men they would be the two most powerful ones in the realm. They would bring with them bodyguards although my uncle had said no servants. This was to be a way of showing Prince Edward the rigours of the campaign. The biggest problem, in my mind, was how I would deal with the Earl of Leicester, and I hoped that King Henry would make that disappear at the meeting to be held at Westminster Hall. The optimist in me hoped that Simon de Montfort would take a knee before his king and our visit to Gascony would be peaceful.

"My love."

I turned and saw a smiling Eirwen, "Yes?"

"Your mother asked if the goose was cooked to your satisfaction?"

I realised that I had been so distracted that I had eaten nothing. My mother had been a widow for a long time and I knew that she always worried about me. I saw it now on her face. I smiled, "I am sorry, mother, I have allowed the worry of the journey to make me rude." I cut a slice from the goose that Dick had placed before me. My aunt had spared no expense and the bird had been cooked with lemons. The meat melted in my mouth. "It is excellent." I nodded to Dick who placed it back in the centre of the table and then retired a pace or two.

My mother leaned across Eirwen and said to me, "Alfred is your brother, and you can rely on him. Share your burden and remember that this is your home; not Aquitaine."

I dabbed my mouth and fingers with my cloth, "The heir to the throne is in my charge and that, mother, is a mighty weight."

She nodded, "It is ever thus with this family. I have watched the knights of the valley leave to serve the king but until now we were not separated by the sea. You be careful and know that I shall be at Elton with Eirwen until you return."

My mother had, since my father's death, lived with my grandfather and grandmother. I could understand why she now chose Elton. There were two ladies in Stockton Castle and she would be of more use at Elton. At my home, she would be a support for my wife. I knew that they would be good for one another and, surprisingly, that thought made me brighten and I put the distractions of the journey from my mind and I began to enjoy the feast. I became louder and funnier. I was not drunk, I drank sparingly but I knew how to tell a tale and a joke. Alfred did too and I watched my mother's face break into a smile as we two became troubadours and entertained.

Thomas also tried to be cheerful but I saw his father had a face as black as thunder. He was not happy. Sir Geoffrey was not family but he had spent so long in this hall that he felt as though he was and I saw Sir Richard of Hartburn giving him what looked like sage advice.

Matthew appeared at my side and said, quietly, "My father asks that you come to speak with him but let not the others know." He hesitated, "He said to say that you go to make water."

I smiled at my young cousin, "Thank you. Where is he?"

"I am sorry, I forgot. He is in grandfather's solar."

"Good. Now you cut along, and I will follow." Matthew was small enough to disappear in an instant. I stood and said loudly, "It must be my age for I need to make water almost as soon as I drink, these days!"

It made all laugh and I slipped out to head to the garderobe that was closest to the solar. My uncle was waiting within the solar with a single candle burning. "You will be leaving early and there will be people around. Since I gave you the command of the king, we have not had the chance to be alone and I need to speak with you. Sit." I did as he commanded. There was no wine for this needed clear heads. "The king is playing games and I know not why. Since the command, I have wracked my brains but cannot fathom the solution. I am not my father who would have worked it all out in a moment. Until the Prince asked to go with you, I thought that you were to be the sacrificial lamb. I wondered if the king thought that Simon de Montfort might harm you in some way and that would make the knights of the north angry enough to fight for the king against the Earl of Leicester. With the prince with you that will not happen."

"Like you uncle, I have tried to see the king's plan but I cannot. I will not worry about that until I have to. I shall do as grandfather did with me. I will try to mould Prince Edward and his cousin, Henry, into warriors worthy to lead the yeomen of England. As for de Montfort? If he acts against the wishes of the king or the prince then I am duty-bound to tell him so."

My uncle nodded, "You are so like your father and yet in your words and your face I see my own father. Perhaps this is meant to be. The Warlord raised Prince Henry to be a great king and it may be that is your fate too. Our family, it seems, has little choice about such matters and a higher power than we determines our actions."

Chapter 3

Henry Samuel

Raised voices in Westminster Hall

The two men who led the archers and the spearmen were sons of warriors who had served my grandfather and uncle. Jack, son of Oswald had aspirations to be a man at arms and he was ambitious. He wore, uniquely amongst the men he led, a hauberk although all of the men had coifs, arming caps and open-faced helmets as well as a spear, sword and shield. He had been an obvious choice to lead the spearmen. Henry son of Harry Longbow was the best archer in the valley. Many men said he was Sir Richard, the Warlord's archer, reborn. Henry did not like such allusions not least because none had seen the famous Dick, buried in the cemetery in the castle, loose a bow. Henry just said that he was content that none could beat him on the long mark at the green of St John's well. On a good day, he could send an arrow over three hundred paces and that was prodigious. None disagreed with him. I was pleased that we had Ralph with us as he was more experienced than any of us. He would be able to help both the squires and the spearmen. We were a youthful conroi and I guessed similar to the one my grandfather had led to the Baltic on his crusade. The more I thought about it the more I realised that the Warlord must have been about my age when he took on the far more onerous task of restoring Empress Matilda to the crown. Both men had far more daunting missions than the one that faced me and that made me feel better.

I turned in the saddle to look at our column as we headed down the Vale of York. We had brought no servants and the squires led our spare horses whilst the spearmen and archers led the sumpters with the supplies. We had not taken war horses; Alan had given us good hackneys and rouncys. The king had not yet told my uncle how we were to get to Aquitaine, but I assumed he would pay for ships. I saw that the squires chatted easily together. Ralph would have to get used to riding long distances again but I knew that Dick and the others would be picking his brain already. Alfred and Geoffrey rode easily together and I heard their laughter that bespoke of a close relationship. Thomas rode alone and I sighed. My uncle's last words had been about his nephew. I was to make him a knight and my uncle knew that would be an even harder task than keeping safe the son of King Henry.

I reined back so that I was riding next to my cousin, "You know, Thomas, that you have the best of squires. Had not your father given up the path to war then Ralph would have become either a knight or a captain. He will help to guide you."

Thomas nodded and lowered his voice, "The trouble is, cuz, that now people call me Sir Thomas and that evokes memories of our grandfather. Will people expect deeds such as the hero of Arsuf might have performed?" Before I could answer he went on, "I have seen you and Alfred fight on the battlefield. You both make it look so easy. I fear for my life each time I draw my sword and I am sure I do not have mail enough to protect me."

I laughed but not in a cruel way; I understood him. "You see that I do not wear a helmet?"

"Aye, you wear an arming cap with a coif held in place by laces and a padded roll. I would not ride to battle without a helmet."

"I have less protection for my head than with my helmet but unless we fight in a battle with serried ranks of charging knights then this affords me more protection. I do not use a shaffron on my horse's head for the same reason. Speed and being able to manoeuvre are far more important. Now my padded gambeson is thick and Eirwen and her ladies have worked many an hour ensuring that blows from a mace or the flat of a sword will not hurt me. Mail links can be broken but unless you are especially unlucky then you will be able to repair them before you fight again. Lastly, think about your shield. See how Geoffrey and Alfred ride as I do with the shield hanging over our left legs?" He nodded. "It means we can pull it up in an instant. Do not try to be brave,

Thomas, protect yourself and bravery will come when you least expect it. The three of us will bear the brunt of the work but you need to watch and learn. Let us say that your apprenticeship as a squire has been extended a little, eh?"

"But I had so much yet to learn, cousin."

"And you will learn it. We have the ride to London and then a crossing to Gascony. I do not think we will be there any time soon. Talk to Geoffrey. He was the last to be knighted and his advice will be sage, despite his youth, and lastly, rely on your squire. Dick is like my rock."

Thomas shook his head, "And I know I was a disappointment to our uncle. He sighed each time he gave a command."

"And that is because you always seemed to question his words. You are a knight now and the men and archers will look to you. Fear not cuz, our uncle asked me to mould you and I shall."

The royal warrant the king had given to my uncle meant we had accommodation in the royal residences along our route. Of course, the lords and constables were not happy about the expense but what could they do? It had an unexpected consequence. They were so unhappy that they spoke more openly about the problems King Henry faced. They seemed happy to revel in the unrest. This was especially true in the midlands where Simon de Montfort was all-powerful even though he resided in Aquitaine. We learned that he had a web of allies all of whom supported his views. Since his public declamation of the king after his disaster in Poitou, it had encouraged the Earl of Leicester to be increasingly vocal in his criticism of the king. His marriage to the king's sister, Eleanor of England, gave him a path to the crown and I now began to see his ambitions. By the time we reached London, I had a clearer picture of this ambitious Frenchman and I still could not see why the king had made him Seneschal. I had enough time to work out that he had sent him as far from London as he could and he hoped that he would fail. It had been a gamble and the meeting at the palace suggested to me that it had not paid off.

Whilst the meeting between king and earl would take place in Westminster Hall, we were accommodated in the Tower of London. It was a fortress and not a palace but that suited us for we were warriors. The king was in the newly built Wakefield Tower in the inner ward and close to the river gate. We were allocated a newly built warrior hall in the outer ward. We were close to the stables and, more importantly for us, the kitchens and bakery. The smell of food took away the stink of the river.

It was as we were settling in that I met the pursuivant who would accompany us to Aquitaine. Robert Williams was, I learned, just four years older than I was but he had a careworn face. I liked the Welshman who had not only a wicked sense of humour but also a great depth of knowledge that would stand us in good stead. He was a pursuivant and so he bowed when he greeted me, "Sir Henry?"

"Aye, I am he and from your garb, you are the pursuivant."

"Robert Williams of Chepstow at your service, my lord." His eyes and demeanour invited conversation but the busy and bustling hall was clearly not the place for it.

Pointing to the walkway I said, "Perhaps, while we talk, we can walk. The king has made many improvements since last I was here."

He pointed out the new towers, the Wakefield and Lanthorn as well as the watergate and the improved gatehouse. We stopped at the recently completed gatehouse at the western end of the outer ward which gave entry to the city and was the best gatehouse I had ever seen. It was a large area and the two sentries allowed us to have some privacy on one side. That meant we could speak more openly. I had to trust this pursuivant for he knew matters I did not and so I was open with him.

"Robert, I fear that my task is doubly impossible. How can I rein in the Earl of Leicester and how do I train the prince whilst keeping him safe?"

He nodded but gave me a comforting smile, "Aye, my lord, you have been set a Herculean task." His eyes flickered to the side and back and he lowered his voice, "I would be honest with you, Sir Henry, for I admired your grandfather and I am truly in awe of your grandsire, the Warlord. I know you not but I believe you are cut from the same cloth as those two heroes. You play chess?" I nodded, "Then you know that sometimes a pawn has to be sacrificed but ofttimes a good player will recognise the sacrifice and ignore it. A knight is a powerful piece for it is quick and can move in a different way from other pieces. It can threaten. The sacrifice of a knight is a bold move."

"We are to be sacrificed?"

"You misunderstand me, lord. I am sorry. You are the knight who tempts the enemy to try to take you. From what I have heard many have tried that and failed. Simon de Montfort is an ambitious man. King Henry, I believe, hoped he would fail in Aquitaine. He has but not in the way the king hoped. Simon de Montfort has used the opportunity to enlarge his fortune and reward his friends. In that, he is not dissimilar to King Henry. Had King Henry wished a knight to be sacrificed then he would have chosen someone other than the grandson of Sir Thomas, the hero of Arsuf and the great-grandson of the Warlord who saved England. King Henry does not think that de Montfort will find you such an easy morsel to swallow. We may be bait but we are bait with teeth. I am just grateful for this chance to redeem my fortunes."

The bitter tone at the end of the sentence made me cock my head to one side, "You have suffered?"

He nodded, "My family had lands in Wales. Those lands now belong to William de Valance."

"And yet you serve King Henry as pursuivant."

"It was a crumb offered to me and, if truth be told, I am less martial than my brother who made the mistake of fighting for his birthright. He died and I live but I have not forgotten. I am a warrior and a knight but I chose the path of the pursuivant." He tapped his head, "I will use my mind and my skill in languages to restore what I once had. If I serve the king well then he will reward me with a manor and as the heir is with us then that does no harm for I am patient."

This was a complex man.

"As for Prince Edward and his cousin, fear not. Both are keen to become knights and they are not pampered popinjays. You do not need to worry about keeping them safe, they come with two bodyguards each. Godfrey, Walter, John, and Kurt are not knights. They are hired swords and they are paid very well. Kurt was a sergeant of the Teutonic Order and your grandfather's story will endear you to him. As for the others, they all served in the Holy Land in one capacity or another. If there is a danger to the prince or his cousin then they will be the ones who will die to save the youths. They swore oaths in Westminster Abbey."

That was all he needed to tell me. A man who swore an oath in a cathedral, especially a crusader, would keep his promise. The rest of our talk was about the politics of Aquitaine and Gascony, the Duchy of Aquitaine. Robert had been in Poitou with King Henry on his ill-fated campaign and he knew it well. "The land is a different country and like any country, there are factions and counties within that land. De Montfort has used the traditional conflicts to create discord. He pays mercenaries and hires swords to ride through the land causing mischief. He likes the land to be unstable while he profits from it."

"Then the king must act."

"And he does. He sends his knight to trap de Montfort and to sweeten the trap he uses his son as bait too. King Henry may not be a warrior but he is the most cunning of men." He stopped and put his head close to mine. "This finery will be left in England before we leave. I will wear plain clothes so that when de Montfort takes the bait I shall return to the king and he will bring an army to deal with his enemies."

"Then you have a task as unenviable as mine."

"Aye, but unlike you, there is the promise of a manor in Herefordshire and that is the honeyed bait King Henry offers me."

By the time we returned to the hall we had an understanding and, more importantly, we trusted each other. Usually, that came through force of arms but we just seemed to like each other and as I had looked into his eyes, I saw a man who would keep his word. I discovered that he had been trained to be a knight and, indeed, had skills with a sword as well as being a good horseman but Robert was a cerebral man who liked books and reading. He had aspirations to write. I did not understand that but I respected it. Alfred, Thomas and Geoffrey had watched our progress from the gatehouse and were waiting for us. I introduced them and then asked, "So, Robert, we are in your hands. What do we do now?"

He smiled, "You are commanded to present yourself at Westminster Hall at terces. Your squires will wait without and others that you brought will remain here. I will accompany your knights into the hall and we will stand close to the king but in the background. The hall is large and can be gloomy. The king wishes us to see but not be seen clearly."

Alfred laughed, "That is a fine trick if you can manage it."

Robert joined in the laughter and nodded, "Aye, it is. All that it means, Sir Alfred, is that we must be seen but not encroach upon the king. His half-brothers and his brother, the Earl of Cornwall, along with The Lord Edward and Henry of Almain will be closest to the king." He lowered his voice, "It will be interesting to see who is brought by Simon de Montfort."

Thomas asked, "And until then?"

"Our time is our own. Cooks will fetch food after vespers and we eat in the warrior hall. Of course, if you wish there is a hall in the tower where we can dine with the high and the mighty."

"No, as you will learn we eat with our men and we do not disparage them because they were not noble-born."

"And in that, you are a world away from those who surround both the king and de Montfort. This shall be an interesting time for me. I will dine with you in the hall if you permit it."

"Of course and my fellow knights can pick your brains as carefully as did I. We are simple country knights who are unused to the ways of court."

Robert was an observant man and as we ate, he was able to add colour to the characters we had already met and were about to meet. "De Montfort's brother Amaury is totally loyal to de Montfort. It was he who, along with the Earl of Cornwall, negotiated his release from his captivity in the Holy Land. The two brothers surround themselves with other Poitevin knights. It is how they manage to control Aquitaine and, I suspect, why King Henry, despite their disagreements, appointed him Lord Lieutenant for he has support from Poitou if not Gascony."

"I do not understand this disagreement." The other three knights were leaning forward to hear this information. I had thought it was some sort of secret but when Robert laughed loudly, I knew it was not.

"You do not know?" We shook our heads. "The king was not particularly happy that de Montfort married his sister but he accepted it. However, when de Montfort ran into financial difficulties, he cited the king as the guarantor for his debts." He shook his head, "He did not ask the king's permission and they fled to France. Tomorrow will be interesting for the de Montfort brothers like the safety of France and Aquitaine to England."

If nothing else we were in for a lively debate in Westminster.

Alfred was thoughtful and asked, "Robert, you speak of Aquitaine, Gascony and Poitou. Are those places interchangeable?"

He shook his head, "Aquitaine is the duchy. It belonged to King Henry the second's wife, Eleanor of Aquitaine. The northern part close to the coast is called Poitou and the lower part, which lies close to the border with Castile, is Gascony. The Gascons are a fiercely proud people and always have been. They do not like the Poitevins and it is they who are persecuted by de Montfort."

We had much to think on that night as we slept in the castle begun by King William the first.

Rising and breakfasting early we ensured that we were perfectly presented. In our blue tunics with the gryphon we would stand out and all men knew the livery of Sir Thomas of Stockton. Eyes would be on us and this far from our home we would be judged. Dick and the other squires rose even earlier to groom and curry our horses so that they looked their best. Robert still wore his pursuivant garb but once we left England, he would become anonymous.

We rode out of the recently constructed western gate and entered the city. There was a market on most days and already carters were pulling their wares to the Cheap that was the place the market was held. It was in the western part of the city and we had to pass close by to get to Westminster. Those who wished to buy were also out and about but fewer of them than there would be later. We were a novelty in our livery and men stared at us. I did not enjoy the experience. In the north, we might have the attention but we would have earned that on the field of battle. Here we were a curiosity. I was also aware, thanks to my conversation with Robert, that there would be men in the city who worked for de Montfort and his brother. We had to look for enemies who wore no livery. The Abbey dominated the hall and I saw that Westminster Hall along with its attendant buildings was not a place to be defended. We passed the area before the Abbey where men could claim sanctuary and then followed the road to the Great Hall. It had been built originally in the time of the Confessor but it was William the Conqueror who had made it the magnificent building it was.

King Henry's guards, on the doors, recognised both our livery and Robert Williams. They parted their pikes and we were allowed to enter. The stone floor seemed to stretch forever and when I looked up, I was amazed at the height of the hall. Light poured through ornate windows at one end and I found myself in awe of it. It felt to me more like a cathedral than what it was, a Great Hall. I had thought that my grandfather had a fine hall but it would have fitted inside this one many times over. Even the one at Middleham was tiny in comparison. I wondered why the king did not fortify the hall and make it his fortress in London then I remembered that he had the Tower. The largest donjon in the land and a river for defence was a safer place to fight off enemies.

We were amongst the first to enter and Robert guided us to one side where a door led to other chambers. There was a staircase that led to the upper floors and our guide pointed out the undercroft of St Mary's chapel where only the most important of religious leaders were buried. He shook his head and said, "It is the most frightening place I have been and despite being a church is not somewhere I am comfortable."

After we entered, Robert identified other knights and nobles when they walked into the huge hall. Each group stayed together. We were not a faction but the nature of King Henry's rule, inherited from his father, meant that men tended to cluster with like-minded souls. When Simon de Montfort and his brother Amaury strode into the hall I knew, before Robert spoke, who they were. The two brothers entered with two boys, I guessed they were Simon de Montfort's sons and half a dozen knights. I recognised the type. They were hired swords and looked to be Swabians. I had fought against such men and knew their skills. The main reason I knew it to be de Montfort, his white gryphon on a red background apart, was his manner. By the way he strode in and waved, regally, it seemed to me that he was giving the impression that he owned the hall and I wondered then why the king had chosen this hall rather than the Tower for the meeting. My grandfather had told me how clever the king was but I could see no advantage to this choice of venue.

The king, his brother, bishops, senior leaders and his son followed soon after. We all bowed as he entered but I saw that de Montfort and his party barely bent at the hip. The king nodded to us and then stood at what seemed to be a prearranged spot facing the de Montfort party. It was only then that I saw that the nobles who had entered early were divided into the king's men and de Montfort's. It was like two battles arrayed before the other. The difference was that weapons were sheathed and any wounds that were caused would come from sharp words. We were to the right of the king and behind him but the ones who were before us were churchmen who were short in stature. We had a clear view of de Montfort and I knew that he had a clear view of us. That was confirmed as, just before the king spoke, he stared at us and then said something to his brother who shook his head. I guessed then that the king was using us to plant doubt in de Montfort's mind. He knew not who we were and that was unsettling him.

When he began to speak it was in a chastising tone which, as I saw from the Poitevin's face, clearly annoyed him, "So, Earl, you have finally deigned to come and explain yourself to me. Know that my son and I are both mightily displeased at the way you have treated our people in Aquitaine. They have implored me to act to constrain your violence."

De Montfort said, easily despite the narrowed eyes and pinched lips, "They are traitors and dissenters, King Henry, and I merely protect the interests of The Lord Edward."

The king turned to the Bishop of London who proffered a parchment, "And you have not profited from such… protection?"

That it was evidence of corruption was clear from de Montfort's response. I saw the corners of de Montfort's mouth turn down as he became angry, "And do I not deserve payment for keeping law and order in Aquitaine?" His voice was becoming louder and I had not yet heard him accord King Henry any kind of title. Was the king allowing de Montfort to dig a hole for himself?

The king was calm as he spoke, "You have not presented to my son yet the accounts of the Duchy. Why is that?"

The slight change of tack appeared to confuse de Montfort who stammered, "Am I a bookkeeper or do you think me a stinking Jew who tots up columns of figures? I do not keep accounts. That is for others."

"Then we will help you. With the Archbishop of Canterbury and the Cardinal, we shall examine your accounts and see if you have acted honourably."

That seemed to set off de Montfort. It may have been that his honour was impugned or, more likely, that he had something to hide, "Do not impugn my honour, King Henry. I was not the king who so dishonourably abandoned his people in France. That was you."

The king reacted angrily for the first time. De Montfort had struck a nerve, "You dare to question me thus. Your words are treasonous."

I glanced around to see what Robert made of all this and I could see that he was as surprised as I was at this turn of events. Would the war of words turn into violence and would Westminster Hall see blood spilt? I forced myself to keep my hand from my sword. I knew that if one man touched his sword then the hall might well erupt into violence.

After a silence that seemed to last an eternity de Montfort said, with a cold smile upon his lips, "Do what you will. I return to Aquitaine to continue to rule that land for your son." He almost spat the words out. I thought for one moment that he would add another insult by turning his back on the king but just at the last moment, his brother made him begin to walk out backwards.

The king had regained his composure and showed masterly timing for as the brothers bent at the hips he said, "And to that end, my son will send, to visit his lands, a most trusted family of knights, the heirs of the Warlord of Cleveland, Sir Henry Samuel, Sir Thomas, Sir Alfred and Sir Geoffrey. They have my son's permission to report on the state of the duchy and their honour is, I can assure you, without a stain."

From his half bow, Simon de Montfort looked up and he looked directly at me. The king's arm had identified us. The Seneschal of Aquitaine was just forty feet from me but the light from the window highlighted his face and I saw it was a mask of anger, "Send who you will. They may look where they will but Aquitaine is a dangerous place and I am not responsible for the rocks beneath which snakes lurk." He was threatening us before we had even left England.

They left and we remained to watch his supporters follow him. There were not as many as had stood behind him. I was still unsure what had just happened but whatever it was King Henry had managed to divide the supporters of his enemy. The king turned to me and smiled, "He knows now who you are. Dine with me tonight at my hall in the tower."

With that, he turned and left. I waited with Geoffrey, my brother and cousin along with Robert until we were the last ones in the hall. I turned, "You say there is a chapel here?"

"There are two, St Mary's and St Stephen's. St Mary's is closer."

"Then let us go there and say prayers for I fear the king has just signed our death warrant."

Chapter 4

Henry Samuel
Choppy Seas

The meal was a small affair and the only ones seated at the table were the king and queen, his son, brother, nephew, Robert and we four. We dined not in the Tower itself but the newly built Wakefield Tower where the king had a small dining hall. It was cosy but the food and the wine, whilst delicious and expensive were the last things on my mind. King Henry was all business and he gave us our commands as we ate. The servants were our squires and they had a difficult task. I felt sorry for Ralph who must have thought his days of fetching and carrying at table were a thing of the past.

"Here is your royal warrant." The king slid over a sealed parchment. "My son's presence guarantees that you will be accorded accommodation, but this warrant gives you permission to raise loyal troops."

I took it, "But sire, I thought that your son would be incognito."

"And he will. Sir Henry, one reason I chose you for this is that you have the ability to think quickly and make good decisions. You will determine which seigneur can be trusted. If they are not to be trusted then you will not need to reveal my son's identity. My son and his cousin will have to act as a squire. I am sure that it will stand them in good stead in the future. As I recall, my grandsire, King Henry did much the same when he tagged along with the Warlord." He took another parchment and a purse of coins, "Here is the warrant for the two ships that will take you to Bordeaux and a purse for expenses. I expect a detailed account of the expenditure." The king was renowned for his penny-pinching.

I took them. The purse was heavy. I was chewing but I knew not what the food was I ate for I could taste nothing.

"My son wishes to see the full extent of de Montfort's terror. Travel as far and wide as you can. My brother and I will be raising an army to rid the land of de Montfort, but I need to know first which lords in this realm are loyal to me and which need to be punished. When that is done we shall bring loyal knights with me. You will need to find the canker in Aquitaine. That is where Robert comes in. As soon as you deem you have the information then send him to me and I will bring the wrath of England upon the head of Simon de Montfort who dares to threaten me in the hall of the Confessor." I heard the reverence in his words and knew that he had chosen the Confessor's hall because the saint, after whom he had named his son, was a hero of his.

His plan seemed to me, a risky one but as I later learned from Robert, assassination was rare and there were other ways of eliminating enemies. He did not rule out kidnap but The Lord Edward would not be harmed.

"You will not leave from Winchelsea as that is too public a port. Instead, you will pick up the ships at Southampton. It is a longer sea voyage, but you have more chance of avoiding any threats that de Montfort might pose."

"Threats, sire?"

He smiled, "You saw that today we angered him and he may react. Your ships will be the equal of any ship you might meet and I do not doubt that you will reach Aquitaine safely. It may be an interesting voyage but that will all give my son and his cousin experience, eh Sir Henry?"

I now understood the trials and tribulations that my grandfather had endured as he had served first King Richard, King John and finally, King Henry. It was not easy and seemed to me, a thankless task.

Before we retired, I spoke with Prince Edward, "I have a fine warhorse, Sir Henry and I will not hold you up."

I shook my head, "The last thing we need is a warhorse, my lord. You and your cousin need a good riding horse, a hackney would be best. You need a beast that can eat up the miles and I can assure you that we will not be fighting from the backs of horses." He looked disappointed and I continued, "If we have to fight then I have failed in my duty.

I need to anticipate any threat to you and deal with it before you can be harmed."

He looked at me thoughtfully, "I will try my best to learn from you. Will I be able to bring my tutor?"

Shaking my head I said, "We need men like your bodyguards, warriors. The lessons you learn will not come from books and you should watch my knights and squires for the lessons. They know their business, none better."

The horse master at the Tower had good horses and the two that were given to Prince Edward and Henry of Almain were amongst the best I had seen. We did not leave as early as I might have wished but there appeared to me, to be no hurry. The two ships would await our pleasure and better to arrive there safely than with horses we had pushed beyond their limits. I set the pattern for our formation early on. I had Henry son of Harry put our best four archers as scouts to ride two hundred paces ahead of us. The rest were behind the baggage. I split my spearmen so that half were with Jack son of Oswald before us. The prince and his cousin were placed behind me and my knights with the four redoubtable bodyguards behind them. Robert rode next to me. Dick and the squires rode before the baggage. I was spreading my experience throughout the column. My four archer scouts had signals to let me know of any danger and they would be my eyes and ears.

I was glad when we crossed London Bridge and left London behind. Simon de Montfort had too many friends in the city and the sooner we were hidden in the countryside the better. Edward and his cousin chattered all the way south and I knew why. This was an adventure for the two of them. Freed from the shackles of court and a tutor it was what every young man wanted. For me, however, it was anything but an adventure. I watched every house and hedgerow that we passed to spy out danger. I knew that it was unlikely, but it could happen. We reached Southampton early the next day having stayed overnight in the royal palace at Winchester. It was no longer the residence of the king but it was a fine old hall and we were treated well. It meant we reached the quayside well before noon and I led us directly to the two ships.

The two cogs were well made, and each had a forecastle and an aft castle. I saw weapons stacked by the masts. The ships' captains were fighters and I approved of that. Captain Joshua Shipwright was the senior captain and he was keen to expedite both our loading and our sailing. "If you would trust me to load your horses, my lord, you can avail yourself of the inn yonder where they have fine ale and good food. It will take a couple of hours to get them all loaded safely."

I think the two young men, not to mention some of the squires, were disappointed not to be able to watch the loading. I knew that the sailors would prefer to load without our stares and I also knew that a few days at sea without hot food was a good enough reason to use the inn. If the captain recommended it then I knew it would be good.

"Thank you, captain. We can leave our mounts in their hands. Henry, have the baggage unloaded and leave a couple of men to watch the horses and the bags. You can have them relieved in an hour. They will not miss out on hot food." The landlord was delighted to see so many rich purses enter his inn. As he shooed away the customers who were nursing their ale and called for his doxies, I said, "Just food. We have no time for your ladies."

His smile faded a little as he saw the chance of extra coins slipping away, "Of course, my lord."

"I will pay the money that is due." I paused and added, "I am on the king's service, and I will scrutinise the amount."

The smile was completely wiped from his face, "Yes, my lord."

My men sat together and the four bodyguards did the same. Robert and the two cousins sat at a long table with me, my squires and knights. The menu was a limited one and the hot food was a fish stew. As a port, it was to be expected but the cook had not scrimped and there were healthy chunks of white fish as well as shellfish both large and small. The ale was passable, but I knew that the archers and spearmen would complain about the lack of body. Of course, it would be better than the small beer they would have on the four- or five-day voyage south. I enjoyed my repast and asked for a second loaf to mop up the juices. It was worth the extra penny and besides the king was paying.

Robert smiled as we four knights and our squires tucked in as though we had not eaten for a week. "You have a healthy appetite, Sir Henry."

I laughed, "One of the first lessons my grandfather taught me was to fill your boots when you could for who knew when you would go on short rations."

He laughed, "I take it, *'fill your boots'* is a northern expression?"

Alfred nodded and used a piece of bread to also mop up the juices, "We shall educate you, Master Robert. We shall learn the ways of the court from you, and you shall learn how to be a northerner. I know that you will have the better of the arrangement."

I saw Edward and Henry of Almain taking it all in. The men around them were real warriors and not the posing lords and their attendants. When my men said something there was no hidden meaning.

Henry son of Harry ensured that those who ate the quickest relieved the ones on watch. All would be equitable amongst my men. I kept a watch on the wax tablet where the landlord marked the drinks, loaves, and bowls of food we consumed. He spied me watching and I knew we would not be rooked.

"Dick, go outside and see how far along we are with the loading."

"Yes, my lord."

He hurried out and I turned to Robert and the two royal cousins, "I am not sure if you have sailed before but performing your ablutions involves hanging your backside over the side. Before we leave here, I would suggest you avail yourself of the facilities. It may well be more primitive than you are used but…"

Godfrey, one of the bodyguards grinned, "I would heed his lordship's advice, my lord. We travelled from the Holy Land, and I can tell you that the sea twixt France and here is the most violent that you will encounter."

The two cousins looked at each other and nodded. They hurried off and I was pleased that Walter and Kurt followed them. The bodyguards knew their business. They had not been back long when Dick came in with the news that the horses and baggage had been loaded and we were to board. I paid the landlord and we headed outside. The sky had darkened while we had been within and there was a biting wind laden with rain swirling. The seas would be rough.

"My lord, the tide is on the turn and the wind will be from our steerboard quarter."

"Then we board." The knights, our squires, Robert, the two royal cousins and their bodyguards would be aboard the larger vessel, Captain Shipwright's, *'The Maid of Plymouth'*. Half of the archers would also travel with us.

As we boarded, I said to Godfrey, "You may choose, forecastle or aft?"

I saw him rub his beard, "If I have a choice my lord, then the forecastle."

I was curious, "Of course, but may I ask why for it is the smaller of the two?"

He grinned, "Quieter. I have sailed in the aft castle and we were constantly woken in the night when the captain ordered his crew to change the tack. This will be cosier but quieter and we can guard our charges better."

I nodded and waved my men to the aft castle. I lowered my voice as Dick and the squires headed towards the stern, following the knights. "You have the harder task in Aquitaine, you know that."

He said, "Aye, but I do not think that any will try to kill our charges. Abduction is another matter and, of course, we have their own wild youth to contend with but we shall manage. Once the two are knighted then our task is done and we can enjoy life once more. Each crown we are paid goes towards that future and we will not risk jeopardising it."

I was satisfied and I turned to Robert, "You can choose your own cabin."

"I will use the aft with you and your knights. Tell me, where do the archers sleep?"

I spread my hand to encompass the deck. "Either below decks with the horses or here with the crew. Neither would be my choice."

The rain began in earnest before we had even reached the sea. My archers and squires were below deck calming the horses. Until they were used to the motion of the water, they would have to take it in turns to calm the animals. I saw that both Prince Edward and his cousin were now nervous because even in the river the motion of the ship was alarming. Their adventure might not be as much fun as they had hoped. Godfrey said, "My Lord Edward, let us retire to the cabin. We should keep as dry as we can. There will be no fire to dry our clothes until we reach land."

I hid my smile as the two young men realised that. My knights and I entered the darkness of the aft castle. Godfrey was right; this was the noisiest part of the ship. The captain and his officers shouted out their orders and even when they were silent there was the creak of the mighty rope beneath our feet as the steering board was moved. I took off my cloak and hung it from the hooks that would secure our beds for the night. We would be sleeping cheek by jowl and it would be cosy. Eirwen had cropped my hair before we left and I rubbed the stubble. Who knew what wildlife lay in the ship? There were upturned barrels in the cabin. I knew that when it rained, they would be taken on deck to be filled with rainwater but for now, they would act as crude seats.

"How long, cuz, do we endure this Stygian darkness?"

Thomas was the nautical virgin. "It could be ten days or more and we are dependent upon both the wind and the waves. A rough sea means we would have to reef our sails and slow. An adverse wind would mean we had to tack back and forth. Whenever it is not raining and there is light we will spend as much time as we can on deck."

Alfred added, "Aye, and we shall get to know each other well, cuz. You will learn that Henry Samuel can snore so loudly that I guarantee any rats or rodents will flee."

We could see faces in the gloom and Thomas looked down fearfully, "Rats?"

Geoffrey nodded, "Aye, they live in the hull of the ship but they will come close to us if we leave food about."

Thomas shook his head, "The task appointed by the king just became harder."

Two of the squires returned after an hour or so and when we neared the mouth of the river. The motion of the river was choppier. Edward said, "Dick and Ralph sent us back to get some sleep. The animals are restless and we are to relieve them in a couple of hours when the captain signals the change of watch."

Another sound we would become used to was the bell used to change the watches.

Edgar looked around, "We sleep here, my lord?"

I nodded, "And while we may not be ready for sleep we should use what little light there is to prepare the cabin for sleep. Edward, hold open the door while we find the beds."

Ships were very organised places and the rolled canvas was to be found stacked in wooden compartments like a sort of ladder. I took one and saw that there were no hooks but just ropes. We would have to tie them. I dropped my almost dry cloak to the deck and tied one end of the canvas bed to the hook. I sought one on the other side and fastened it too. "There. Edward and Edgar, I would suggest that you take the two closest to the cabin door."

Thomas asked, "How do we sleep?"

I knew there was an art to mounting these swinging beds and I searched my memory for the technique I had used. It came to me and, placing my hands on the two sides to spread the canvas, I rolled into it. There was a generous amount of canvas and I was cocooned within it. I began to take off my boots. "And now that I am here I will avail myself of some sleep. I cannot command it but I suggest you all take advantage of the gentle motion."

"Gentle?"

"Yes, Thomas, it will get worse when we reach the sea beyond the sight of land."

In truth, the motion encouraged sleep and I was soon in a deep sleep. My bladder woke me or perhaps it was the bell that must have sounded for feet pounded on the deck. I rolled out of the bed and contemplated, albeit briefly, donning my boots. Then I remembered that sailors went largely barefoot. I took off my breeches and then my hose. I placed the hose in one of the compartments and put on my breeches again. It might be undignified, but I would emulate the sailors. I dipped my body beneath my swaying and sleeping companions.

As I neared the door Ralph's voice spoke, "The horses are calmer now, lord, but Edward and Edgar will stay with them until dawn."

"Thank you, Ralph."

The chill breeze flecked with rain came as a shock to me and I regretted not donning my cloak. I had many lessons to relearn. I went to the leeward side of the ship and dropped my breeches. I had forgotten to tell my charges that the leeward side was the toilet. I hoped that Godfrey would remember. By the time I slipped back into the cabin I was chilled to the bone and I picked up my now dry cloak and used it to cover me. The ship sent me to sleep once more.

Dawn brought two pleasant surprises: first, the rain had stopped and there was a weak sun peering from behind scudding clouds and secondly, the captain had brought aboard hot food and with the pots wrapped in hay, which, when it had cooled, would be later fed to the horses, we had warm porridge. Served with dried apple and honey it was as fine a breakfast as I could remember.

We ate on the deck and I saw that Alfred had copied me and was barefoot. The others would learn. From the forecastle, I heard the sound of retching and saw the two royal cousins vomiting over the side. Some men, like me, appeared to be natural sailors. The royal pair were not.

The first four days at sea, after we had left the land, were a mixture of sun and showers. The sea was choppy but not wild and we all learned to become sailors, even Prince Edward and his cousin. They were young men and learned that if they wished to eat then they had to learn to control their guts. Captain Shipwright gave them the invaluable advice to stay on deck as much as possible and to watch the horizon. When the seas permitted it my knights and I brought our swords out for some practice. With the horses calmer the archers and squires also joined us on the deck. Of course, as soon as the crew had to adjust the sails then we were banished to the places we would not get under their feet. The Lord Edward could not believe how skilled were the lithe men who leapt to the top of the masts as though they were climbing stairs in a castle.

"Sir Henry, how do they manage that?"

"They spend long hours learning the skill. If you were to face them with a horse, whilst it is much lower than the masts they climb, they would find it a daunting experience."

We were on the larboard side of the ship and somewhere to the east of us lay France. The islands that England controlled still guarded that part of the land but once we passed them then until we reached the Garonne, we would be closer to the French than the English.

"My tutor told me that the land to the east used to belong to the crown until my grandfather lost it."

Bartholomew Pecche was treading a dangerous route if he was telling The Lord Edward the truth. I saw no reason to be dishonest. The prince had to trust me, "Aye, he did. Your grandfather made mistakes and while all men make mistakes, those made by kings have ramifications until the end of time."

"Like my father when he lost his war in Poitou?" I let my silence answer him. He nodded and said, "The Earl of Leicester is a dangerous man, is he not, Sir Henry?"

"He is but I think your father believes he has the measure of him."

"Do you?" I said nothing. "How would you deal with him?"

"Simple, strip him of his office and put him in the Tower as my guest."

He laughed and Henry of Almain who had joined us also laughed. "You are a direct man then, Sir Henry."

"Yes, my lord, for I have been a border knight my whole life and I know that compromise never works when you deal with one who seeks your home or," I added, "your crown."

"Then I am glad that you are with me. Know that I shall not be as unnecessary baggage. I might not be able to clamber up a mast but I can ride and do not fall off. You must do what you must do, Sir Henry, and let my bodyguards protect me."

I nodded, "Easier said than done, my lord, but I thank you."

The Norman coast jutted out into the sea and was like the jagged mouth of a shark that would rip out our keel. The captain was forced to head further into the bay and we met a storm that almost did for us. Even in the swinging beds, sleep was almost impossible and the neighing horses meant the squires and the archers lost any chance of rest. After a torrential and stormy night and half a day it abated and we found ourselves alone in the ocean. Our consort had gone.

I joined the captain, "Is there a plan for such an eventuality?"

Captain Shipwright nodded, "Aye, we repair our sails and then edge in to the east until we see the smudge on the horizon that is the coast and then we sail in a circle until either we see our consort or she sees us." he gave me a sad smile, "Our voyages are never easy my lord, and we shall get there when we get there. Trust to me and I will trust to God."

Ropes had been frayed and one of the sails had to be replaced. We kept out of the way as much as we could while the repairs were made and the captain edged gingerly towards the coast. It was slow and laborious but we could do nothing about it. I was just grateful that not a man had been lost and that must have been thanks to God watching over the heir to the throne. There was a crewman at the masthead helping to replace a rope and it was he who shouted the warning, "Sail, ho to the east." There was a pause. Seamen had good eyes and knew the lines of ships far better than we landsmen, "It is *'The Maid of Lewes'* and she is under attack from pirates."

The ship was our consort and the captain took decisive action, "Forget the repairs and make all sail. We cannot let these devils have English sailors."

I turned and shouted to my men, "Arm yourselves."

We hurried to the cabin and our chests which lay around the side. I took out my coif and arming cap. That would be my defence while I had my sword and long dagger for offence. The archers went below decks to fetch their war bows.

The Lord Edward asked, "Should we don mail?"

Godfrey answered for me, "Not unless you would like to see what the bottom of the sea looks like, my lord. Arming cap, coif and sword." The two youths nodded, "And keep behind us. If they are pirates then you will not be spared because of your youth."

I ran to the forecastle and shaded my eyes against the light. I could see the smudge that was France behind the cog and the French ships. I turned to a sailor who was tightening the forestay, "What ships are they?"

He glanced up and then resumed his work, "They are oared vessels, my lord. They have a small sail. When they are employed peacefully, they fish the waters close to the islands hereabouts but they are French and prefer to be pirates when they can."

"Can *'Maid'* hold them off?"

He looked up and nodded, "Your archers are aboard and, with your spearmen, perhaps they might. The low freeboard of the pirates means that *'Maid'* has the advantage of height but we must hurry." He finished his tightening of the stay and then hurried off to arm himself like the rest of the crew. They had boarding pikes, axes and short curved swords called falchions.

Dick joined me and he handed me a throwing spear, "I found these, my lord. You have a good eye and arm."

"Thanks, Dick, did you get one for yourself?" He nodded, "Then let us hope we are in time. We cannot last long in Aquitaine without spearmen."

That the pirates had not had long to assault the ship was clear. Our consort's captain had managed to try to sail away from the danger and the pirates had been forced to row further than they wished. However, as we closed with them, I saw that one pirate had placed his ship at the bows and that meant the cog was going nowhere. A second was at the stern while the third was trying to sail around to the steerboard side. They were trying to push the ship into the shallows where they would have the advantage.

Leaving my brother to keep watch on the pirates I ran back to the captain, "Do you have a plan, Captain?"

He nodded, grimly, "I cannot let my brother die at the hands of those murderers. I will sail as close as I dare."

"Your brother?"

He said, "Aye, Edward is my younger brother."

"Do you trust me, Captain Shipwright?"

"If the king trusts you with his son, then aye."

"Then lay us next to the pirate to steerboard. I will board with my knights and squires. First my archers will clear the decks and when that one is disabled, we will board. Jack and Henry will fight to the end and I will not see my men killed by French pirates."

"If you are willing then I will risk my ship."

I hurried back to my men and when there explained my plan. Whilst they all nodded, I saw the look of fear on Thomas' face. This would be a baptism of fire.

The Lord Edward said, "Take our bodyguards with you, Sir Henry. They are doughty men and will help you."

I shook my head, "This is our task and theirs is to guard you."

Robert had strapped on his sword, "And I will earn my passage with you if you will." I nodded.

We were closing rapidly, and I could see the last pirate had grappled the cog. The men were waiting at the waist. Henry of Almain, who had counted the pirates in the first ship, said, "There are more than twenty of them, Sir Henry."

I nodded, "And that means the odds are more than two to one in their favour. They are acceptable odds." I turned to the senior archer. Senior was a misnomer for Rafe was but twenty-two years old but he had arms like young oaks. "Rafe send your first arrows at the men towards the stern. They have a hard climb and if we kill enough then we can discourage them. Worry not about wasting arrows. We can have more made in Aquitaine."

"Aye, lord and do not worry. Not an arrow will be wasted. These pirates are the rats of the sea."

"Squires, stay close to your knight and watch their backs."

"Do we not need shields, cuz?" Thomas' nervousness was clear.

Shaking my head as Rafe and the archers each nocked an arrow I led my men to the waist where sailors had grappling hooks ready. "It will encumber us. We have better weapons, and you have the skill, Thomas. Hack, slash and stab as quickly as you can. Rafe and the handful of archers will aid us and you have Ralph to watch your back."

We could now hear the shouts of the French as they began their climb. Henry and his archers were on the forecastle and sterncastle while Jack and the spearmen ringed the mainmast. For the moment they were holding their own but as soon as the stern and steerboard side boarded then the slaughter would begin. I heard the twang of bowstrings as the French who were climbing the stern were picked off by the best archers in the north of England. I knew that the deaths would delay an attack over the stern and I concentrated on the men in the waist. Half were already clambering up ropes and the other half were waiting. Laying my throwing spear by the gunwale, I put my long dagger in my belt and pulled myself onto the gunwale with my left hand. I used the forestay for support and I balanced myself. Surprisingly enough we approached unobserved. We had not shouted. As Rafe's targets shifted to the men at the stern of our enemy I prepared to jump. I heard Captain Shipwright order the sails to be reefed as a flurry of goose fletched arrows cleared the stern and I saw a throwing spear, no doubt sent by Dick towards the steering board. The French helmsman and his assistants died.

I leapt down to the deck. It was a longer jump than I had anticipated, and I mistimed it. I was lucky for I landed on the back of a Frenchman and his body broke my fall. I heard his spine break as I landed and then I swung my sword in an arc as I drew my long dagger to stab almost blindly at the men before us. Blood spurted and a shout went up. Rafe and his archers began to slay the Frenchmen who were climbing the ropes and the ones who had yet to climb turned. The leader, who wore a mail shirt and helmet, turned first and I slashed at his chest with my long dagger whilst bringing down my sword. I allowed him no time to react, and my sword cracked into his helmet, stunning him. I saw a knee buckle and I drove my long dagger into his eye. Henry of Almain was right, we were outnumbered but in those few moments when we attacked men who were not expecting us, we changed the odds in our favour and Rafe and his archers completed the task. Two or three tried to surrender but Ralph and Dick were in no mood for mercy and the Frenchmen died.

"Up the ropes! Our brothers in arms need us."

I sheathed my weapons and grabbed a rope. It was slick with sticky blood. I began to walk up the side of the *'Maid.'* Above me, a nocked arrow and bow appeared and then retracted. Long Peter's face peered over the gunwale and he shouted, "Sorry, my lord!"

I kept climbing and when I reached the deck saw that we had arrived just in time. Jack and his men had made a shield wall, but the number of Frenchmen had tightened around them like a noose. Even as I stepped onto the deck and drew my sword, I saw a Frenchman with a boarding pike raise it to try to smash down onto the head of Martin Redbeard. I launched myself at the Frenchman and his swing exposed his side. My sword went into his armpit and came out on the other side. The pike fell from his lifeless hands and as I withdrew my sword Dick and Alfred materialised at my side. As more of my knights and squires joined us and Rafe and his archers sent their arrows towards the Frenchman at the stern, so we began to win.

I saw that Captain Edward had been wounded and it made me angry, "Drive them into the sea! No prisoners!"

The crew of the *'Maid'* needed no encouragement and Jack and his spearmen had endured enough already. The pirates were swept over the side into their ship. There were stones laid at the side of the gunwale. They had been brought up when the horses had been loaded. The crew of the *'Maid'* began to drop them onto the deck. Within a few moments the pirate had begun to sink and the men who could, were busy swimming for the last French ship which had abandoned the attack.

I looked around and saw that while many of my men had wounds we had lost but one. Young James of Oxbridge had a skull split in twain by a French axeman. I was glad I had shown no mercy. After the bodies had been searched Captain Shipwright had his men hew holes in the hull of the first Frenchman we had taken and when it sank, he secured our two ships together.

As we approached his wounded brother he grasped my arm, "Sir Henry, I am in your debt and should you ever need my ship or my brother's then it is yours."

"There is no need for thanks. We were all one body and we fought as one." I looked back to *'The Maid of Plymouth'* and saw that most of the crew were with us. Just the two royal cousins and their bodyguards remained on board. "We will get back to our royal charges."

As we crossed over the gunwales, I saw that my cousin was smiling, "Are you happier, cuz?"

Thomas nodded, "You were right and worrying about death did nothing to help me. Once I saw your mad charge and how well you fared, I did not fear for myself as I was sure that you would be killed before me."

As I dropped onto our deck I laughed, "It is good, cousin, that you took my impending death so well."

The two royals approached us, and The Lord Edward shook his head, "Impressive, Sir Henry, and just to save archers, sailors and spearmen. How much harder would you fight for your king?"

I looked at Godfrey who rolled his eyes. "Let us hope, my lord, that I never have to but the men you spoke of were largely my men and there is a duty not only for the men to protect their lord but for their lord to do the same. The Warlord began the system and it is now part of our lives. The men of Cleveland are one band."

Godfrey nodded, "Amen to that, Sir Henry, and that was handy sword work. I see you are a fighter and not a tourney knight."

"I take that as a compliment, and you are right. I do not think I would fare well in a tourney for when I fight it is to win and that usually means killing my opponent."

"You would have made a good sword for hire, my lord."

I nodded, "Aye, that was the life of our grandfather. When he lost his lands, he became a sword for hire and he never forgot that life." I swept a hand at the wreckage from the French ships. "And what intrigues me is was this happenstance or had someone sent the French to do their dirty work?"

Robert said, "De Montfort?"

I shrugged, "You know the man better than I, what do you think?"

"I think, Sir Henry, that you have a keen eye into the enemy of the king and you may be right but there would be no way to prove it."

I laughed, "I need no proof. De Montfort will learn that if he makes an enemy of one of the Warlord's heirs then he has an enemy for life. Let us say that I have given de Montfort his one benefit of the doubt but I shall keep a close eye on him from now on."

Gascony 1254

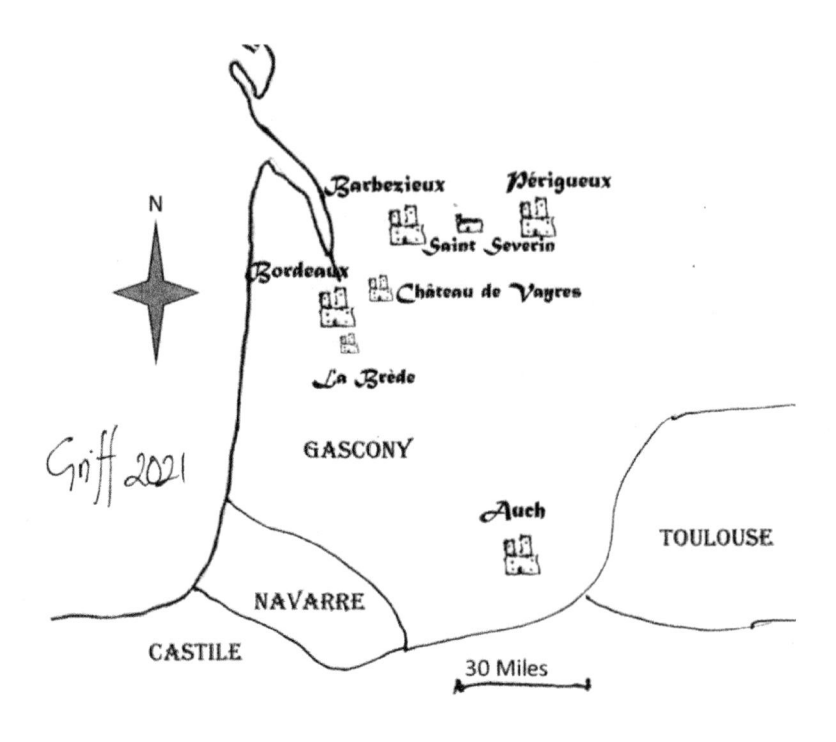

Chapter 5

Henry Samuel

Castilian connections

We arrived in Bordeaux after a two-week voyage. The horses would have suffered, that we knew and before we could attempt to reconnoitre the duchy they would need a rest. Before we had left England we had established where would be the best and safest place for us to lodge. We had the royal warrant and rather than staying in the castle on the Garonne we took over Château de La Brède. It belonged to the duchy and as it was south of Bordeaux and away from the city was almost a retreat, a hunting lodge close to the city. Duke Richard, later the Lionheart, was the last Duke of Aquitaine to use it and since then, during the time of King John and King Henry, it had been forgotten. It was Robert who had discovered it. While it was a rundown castle it had a good ditch and a river for protection. More importantly, it belonged to the Duchy and with just a castellan and eight retainers it was ours. We would be able to come and go as we pleased and as it was a small castle then it would be easier for us to defend. Bordeaux lay fifteen miles to the north and we would be able to control our own defences.

When we reached the castle we saw that the neglect had begun to show. The ditch was no longer sharp-edged. Some of the mortar needed to be replaced and the wood on the gates was showing the effects of time. The castellan, Jean de La Brède was embarrassed at the condition of the castle which had been allowed to become almost derelict. He and his family came from the village. He had been the sergeant at arms and became the castellan by default for he was the most senior of the handful of men who lived there. Money from the duchy had not been forthcoming and that explained the dereliction. I suspect that had we not come then within a few years it would have been abandoned or destroyed. It had been the villagers who had kept the garrison fed and it was they who had made the repairs. While our horses were stabled Alfred and I walked the walls to inspect our new home.

The road ran along the river and was only separated from the castle by a few houses. Those houses fished the river. To the north and south were the farms of the village. The outer wall was made of stone but was not high enough. There was a fighting platform but there were no embrasures and the only towers were those on the inadequate outer gate. The outer ward was small but it had a ditch before the inner wall. It was too shallow but it was a ditch. The inner wall was more substantial and the two towers of the gatehouse had embrasures. At the four corners of the castle were towers that could be used for defence. Finally, there was the keep. It was a small one, just three floors high and with small towers on the four corners. The stables, warrior hall, kitchens and bakery were all far enough from the keep to give a good line of sight. There was no church. As we headed into the keep I asked Jean about that.

"There is a small chapel close to the large bed-chamber. I used that but I will have it emptied for you, my lord."

I shook my head. I had already surmised that this was a loyal man. The livery he wore was old and faded yet he wore it proudly. I decided to confide in him. "Jean, this is for your ears only but I shall not be using the bed-chamber. I will sleep with the garrison and my men in the warrior hall. The young man we brought here is Prince Edward, the king's son and the future Duke of Aquitaine."

He looked shocked and I think it was because of the condition of the castle. It was not his fault but he showed his true colours. He was a loyal Gascon.

"I am sorry, my lord. Had I known…" his voice tailed off because we both knew he could have done little, having no funds.

"There will be money made available to you. Choose some of those in the village you think would make good servants and they shall be paid. They might as well be rewarded for their loyalty." I would have Robert keep the accounts for presentation to the king.

The first evening when we dined in the former Great Hall with hastily cooked food Robert offered an explanation. "De Montfort has taken over the great castle in Bordeaux and allowing this royal castle to fall into disrepair would suit his purposes." He shrugged, "I suspect that King John began the process but the Earl of Leicester should have made good the castle."

The Lord Edward listened attentively to our conversation. The fight with the pirates had reinforced his trust in us for we had all risked our lives while he had looked on. I nodded, "And unbeknown to the Earl of Leicester it suits ours for our horses will need time to recover and we can set to work making the castle stronger. I know that he will hear of our arrival but I had Egbert and Paul ride half a mile behind us to ensure that we were not followed so the only word he will have is that we headed south. I do not think he will even suspect that we might stay here for I do not think he would. Its very meanness is the best disguise." I smiled at Prince Edward, "And it can do no harm, my lord, to improve a residence for you."

"Should I begin to hire men to defend it, Sir Henry?"

"No, at the moment, we have enough and our purpose is to travel your Duchy so that you can see what problems face your subjects. We will wait a week or so and then visit with the earl. He will know that we have landed despite the fact that we did it quietly. He will have spies watching shipping and if he had anything to do with the attack, he now has time to put on a face to meet us. They did not follow us here and so we have a little time. We use that time well. Let him make assumptions about our purposes."

Thomas said, as the newly hired servants brought in the food, "You are so confident, cousin. When did you think all this out?"

"You did not spend a great deal of time with grandfather, did you?"

He shook his head, "I envied you and your time with him."

"I learned that he was always thinking and planning. He did not let his mind remain idle. I was lucky for he told me of men like Birger Brosa and Bishop Albert whom he met in the Baltic and of King John, William Marshal and Bishop Puset in England. He saw the good and the bad in leaders and he taught me to use their strengths and weaknesses when planning. Simon de Montfort wishes to be king. That much is clear to me. When we met in Westminster I saw it there. He can only be so indirectly, through his wife, the king's sister. He will not risk a civil war but he will foster discord here in Aquitaine. After that, he will move on to England. What I need to do is find proof for the king. That will not be easy. To answer your question, Thomas, it is that while I lead this conroi I will never stop thinking. Even when I sleep my mind will be planning. It will be when I return to Elton that I can give my mind a rest."

The Lord Edward looked at me with perception in his eyes, "I am sorry that I have taken you from your home, my lord. I now see that regal decisions have ramifications for all."

"And it was not your decision, my lord. Your father has used me and my family. I cannot yet see the purpose properly but I will. All I ask is that when you are king you weigh these decisions before you make them."

We did not waste our time while we waited for the horses to recover and used the delay to improve our castle. As we did so Robert walked amongst the villagers to ask about their lives. On that first evening after a day of hard labour Robert and I sat with the cousins and the castellan where we spoke. It gave a clearer picture of who was loyal and who was not. The villagers were all loyal but as the road to Bordeaux passed close to the village and travellers often stopped to water their horses, they were able to tell Robert about the varying views of those who lived in Gascony. It was illuminating. There were genuine enemies to English rule amongst the Seigneurs, the lords of this land. Many of those owned lands in France as well as Aquitaine but there were others who had been loyal but had been turned by the misrule of Simon de Montfort. It was they we would need to turn back to follow the royal path. I saw Prince Edward's face as he realised the enormity of the task and the result of not only neglect in the duchy but also the disaster that had been the appointment of Simon de Montfort.

Four days was enough for the horses to have recovered and I decided to split my small force into two. One half would continue to make our home stronger while I would take Prince Edward to do as his father had ordered and ride abroad. I decided to head south, not least because that was far from Poitou and the heartland of support for Simon de Montfort. It was where we could get a clearer picture of the opposition to English rule.

"My lord, let us take your bodyguards, my knights and a small escort and visit Auch."

"I thought you wished us to visit the Seneschal, Sir Henry?"

"I did but my mind has devised a better strategy. We have seen no strangers watching the castle for men have watched as we worked. That means that while de Montfort knows we are in Gascony he knows not where. Let us use this ride south to disappear and make him wonder. We will try to do that which he does not suspect."

"I am in your hands and I can now see why you were appointed by my father. You seem to think the reason was sinister but I believe he chose the best men for the task."

I nodded, "I thank you for the compliment, my lord, but if that was true then he would have sent more men."

As I came to know the prince better so I was able to read him. The look on his face told me that my words had pricked his mind and he was now ruminating about them.

We had learned that the Seigneur of Auch, Reynard d'Eauze, had been loyal to the duchy but when his lands had been raided, he had, it was said, begun to make overtures to the rulers of Navarre and Castile. Whilst that was better than an alliance with Toulouse, Robert was alarmed enough to suggest we speak directly with the Seigneur and that determined who we would speak to first.

As we prepared to head south on the journey of days rather than hours, Prince Edward said, "My great uncle, Richard, married a Castilian, did he not?"

The question was asked of Robert rather than me and he nodded, "Berengaria, who neither bore the king any children nor ever set foot in England. Why do you ask, my lord?"

"I am curious why a land which has no borders with Aquitaine should seek to make inroads into my land."

Robert nodded and, like a schoolmaster, explained, "The ruler of Navarre, which does border Aquitaine, is the Count of Champagne and a Frenchman. He is rarely in Navarre and the new King of Castile, Alfonso, is keen to expand his lands. He has a claim to the lands of Aquitaine. He is young and ambitious. The southern part of Aquitaine is called Gascony and is closely linked to the Iberian kingdoms." The prince looked confused by the answer and so Robert elaborated, "If he can claim Gascony and gain the support of Gascons then as Lord of Gascony and King of Castile, he would surround Navarre. At the very least he could make it a vassal kingdom."

That made sense to the prince who nodded and then looked at me, "Is it not a dangerous journey, my lord?"

"We landed without fanfare my lord but despite what your father wished I cannot keep you hidden. Simon de Montfort will know we have landed. The castellan knows it too and the villagers are no fools. They will all know you are here. If we travel south with a small number of men then we will not be seen as a threat and perhaps diplomacy might strengthen your lands. Besides the Seigneur of Auch is a powerful man and with him on your side then that part of Gascony would be safer. King Alfonso is only belligerent because he sees weakness. Just as we shore up the defences of this castle so you need to do the same with your Duchy."

He nodded, "And you think I can do it?"

I smiled, "My grandsire, the first Earl of Cleveland had young King Henry the second ride with him when he was your age and from what I have heard the young Prince Henry learned how to be a great ruler while doing so. Let us say that your time with your tutor gave you skills in languages but you are about to get skills of a more martial nature. You are too young to use a sword so let us use your tongue. I have no doubt that an appeal from you might result in success where a force of arms might fail."

I think he was persuaded already and with just four spearmen and four archers we took the road south. The religious houses were more than happy to accommodate us when I showed my royal warrant and once we had established that the churchmen were largely loyal, then The Lord Edward's identity was revealed. It was from them that we learned that abbeys had been raided by men sent by Simon de Montfort. They had not worn livery but the monks, canons and priests were clever men who had worked out the hand behind the raids. Robert kept a written record ready to take back to England when the time was ripe.

Auch was a mighty city with a strong wall and a beautiful cathedral. Hitherto on our scouting expedition, we had just met churchmen but now we would face a potential enemy. We halted just two miles from the citadel to ensure that we looked presentable. My knights and I would be seen from the walls as we approached and our livery identified. I was glad that we wore no red at all. De Montfort's silver gryphon on a red background was distinctive.

My royal warrant gained us entry to the town and we wound our way through the streets towards the castle. There, our progress was halted. I had suspected something when the guards at the town gate had insisted upon reading the warrant carefully. I doubted that they could read. I had seen one of the watch race to the castle where we were halted.

"The Seigneur has important guests and asks that you return tomorrow."

I nodded, "And where should we stay?"

The sergeant at arms shrugged, "I was not told."

Robert had read about this land before we had left England and he nudged his horse next to mine, "Sir Henry, let us ride to the cathedral."

I had learned to trust the Welshman and I nodded, "We will return at terce on the morrow when I hope for a better welcome."

We rode to the cathedral and its attendant buildings. It was close to the castle walls. We dismounted at the church and a Dean came to speak to us, "May I help you?"

"We have travelled from England to speak with the Seigneur but he is unavailable until the morrow." The Dean nodded. "Would there be accommodation here?" I took out the parchment, "I have a warrant from the King of England."

"If you would wait here, I will speak with the archbishop."

It was hot but there was a water trough, and we watered our horses. This was all new to me. I was more used to negotiations with a sword rather than words.

Archbishop Hispanus de Massanc was an old man and with old age sometimes comes wisdom. In the archbishop's case, this was true. I was summoned to his chambers where his eyes searched my face as he spoke. He gestured towards the parchment, "The warrant you hold has bought you an interview with me but I need more reason than that to allow English knights to stay within my walls." He gestured for me to sit. "Your king's eye has strayed from this land and allowed a tyrant to rule in his stead. Have you come to end that rule?"

He was so astute that it frightened me, "No, your grace." He had flustered me and I wished that Robert had been allowed to accompany me. I recovered my wits by thinking how I would combat the archbishop if we were using edged weapons and not words. "I do, however, bring hope."

"Hope is good. We all have hopes of heaven and that our good deeds in this world will ease our passage into the next. Is your soul clean and have your sins been forgiven, Sir Henry?"

The clever prelate had me off guard again, "I believe so."

"Good. If nothing else we will afford your men the opportunity to confess to my priests so that whatever happens their sins are forgiven. Now, what is this hope you speak of?"

"I bring, in disguise, King Henry's son, The Lord Edward. He is the heir to the Duchy of Aquitaine and we are here so that the future ruler of this land can meet its people and see its problems."

"In disguise. That often hides ill intent."

"There is none here and the disguise is necessary, for the moment, your grace for we both know that if his identity was known then men would present a face and offer an opinion that might well be biased."

"You are clever, and you choose your words well. Henry of Elton; that is close to Stockton is it not?"

I nodded, "My uncle is the Earl of Cleveland."

"And that makes your grandfather the killer of a bishop." The man knew much that lay beyond his own lands.

"For which act he atoned and was forgiven by Bishop Albert."

"Indeed. I shall grant your request and this evening, at our humble feast, I will speak with the heir to the English throne. I am too old to worry what a stripling youth might do sometime in the future. By then I suspect I will be dead. Perhaps I might give you an insight into this land and the misrule of King Henry's Lieutenant. I have never met the man but had I done so I might have looked into his soul as I have with yours to divine his purposes."

I left a relieved man for the archbishop was disconcertingly perceptive. I rejoined my men in the courtyard as one of the archbishop's servants came to show us first to the stables and thence to our accommodation. The spearmen and archers had been chosen for their skills not only with weapons but their quick minds and I put my finger to my lips so that all would remain silent. Even The Lord Edward had learned to heed my commands. The fight on the ship had served many purposes. The cathedral had a hospital attached to it, for pilgrims travelling to Santiago di Compostela, often stayed in the building. There were few visitors on the day of our arrival and we were given the whole of the hospital for our chambers. Godfrey, whom I had learned was the senior bodyguard told me that two of the bodyguards would act as chamberlains and sleep behind the door while the other two would sleep at the foot of the beds of their charges. He was a diligent man and it meant the rest of us could sleep easy.

We washed and changed and used the pot in the corner to make water. I learned from Robert that they still used the urine to cleanse the clothes of wildlife. The speech we had was about such mundane matters. Robert reminded them that the only edged weapons we would be allowed to take with us to the feast would be our eating knives. We were summoned by a robed priest and taken to the hall where the archbishop dined. I suspected that the food they were eating would have been the same even without our presence for it was very simple. There were more prayers than was normal and our squires, to their delight, were seated with the spearmen and archers amongst the lowlier stations of priests. The four bodyguards, none of whom wore spurs were also relegated to the lower table along with Robert. The look that Godfrey gave to me left me in no doubt that I would be responsible for keeping the royal charges safe from harm although I was certain that within these walls we would be free from danger.

Hispanus de Massanc was seated between the heir to England's throne and me. His dean was between my brother and me. All of us were separated by men chosen, no doubt, by the archbishop to gather information. This would be a testing meal for us all. "So, Prince Edward, you are to be the man who rules this land?"

"I am, your grace."

The fish we ate was river fish and there were many small bones. The archbishop fastidiously fished them out, "You know that the King of Castile, Alfonso, has a claim to the land of Aquitaine and Gascony through his great-great-grandmother, Eleanor of England who was the daughter of your King Henry and Eleanor of Aquitaine?"

I saw from his eyes that the prince did not but he nodded, "King Henry had many sons and daughters and I do not doubt that there are many with King Henry's royal blood coursing through their veins."

The archbishop nodded and wiped his fingers. A priest whisked away the platter, cleaned it and placed it back before him, "But those nobles do not live so close to Gascony that they could ride here within a day."

He was speaking to Prince Edward, but the words were meant for me and were a warning. I decided to be blunt, "You are telling us that King Alfonso has designs upon Aquitaine?"

"Not immediately but Gascony, lying so close to the prize he desires, Navarre, is a land he would have for his own and the discord that brought you here means that he sees a plum that is ripe for the picking."

This was confirmation of the news Robert had already gleaned and I knew that it had to be relayed to King Henry sooner rather than later. The archbishop was being as clear as he could be and I had no doubt that he had the information from the many travellers who would pass through Auch.

Edward was a clever youth and he asked, "And the Seigneur of Auch, what is his position on the matter?"

The archbishop took a small fowl from the platter proffered by a priest and carefully carved off the two small pieces of meat from the back of the bird known for their sweet taste. He sliced them into smaller pieces and savoured each one as he ate it. Wiping his hands and then drinking a little of the wine he said, "You would have to ask the Seigneur for any knowledge I might have of the lord's mind would come from the confessional, however, I do know that there will be room for you tomorrow in the castle when the Castilian guests he entertains this night have left."

The twinkle in his eye told me that he knew what he was doing and his words were a deliberate warning. "And how, Archbishop, would you view the rule of this land from Castile?"

He nodded as though he appreciated the blunt question, "I am an old man and I will soon be dead. This land came to England through Eleanor of Aquitaine and her antecedents would not have appreciated Castilian rulers." He did not wish Castilian overlords. He wiped his hands, "And now I am tired. Forgive an old man who needs his rest before he rises for compline, matins and lauds." We all began to rise but he waved us back to our seats. "You need not rise. I may have the appetite of a hermit but you are young men and it does not do to waste God's bounty."

Three priests, including the Dean, left with him. We were seated on benches and when the empty platters were taken away, we slid to be closer together. I was able to speak to Prince Edward, "You will need all your skill on the morrow, my lord, to try to divert the Seigneur from a path that takes him to Castile."

He shook his head, "I have not the skill."

"Then, my lord, use honesty. You wish Aquitaine to be safe do you not and the people happy?"

"Of course."

"Then make the wine you sip the last of this night and when you retire put your mind to how you might attain that. It is clear to me that your identity is known, why else refuse us entry to the castle? The archbishop made no secret of the fact that the reason we were denied entry to the castle was because of the visitors who were there. My guess is that they are Castilian envoys. Be bold and use this as a test of how you might rule not only Aquitaine but England."

Robert nodded, "Sir Henry is right. The Seigneur will be guarded in his words but the archbishop has given us knowledge that the Seigneur sought to keep hidden. It is a weapon, my lord, that we can use to our advantage."

I did not envy the prince his task. That night with two bodyguards at the door I was able to talk to Robert and Prince Edward. When I told Robert what I had learned he nodded, "Aye, we were at the lower end of the table but the priests there knew of the Castilian delegation. What the archbishop did not tell you is that King Alfonso is offering his sister, Leonor to marry Theobald of Navarre. He is younger than your brother, Prince Edmund and as Leonor is older would give King Alfonso the opportunity to rule Navarre and give him direct access to Gascony."

The Lord Edward nodded, "Then when we are done here you need to return to my father as soon as you can. We have learned much in just one visit and the Castilian news changes everything."

I asked, "And what do you hope your father will do?"

"We both know, Sir Henry, that my father is not the warrior his namesake was but he knows how to use diplomacy. Knowing what is in the Castilian minds helps us and he can also bring my uncle, Richard, who is a warrior, to lead an army to right the wrongs of Simon de Montfort. On the ride south I saw enough evidence of malfeasance to know that the man asked to rule in my stead has not done as either my father or I would have wished."

At that moment I saw a future king of England and I had hope that this one would be a good one.

The Seigneur of Auch was a haughty man who knew that his city was one of the strongest in the area and that when Gascony had been a sovereign country with its own ruler it had been the centre of power. As soon as we were ushered into his presence, I knew that he felt he was not the inferior of Prince Edward but at least his equal. He made it quite clear that he knew who Prince Edward was. He gave a slight bow, "Prince Edward, it is good that you have decided to visit your Duchy and, if I might say, it is not before time. This land has been ravaged by those who should have protected it."

It was a criticism not only of Simon de Montfort but King Henry too. The Lord Edward had heeded my advice and his response was measured and, for the age of the prince, mature. "Know, Seigneur, that I have just come into my inheritance, and I have availed myself of the first opportunity to visit this land. Be in no doubt that all that I see will help me to rule this land in a fair and equitable way and any who have transgressed against my people will be punished."

His words rang of sincerity, and I could see a slight change in the demeanour of the Lord of Auch. I noticed that the archbishop was not present and knew that was deliberate. The wily prelate did not wish to be seen taking sides. I think Sir Geoffrey and my cousin were a little bored with the proceedings but Alfred and I watched every move the young prince and the Seigneur made. My grandfather had told all his grandchildren that there was no such thing as useless knowledge. There was just knowledge you had yet to use. Sir

Thomas had obviously not heeded the lesson as well as my brother and me.

We were taken on a tour of the town where the four bodyguards were augmented by ten magnificently mailed men at arms. The Lord Edward was not identified but the people we saw must have known that he was a figure of importance. We dined well and that evening, after we had retired to our quarters, I used the time to speak to the others. Our charge had no opportunity to look around him. Neither had Robert who was busy mentally recording all the comments by the Gascon lord. With my men watching the doors I sat with the bodyguards and my knights around the long table.

"How do we see the Gascons of Auch? Are they friends or foes?"

Alfred was astute, "I think that before we came the lord was a foe but your words, Prince Edward, may have moved him a little more into our camp. I noticed a difference in his tone."

"Robert?"

"Your brother is right. The very fact that the prince came here to speak to him has helped. I am wondering if, perhaps, the Castilians who were here did not offer all that the Seigneur hoped. If so then this was a judicious choice, Sir Henry, for the first visit to a Seigneur."

He had seen what I had not that the Iberian king might not be as welcome as we had thought. De Montfort had much to answer for. "Thomas?"

"I saw nothing. The day was tedious."

"Geoffrey?"

"The men we saw on the walls and those who came with us are fighters. I noticed that the city itself had not suffered any attacks from de Montfort's brigands and I can see why."

"Aye, the picture is becoming clearer. When I spoke to those at Château de La Brède I was told that the raids were by small groups of men, no more than fifty or so. They attack the larger manors that do not have walls."

Godfrey had been silent and coughed before he spoke, "My lord, there were spies in the town this day."

I turned, "Spies? You are certain?"

He smiled, "We are bodyguards, and we look not only for danger but also suspicious behaviour. I saw men at arms watching us as we moved through the town. They were not the men of Auch for our escort viewed them with suspicion. They looked to me to be hired swords and they were trying to remain hidden."

"How many?"

"I saw three, my lord and my fellows, another two. They were not together. If we saw five then who knows how many others there are? I know not if they were hired by the King of Castile or Simon de Montfort. From what I have heard both have a reason to send spies into this land. Even if The Lord Edward has escaped notice up until this moment, I fear that now, having walked next to the Seigneur, then his identity will no longer be a secret."

Part of me wondered if this had been at the back of King Henry's mind. Was this like the hunt at Pickering? Were we a bait to lure out the enemy? If so, the king had miscalculated or I had made a mistake. With a handful of men to protect us, I risked capture or worse. I had to be the decisive knight my grandfather had taught me to be, "There is no point in worrying about that now. The carrot is out of the ground. We will beg leave to depart on the morrow and ride as fast as we can for Château de La Brède. When we get there Robert, I want you on the first ship out of Bordeaux."

"And Simon de Montfort, my lord? He may try to stop me."

I smiled, "Then we will have to try a subterfuge of our own. Let us get back to La Brède in one piece and then we will try to outwit the wily earl."

Chapter 6

Henry Samuel

The spilling of blood

    We knew from our questions to the Seigneur that we had twenty miles to travel until we had a choice over our route and after that, we had three ways we could travel back to Bordeaux, each one the same distance. Heading south we had chosen the route with the best accommodation but knowing that men had been watching us made me wary. I intended to make us hard to find and so I made the decision to wear our mail and ride the first twenty miles in under two hours. I wanted to be as far away from Auch as soon as possible. I hoped to surprise our watchers. It would be a hard ride, especially for the royal cousins but it was necessary. The spies in Auch might just have reported to their paymaster and he may have been in Bordeaux or Leon; it mattered little to us until we had the walls of our small castle to protect us. This time we rode in a tighter formation. With two archers at the rear and two at the van, we trotted out through the gates of Auch as soon as they were opened. There was no way to sneak out and I knew that if any of the spies remained in Auch then they would know we were heading north. The first waypoint would be the Petite Baïse, a small river close to Valence-sur-Baïse. There we had a fork in the road and we could either cross the bridge north or take the road to the east of the river and avoid the bridge.

    We were just a mile from the hamlet of Valence-sur-Baïse when Egbert, one of the archers at the rear shouted, "My lord, there are hooves thundering up behind us." The urgency in the normally calm archer made me heed his words instantly.

    Without slowing, I shouted, "Godfrey, protect our charges and take the two archers with you. Ride to the bridge and try to make an ambush. We will delay them. Robert, follow them. You have to get to London."

Raising his arm to show that he had heard me he shouted out orders.

Alfred said, "And what if these horsemen are intent on driving us into an ambush?"

"Then we have failed, Alfred, but I think we have ridden so quickly that such an outcome is unlikely." I turned in my saddle, "Squires, overtake us and follow Godfrey and the others to the bridge. We ten will slow them."

They, of course, obeyed but Thomas asked, "And what if they outnumber us?"

I smiled, "As they did on the boat cuz? We fight for that is our only choice." He nodded and I said, "Let us slow and draw weapons. On my command, I want you, Egbert and Paul, to dismount, nock an arrow and prepare to knock the pursuers from their saddles. We will turn and charge them."

My archers and spearmen shouted that they had understood. Now that we had slowed, I heard the hooves more clearly and from the sound, we would be outnumbered. I was not as worried as Thomas for we had the edge in that we had two archers and they could each send ten arrows in a minute at whoever followed us, we were prepared and we had mail. Of course, the hooves might be innocent and may have been men riding north on an urgent mission. If the men pursuing wore the livery of Auch then I would give them the benefit of the doubt. We passed around a bend and the road began to climb a little through some sparse trees. I reined in my horse and walked him up the slope. The others slowed with me and when I reached the top of the slight incline, I turned him and drew my sword. I saw the horsemen. They were mailed and they had lances and shields. As they turned the bend we had rounded, just three hundred paces from us, I counted fourteen of them. They wore no livery and were not men from the Seigneur.

My grandfather had taught me to be decisive and to trust my instincts. "I think they mean us harm. Egbert."

My archers had already dismounted and tied the reins of their horses to the trees. They leaned on the bows to string them. We had time on our side and the rest would do our horses good. The men pursuing us spied us and had seen that we had stopped and awaited us. I saw the leader point his lance at us as they formed an arrow to charge us. They must have thought they had the advantage as they had lances and we did not. The spearmen had the shorter spears.

"Await my command and then the four of us charge together. Garth, have the spearmen form a second rank."

"Aye, lord. You hear Sir Henry, now couch your spears. We will give these bandits a lesson in spear work and show them that we can beat longer lances."

My spearmen had been delighted when I had chosen them to come to Aquitaine with us and they had practised when they could. They were ready to show me that they could become men at arms.

Egbert said, "Ready, my lord."

"Then loose. Hit them on the flanks and we will take the centre."

I think that the men charging up the road expected us to flee and when we began to trot down the cobbles towards them it must have come as a shock for they slowed a little. That could have been due to the slope or the tiredness of their mounts but either way they were not charging as fast as they had been. I was in the centre of the line with Alfred on one side of me and Thomas on the other. Geoffrey was on Thomas' right. My novice cousin would be well protected. I pulled up my shield as we headed down the road and as the first of the arrows flew. The two archers were using their precious bodkins and the two men on the extreme left and right were hit in the shoulder. My archers had practised regularly at the mark and I knew that they were accurate up to three hundred paces. The range was well within their ability and I could trust them not to hit us.

As we neared them, I saw that the pursuers were not knights. There were no spurs to be seen and they had no single livery. The tunics were plain ones. From the faded designs, I guessed that some had been sergeants in the religious orders or perhaps they had simply taken them from their dead victims. We would not be able to identify their master and that tallied with the information we had already gleaned. The men who attacked and pillaged disguised their identity.

I spurred my horse when we were just twenty paces from the lances. Three more of the enemy had been hit and a horse and rider were down but we would still be outnumbered and they were riding closer together and enjoyed mutual protection from their shields. The leader and I were closing and this would be all about timing. I had told Robert that I was not a tourney knight but I had practised on the green at Elton with Dick and Alfred. I knew how to deal with a lance. Charging uphill meant that the horseman would be more likely to lean forward and perhaps to stand. When we were just ten paces from each other I spurred my horse hard and he leapt forward. The sudden move took the horseman I had chosen to fight by surprise and he tried to stand and thrust at the same time. Relying on Alfred to protect my right I stood and swung my sword at the horseman's head. He wore a helmet and I did not but his helmet had a visor and limited his view. His late strike with the lance made it glance off my shield doing no harm whatsoever while his shield did not rise quickly enough to slow down my sword. I smacked it into the top of his helmet. The metal cracked and the arming cap did not work as well as it might. He began to slide to his right and ignoring him I swung at the man who was following him. When Alfred's opponent fell from the saddle and another was felled by an arrow the others decided that they had fought enough and wheeled their horse around. Before they were out of range three were hit in the back. They kept their saddles but they knew that they had been bested.

Dropping my shield back to cover my leg, I reined in and rode towards the three men who lay on the ground. Two were clearly dead but one still moved. I dismounted and sheathed my sword. Without looking up I shouted, "Collect the horses and search the dead for clues as to their master." I knelt next to the warrior who lay on the ground and whose eyes were fixed on me. Unlike the other two, who had bled out, there was remarkably little blood to be seen. "Can you move?"

His French, when he spoke, was accented and I guessed he came from the Flanders or close to it. His face contorted and he gave the slightest of shakes of his head, "I fear my back is broken. Give me a warrior's death, my lord, I beg of you."

I nodded and took out my long dagger. I would have done the same for a horse and this grizzled warrior who lay on the ground looked to be of an age with my uncle, "Who sent you?"

"I know not." I stared at him, and he pleaded, "I beg of you, my lord, end my life. I know not who sent me and I will not make one up and go to God with a lie on my lips. A cross."

I took out his dagger and placed it in his mailed hands.

"Then tell me all you know."

His face twisted showing that he was clearly in pain. "We were hired in Bordeaux. The inn with the cockerel's feathers by the river. We knew it was a place where a sword for hire could find work. We were hired by a man called Alain and taken to a hall south of the city. A week since we were sent to Auch and told to look for English knights with two English youths. Our leader," his eyes flickered to one of the bodies, "Jean de Marin, quartered us around the city and we waited. We were told that the knights and men at arms could be killed and their treasure ours but the two youths were not to be touched or harmed in any way." His eyes closed and I thought that his wounds had taken him but he opened his eyes and gave a wry smile. "The days, while we waited for you, were good ones. There were women and the wine was good. It was Jean de Marin who found you and we took your trail this morning. I swear."

A paroxysm of pain raced through his body and, taking my dagger, I said, as I slit his throat, "Go to God. You have spoken the truth."

I stood and it was then I realised I had been remiss. I had not asked if any of my men had been wounded. As I looked around, I saw Geoffrey and Alfred kneeling over a recumbent form. I saw the spurs, it was Thomas. I had information but family was more important, and I ran to join them. To my relief his eyes were open, and he was smiling. I looked at Alfred who said, "He took a lance in his left shoulder. It did not penetrate deeply and as far as I can tell it struck neither bone nor vital part but he is in pain. I had staunched the bleeding and we have bandaged it but he needs a healer."

Thomas looked up at me, "You told me to keep my shield high. I should have listened."

"These were professional warriors, cousin and you did well." I stood and saw that Egbert and Paul had collected two horses. A third had wandered in some fields. The locals would have an unexpected gift. My spearmen had collected the weapons from the dead. "We have a more important duty than to bury these hired killers. We must get Sir Thomas to a healer. Egbert and Paul, lead the horses. Alfred and I will flank our cousin. Sir Geoffrey, take the van and lead us to the bridge."

Thomas was pale as we helped him onto the back of his horse. The high cantle would help to hold him in place but to be certain I took his horse's reins and we made sure our legs touched his. We did not gallop for it soon became clear that each hoof clattering on the cobbled road hurt Thomas. We would have to find a healer. My other archers stepped out from the trees as we approached the bridge, "Robert and Prince Edward are beyond the trees close by the houses of the hamlet."

"Good, You two form the rearguard."

"How is Sir Thomas, my lord?"

"Wounded but alive."

When we reached the others, they had heard our horses and had mounted. I spoke not to Prince Edward but Godfrey and Robert, "We killed three and hurt others. They will not follow again for we killed their leader. My cousin was hurt, and we need to find a healer. Robert, ask one of the villagers if there is a house of healing close by."

While he did so Godfrey took a flask and held it to Thomas' lips, "Drink this, my lord. It is a spirit they distil in Poitou. It warms from within." He took a mouthful and started. Godfrey chuckled, "Aye, it will do that to a man but it helps."

Robert returned and he had a smile upon his face, "The Abbaye de Flaran lies just half a mile up the road. They are Cistercian monks. We should find help and shelter for the night."

I looked up at the sky; the fight and the aftermath meant it had passed noon and by the time Thomas was attended to, we would have no time to travel. "Lead on."

Alfred asked as we rode up the road to the abbey, "Did you learn anything, brother?"

"Some but now is not the time to speak. Thomas' blood lies on the road and that is more important than anything at the moment."

My brother lowered his voice, "More important than the prince?"

"What I can tell you is that they will not harm the prince. Their aim was to take him and we have ended that threat. I believe that we can disappear on the road and reach our sanctuary at the castle. We will talk more in the abbey."

We passed fields filled with toiling monks. The Cistercian order had decided that the Benedictines had forgotten the original ethos of the order and had split away to form a new order. I hoped there was a healer. We were admitted through the gates and into the courtyard. Sir Geoffrey and Alfred helped Ralph to lower an almost unconscious Thomas from the saddle. I handed my reins to Dick and took out the warrant.

The prior approached with two other white-robed monks. "I am Prior Nicholas. I see that you have a man who is hurt."

I nodded. This was not the time for deception. "We are escorting Prince Edward, King Henry of England's son to Bordeaux. Just a mile from here, we were ambushed by hired swords. Sir Thomas, my cousin was wounded but they fled leaving three men dead."

The prior turned, "Brother Stephen, take some men and fetch the bodies. We shall bury them here. Whatever their sins they deserve a burial."

The monk hurried off. I noticed that he just tapped the monks he wished to accompany him on the shoulder. The Cistercian were not a silent order but used as few words as possible.

The prior said, "We will tend to your cousin and you are welcome to stay the night but know that we are a simple order and our food is plain. The heir to the English throne will be disappointed if he wishes a feast."

I smiled, "Prior Nicholas, part of my task is to make a man of Prince Edward. This will do him no harm."

Monks took Thomas away and Edgar helped them carry his master. With our horses stabled we were led to a simple hall with no beds as such but straw-filled mattresses on the floor. The monk who took us there said simply, "This hall is kept for visitors such as yourself. We live simply here. I will return when it is time to eat. The prior suggests that you use this time to contemplate your lives and how you might serve God better."

I knew that Prince Edward and his cousin Henry were desperate to know what I had learned and as soon as we had washed and drunk some of the watered wine the monks fetched for us I gathered all around me to tell them. It was not just the royal pair whose lives were in danger. All of us could have died and they all deserved to know the danger.

I told them what I had learned from the dying man. "It answers one question; whilst Castile might have designs on Gascony the threat to the prince did not come from there and I believe that although we have many miles to travel, we will be safe until we reach our castle. While we do not know the name of the man who paid Jean de Marin we do, at least, know where to begin our search, the inn and the man called Alain. Once we have ensured that Robert is safe on his way to King Henry then my brother and I will visit this inn, in disguise, and offer our swords to whoever will pay us."

Prince Edward said, "Why you, Sir Henry?"

I sighed, "My lord, you and your cousin must be protected. I will not send a spearman or an archer to do what I fear to do. Your father gave me this commission and as the leader, I will take the risks."

Godfrey said, "These are men without honour, Sir Henry. It will be dangerous."

I laughed, "And my family have been courting danger since Sir Aelfraed returned from Constantinopolis. I know the kind of men with whom we will be dealing, and I will be in disguise. My brother and I will not wear spurs, nor will we wear a livery. When we have investigated the inn then we will, while we await word from England, beard the Earl of Leicester in Bordeaux. We will not alert others that we have returned to the castle. I intend for us to sneak in. I would see the surprise on the face of de Montfort. If, as I believe, he sent men to kidnap Prince Edward and his cousin, then he will be awaiting the return of his men. The longer he waits the more doubt there will be."

Godfrey nodded although I could still see the doubt on Prince Edward's face, "It is a sound plan, my lord, but the hard part will be keeping our presence a secret."

I nodded, "I intend, when we near Château de La Brède, to send Dick and Robert to alert the castellan to our plan. Two plainly dressed riders should not alert suspicion. We will arrive at night, before Lauds. We will walk our horses into the castle and, hopefully, none shall know."

Sir Geoffrey asked, "And Sir Thomas? He is wounded."

"And he is the grandson of Sir Thomas. This is a test for him every bit as much as a nighttime vigil. Do not worry about my cousin, Geoffrey. The wound will be the making of him."

Godfrey nodded, "You are right, my lord. I remember the first time a blade sliced into my leg. I determined after that never to allow an enemy to get that close to me again."

The silence when we ate in the refectory was strange. We were used to the buzz of chatter. We all respected the unwritten rule. There were just three reasons to speak: a question that would help a monk to perform some duty, a conversation about spiritual matters or, on a special occasion a spontaneous conversation. I found it soothing and helped me to reflect on my life. We had visited Thomas before we ate and he seemed in good spirits. The wound was not a deep one but he had lost blood. The monk in the hospital recommended a rest of a few days. That would not happen.

It proved to be true for Thomas seemed in a more positive mood as we headed north. He had been wounded and survived; more he had not let his family down. Garth had said that he saw Sir Thomas lanced but that Sir Thomas had managed to wound his opponent. It boded well. We had an uneventful journey back to Château de La Brède and we timed it well so that it was dusk when I sent Robert and Dick to speak with the castellan. We waited in the woods by the river. It was a pleasant place to wait and as darkness fell, we were surrounded by the sounds of the night and of animals and birds. We were so still that a fox approached and then fled when he caught our scent. A nearby monastery's bell told us when it was matins and we prepared to leave. We walked our horses through the woods and instead of using the road made our way through the wine yard that lay close to the river. We saw no one and we were helped by a cloudy sky that hid the moon. The gate loomed open, and we slipped silently in. Kurt quietly closed the gates behind us. After stabling our horses we went directly to bed. The castellan and his loyal men would watch the walls and we needed our sleep.

We woke before noon and there was food for us. The fact that we had left the bulk of our men in the castle had helped maintain the illusion, to the villagers at least, that we had not left. Henry son of Harry and Jack had kept the men working on the defences so that any watchers would have seen them at work. The castellan and I spoke and I learned that Simon de Montfort was in Bordeaux and his minions were still causing havoc. Trade had suffered and fewer ships were leaving the river.

"Sir Henry, the king must do something about this situation. I am a loyal knight and I fought alongside King Henry but even I tire of the misrule."

"And it will end." I pointed to Prince Edward, "Therein lies our hope. He seems to me to have potential. He is raw clay but already I see it being moulded into a man whom men can follow."

The next day Dick, Robert and I shed all accoutrements of nobility. With just our swords and a haversack containing that which a sword for hire would carry, we trudged into Bordeaux. We had used the clothes and buskins of the spearmen and we left our hair unruly. We had found two very old hauberks in the castle armoury and they showed age. Some links were missing and there were patches of rust. They were just the sort of armour struggling warriors might use. With our helmets hanging from spears the three of us headed to the port. I intended to visit the inn where men were hired but my priority was to secure passage on a ship. We were anonymous in Bordeaux for we were like many others who either sought work or a ship back to England. The advantage we had was that my purse was full and we could pay whatever extortionate price was asked.

To our great delight and surprise, Captain Shipwright was in port. Our disguise was so effective that it took some moments for him to recognise us but, being a clever man and knowing the disguise was for a purpose, he led us directly to the sterncastle where we could speak. I just said that Robert needed passage back to England and he did not hesitate.

"If you wish him to remain hidden, my lord, then best that he does not leave with you. I will keep him hidden until we sail on the evening tide."

"Thank you, Captain, and this pays all debts."

Shaking his head he said, "Until I have saved the life of one of your family, Sir Henry, then I have not."

Our farewells from Robert were brief. He knew what he had to do and if we remained aboard much longer then those who hung about the quay might be suspicious. As Dick and I left we acted out a little scene to explain our departure.

"We need more coin, Dick, if we are to sail to England. The prices that they charge in these challenging times are too high for us."

"Perhaps we can find work here in Bordeaux."

I laughed, "Aye well so long as it is sword work and not hoisting barrels aboard then I will take whatever is offered. Come let us find an alehouse."

I deliberately used the English word so that any listeners would be in no doubt as to our nationality. It proved to be wise as a furtive looking fellow suddenly roused himself from the coiled ropes upon which he lay, "If you seek work, master, then try *'The White Cockerel'* there are men such as you who congregate there."

Still playing a part I said, "And what is in it for you, weasel?" It was the right response for men such as us.

He recoiled and held up his hands, "Nothing, master, just being friendly."

"In my experience, there are few friends this side of the sea!" As we headed for the inn, I guessed that this might be the same inn we had been directed to on the road from Auch. I also now had the weasel to question should my plan fail. I turned to Dick, when we were out of earshot, "We play a part; say little and scowl whenever possible. Forget being polite. That Dick does not exist while we scout out this inn."

He nodded but I saw the fear in his eyes. He was not Thomas and I knew that even though afraid, Dick would do the right thing at the right time.

Chapter 7

Henry Samuel
The mercenary

I did not know if this was the same inn that the dying man had told me of but when I saw the cockerel's feathers then I knew we had found the right place. It did not front the quay and there were houses before it as well as some merchants' warehouses at one end. The wine merchant at the end did front the quay for the river curved. The inn lay close to the quay but far enough away so that at night it would be a poorly lit place where men could come and go undetected. I understood that arriving during the day we might not be able to find the men we wanted but that was all part of my plan. I knew that the kind of people who hired knives in the night would be careful. I wanted us to establish our story and then leave. We would return after dark but the next time I would have men watching outside. I was not a fool and I realised the men I would be dealing with were desperate ones and more likely to kill to silence one they thought threatened them.

The outside of the inn looked in need of repair and I saw cracks in the wooden lintels over the doors and wind holes. It looked seedy and run down. It was a small door and I had to duck to get in. That would also suit those who sought men here. It would slow down any escape from an informer or one who worked for the town watch. The door was also ill-fitting and I had to lift it to open it. I stepped into a dimly lit room. The candles were smoky tallow ones and that added to the gloom. I wondered what it would be like at night when there was not even a glimmer of light from the outside. The tables were old upturned wine barrels and the benches were crudely made. There were fewer than five men in the place and they were all drinking wine. Each one had a small earthenware jug. There was a smell from the rear that suggested food. Every eye swivelled to us as we entered and silence descended like an executioner's axe.

Dick and I had practised our story and rehearsed how we would play it, "Well, little brother, I think we would find more cheer in a graveyard. Perhaps this is not *'The White Cockerel'*. Let us go and find the place the gutter rat recommended."

The swarthy man who was behind the bar gave me a grin that showed he had lost teeth, no doubt in fights. His eyes appraised us as we neared him, "No, my friend, this is the right place. Welcome, I am Jean the owner. Take a table and I will bring you a board showing our fare."

As we sat, I said loudly, "We have little money to waste. Just bring us some ale, if you serve it."

"Of course, but I will bring you the wax tablet for not everything is expensive and if you need food then you will not find a cheaper place to dine in the whole of Bordeaux."

Sniffing and pointedly wiping the chairs, we sat. The owner brought over the jug of beer and we held out our costrels. A knight would expect a beaker but a sword for hire carried his own beaker for drinking. A costrel would hang from the belt of every archer, spearman, and crossbowman in the land. I sipped the beer and then wrinkled my nose, "I have drunk worse, but I cannot remember when."

The owner laughed but it was the false, hollow laugh of one trying to put us at our ease, "You English! Why you do not like our wine I do not know. Here is the bill of fare." He showed us the wax tablet. The prices were cheap and only a fool or a spy would not take advantage. I spied the cheapest item on the board, mussels cooked in wine and served with local bread. "A wise choice." He held out his hand and I counted out the coppers as though they were the last we had. My full purse was back in the castle and the one I carried had but one silver coin in it and that was a French one we had taken from one of the dead warriors who had tried to ambush us.

As it was almost noon more of those who worked on the river came to eat and to drink. The place filled up and, as we were strangers, we were scrutinised. We ate the mussels slowly although they were tasty. That is what those who are hungry do. They make the food last as long as possible. We mopped up every last drop of the broth and ate every crumb of bread. I noticed that most of those who entered chose the same meal.

The innkeeper came to collect the bowls and he also brought the jug of ale, "More beer?"

I pretended to examine my purse, "Just one more. Until we find employment, we have to watch every copper."

He poured the beer and took the coins. Nodding at the swords we both wore he said, "Warriors?"

"Aye, when we can get the work but there seems to be little left here in Aquitaine. We went to Gascony, but they are not hiring Englishmen. This is our last attempt to find work before we head home. There is always work to be had fighting the Scots or the Welsh."

"Aye, well you English are not as popular as you were in the time of the other King Henry. Still, there is always work for those who need it." Enigmatically he left.

We made up a conversation about visiting the castle in Bordeaux just to add colour to our story. We nursed our ale and then, after draining our costrels took our spears, helmets, and haversacks to leave. The innkeeper shouted, "If you do not find work this afternoon then return this evening. I will spread the word. I may have news. There are some lords who prefer to hire English swords."

I nodded. As we opened the door, I saw the weasel from the quay. He grinned at us, "You found it then?"

I nodded and pushed past him. He shrugged and after Dick had joined me, he entered the inn. I was aware that we might be observed and so we headed for the castle. There the livery was all the red of the Earl of Leicester. The men who stood guard at the gatehouse were mailed and well-armed. They spied us and did not even let us approach to ask a question.

"Be off with you. We have no need of gutter rats like you!"

"But we are English!"

He laughed, "And that does not afford you any courtesy here. Try the river. They need men to lift barrels."

We left the castle but did not head towards the river. Instead, we lost ourselves in the busier parts of the town. We backtracked and took side alleys until we were sure that none was following us and then headed for the village and the castle. Getting back into the castle unseen proved easier than I had expected. A column of wagons lumbered up the road with barrels of wine intended for England and when we stepped out of the way we were able to slip into the castle unseen.

My cousin laughed as we entered the inner bailey, "That was harder work cuz than fighting in a battle. I felt sure that someone would know us and all would be lost."

"We had luck on our side but this night we will have more than luck. Henry son of Harry and Jack shall choose half a dozen men to come to the inn and they will give us help if we need it."

Prince Edward was relieved that word would reach his father, "I am sure that when Robert tells him of the threat from Castile and the harm that de Montfort has done then he will bring an army to deal with him."

Godfrey snorted as did the other bodyguards and I shook my head, "My lord, it takes time to raise and transport an army. Even if the king, your father, acts immediately, then we have at least a month or six weeks before they can reach us."

"And do you need to take this risk tonight, Sir Henry?"

I nodded, "It is a calculated risk. If we are to make a connection between the unrest in the land directly to the Earl of Leicester, then we need evidence."

Henry of Almain was a quiet and thoughtful youth. Older than his cousin he was a little more mature, "My lord, it will be the word of a hired sword against that of a noble."

I smiled, "I have thought of that but if I can get one of these hired men to give his confessions to a priest and to The Lord Edward…" I let the words hang in the air.

We left after dark and we allowed our men to go first. Three would secrete themselves inside the inn while the rest remained outside, hidden. This time Dick and I did not take out sacks, helmets, and spears. We would let them think we had found somewhere to stay as well as which I wished to be unencumbered. We used some ale to make our clothes smell of drink and Dick and I would affect a slightly drunken attitude. I found the inn more sinister after dark. Still dimly lit, even when the door was opened it was hard to see much light but inside it was now packed. As we ducked beneath the groaning door, I spied our three men. Each was on his own and had his back to a wall with a beaker of ale in his hand.

    I have never seen such a collection of miscreants and villains outside of a gaol. Perhaps it was the dark but I felt it to be a more sinister place than when we had eaten there at noon. We made our way to the bar which now had the innkeeper and two women serving ale. We adopted a meandering and weaving gait to simulate drunkenness and I saw the innkeeper smile knowingly. He waved an arm to clear away a space and greeted us like old friends, "English, you have come back and without your helmet and spear. Did you sell them or have you somewhere to sleep?"

    I still feigned wariness, "They are safe and as we have no employment yet I thought we would return here. The ale in this town is expensive."

    "Then you have come to the right place. There are no tables but have two drinks on me while you wait for the man who comes to offer you a job."

    I smiled, "Then we are in your debt."

    He laughed, "You can pay me back when you are paid by my friend."

    Dick and I raised our costrels to the innkeeper and then began a fiction about what we would do back in England when we were rich. All the time we spoke I watched our three men who had managed to become almost part of the furniture. Unless you knew where they were they were invisible.

    The man, when he came in, looked different to the rest. He reminded me of Ralph. He was a soldier and wore mail with his coif hanging down but he had on his arming cap.

His sword was a long sword. Usually, the sword chosen by a knight, it was long enough for most men to have to use two hands to wield it. I saw no spurs and this did not seem, to me, to be a knight. The warrior looked powerful enough to use it one handed. I saw him scan the room before he stepped in. He was looking for danger. He had the easy gait of a wolf and almost loped across the room. Men made way for him. The clients of the inn were tough men but the one who strode through them made even those predators fearful.

The innkeeper gave a slight bow. "Welcome master, the two men I spoke of are here." I saw then that the innkeeper had kept us deliberately close for that reason.

"Wine!"

He looked at me and then Dick. Nodding he said, "You, I can see are a warrior although you seem to me a little young to have seen much fighting," he gestured to my cousin, "this other is a stripling."

Dick flushed and I defended him, "He is my younger brother and while he may not have age on his side, he can handle himself in a fight,"

"The man I work for wants experience. He pays for experience and you look to have it although had we not lost men recently then I might even have ignored you. I can pay you six pennies a day but your brother is worth but four to me."

I made my eyes narrow, "I do not like you and I would be tempted to seek another master but at times like these, even the devil would seem attractive. What is your name?"

"It is Alain of Auxerre and yours?"

"Henry of Prescot." I had chosen the name of a place that was far away from the lands of the Earl of Leicester and far enough away from Stockton.

He seemed satisfied, "Where is your war gear?"

I gave what I hoped was a cunning look, "We have hidden the weapons and our helmets."

The man nodded and flipped a coin at the innkeeper, "Come, we go."

My three men had seen our move and as we headed for the door they began to surreptitiously move towards it too. I had not expected my plan to have worked so quickly and the thought passed through my mind that the lost men might have been the ones we killed and wounded. We might have only left three bodies on the road but I knew from the skirmish that the wounds the others had suffered would impair their ability to fight for some time.

 The man called Alain led and I followed. My three men were also almost at the door. It was as I raised my head, having opened the door that the voice from the dark street shouted, "Alain, that is the knight who slew Jean de Marin!"

 Things happened so fast that all my actions were reactions. Alain moved away from me, drawing his sword while the man who had shouted lunged at me with his short sword. I barely managed to get my sword out of its sheath before his sword slid along the mail links of the old hauberk. It saved my life. Dick's sword was out so quickly that he was able to ram it up into the skull of the man from the skirmish. My hidden men stepped up and Alain of Auxerre realised it was a trap and he turned to run. He must have had two more men waiting with him for I heard the clash of steel as the three men who had been in the inn with us blocked sword thrusts and ended the men's lives.

 I turned to look for Alain of Auxerre and spied his body lying ten paces from us. Henry son of Harry stepped from the dark and patted his club into the palm of his left hand. "I tripped him, my lord, and then clubbed him. I assumed you want a prisoner?" I nodded and he went on, "Then we had best disappear for the noise and the blood will bring the town watch."

 He nodded to his archers and they hefted the unconscious mercenary on their shoulders like a coffin at a funeral and I led them away from the bloody alley. I did not use the same route Dick and I had followed earlier for this was now night and we needed speed. Jack and his couple of spearmen were the rearguard and we raced through dark streets knowing that they would deter pursuit. Behind us, we heard the furore as the bodies were discovered. It had all happened so quickly that none in the inn had seen the fight. I hoped that by the time the town watch arrived the bodies would have been stripped by the carrion in the inn and that they would put it down to a drunken fight. If we were seen then it was only briefly because we ran as though the devil himself was behind us. My brother and Sir Geoffrey had the gate manned and we were inside with it barred before the owl that swooped down on the mouse we startled had returned to its nest to enjoy its feast.

"Geoffrey, have men keep watch from the walls to see if we were followed. I do not think we were but it is as well to be careful."

The castellan was at the entrance to the keep, "We have a prisoner and we need him both secure and where we can question him."

He nodded, "Follow me." Taking a lighted brand from the sconce he spoke to me as he led us through the hall to the steps that led to the storerooms. "When this castle was more important than it is now, we kept a good supply of wine. There is a second wine cellar that we no longer use."

"Good. Dick, find some bedding and some clothes for the man." He might have wondered at my request but he was a good squire and he obeyed instantly. The twisting stairs made it hard for the archers. Alain of Auxerre was a big man and he wore mail. Had they not been archers it might have been an impossible task. As it was it merely slowed them and allowed the castellan, Alfred, and I to enter the damp cellar. It was large enough to hold a dozen or so firkins of wine. There was, of course, no wind holes and the only entrance was the door through which we had come and that had a bolt on the inside.

"We will need bedding for him."

The castellan handed the brand to Alfred and said, "I will have some fetched."

I shook my head, "Dick is fetching some but we will need a pot for him to make water."

He paused, "Do we act within the law here, Sir Henry?"

I nodded, "The warrant from King Henry gives me all the authority I need." He left and Henry and my archers manhandled the unconscious warrior into the cellar.

"Quickly before he wakes, I want him as naked as the day he

was born. The man looks to know his business and I want no secreted weapons."

By the time Dick returned with a selection of clothes the man was naked and it was as well we had done so. There was a small knife in a sheath hidden beneath his hose. I saw the scars from wounds of battles past. This was a warrior. He began to come to as we put on the last of the clothes. Without opening his eyes he put his hand to his bloody scalp and felt the blood. He opened his eyes and we all stood. Henry had a short sword drawn even as the man tried to rise.

"Friend, stay where you are until his lordship says that you can rise."

He glared at me, "You cannot do this to me."

I smiled a cold smile, "And yet we have. Come, you and I know that you have been working against the interests of King Henry. The men who recognised me tried to ambush the heir to England's throne. One of the men we killed on the road from Auch gave your name, Alain of Auxerre. Denial will avail you nought. You are guilty of treason and any rights you may have had disappeared when you took this path." His eyes had become adjusted to the dim light and he saw that there were seven of us in the cellar and there was no escape. "Tell me the name of your master and have your statement witnessed by a man of God and you shall go free. You have my word."

He laughed and in the eerie cellar, it echoed and sounded terrifying, "You fool! Do you think my master is a robber baron? He has power and he has ambition. More, his arm is long and if I speak then my life is ended. Do your worst. I can endure torture and I am a patient man. You may decide to kill me although if you are the man I believe you to be then you will not because you have what you call honour." He spat blood onto the floor, "That is what I think of honour. You will tire of watching me and then I shall escape."

I was not sure if this was bravado, but we would learn nothing immediately. I nodded and, as the two servants came in with a straw-filled mattress and a piss pot I said, "Then reflect on your future for if you are patient then I am more so for I fight for a just cause and not thirty pieces of silver."

Without turning our backs on him we walked out of the cellar, taking the brand with us. I saw his hand go to his back and a mask of anger descended on his face as he realised we had taken his hidden knife. The door was shut and I slid the two bolts across. "Jack, Henry, I want two men here from now on. Use a mixture of our men and the garrison. Each pair watches for two hours. Others will come with food so that when he eats there are four pairs of eyes upon him. Make no mistake this man is dangerous."

"Aye, lord. Do you wish us to torture him?"

"No, Henry, son of Harry. It is against my nature, and I do not think that it will work. We have him and I now need to plan how to use his capture to our advantage."

We reached the Great Hall where the bodyguards, squires, Sir Thomas, and the royal cousins awaited us. I waved over the castellan, "We will keep two men on watch at all times. Every warrior in the castle will share that duty."

He smiled, "Sir Henry, my men and I are grateful for the opportunity to serve the crown again and we are honoured to have the future Duke of Aquitaine here. All will be done as you wish."

"Have Sir Geoffrey and my men relieved. We need to talk. First I will make water." I headed for the garderobe and when I returned saw that Dick had been speaking to the men around the table. I sat and Edgar fetched me some wine. They sat expectantly around the table while we waited for Geoffrey. He arrived and I smiled, "Well, we have our evidence, Prince Edward, for your father. The trouble is that it may be hard to extract."

He said, "Dick has told us that the man who recognised you was at the ambush, and he was with this Alain of Auxerre. Surely that is all the evidence we need."

"If that was all we needed then aye and we could execute him but we need, Prince Edward, the name of the man who hired them."

"That is obvious, Simon de Montfort."

"And how do we prove that?" My words silenced them. "The fox has attacked the henhouse enough and it is time that we visited him in his den. Tomorrow, Prince Edward, we dress in our finery and, leaving my spearmen and archers here, along with Sir Thomas and Sir Geoffrey, we will visit the Earl of Leicester."

When Thomas spoke he showed his new maturity for his question was not petulant but considered, "And why do you leave Sir Geoffrey and me behind, cousin?"

I smiled, "Firstly you were wounded on the road and such a wound needs time for healing but, mainly because Simon de Montfort must know that we are in Gascony and, probably, where we are staying but thanks to our cunning, he cannot know how many of us there are. The men who survived the ambush and reported to Alain and the earl may well have been careless with the truth. They may have said that they did not wound a knight but killed him. When the bodies of his men are discovered, he may assume that some of our men were hurt. Let us take the smallest number we can so that he underestimates us. We go and speak to him, Prince Edward, to ask him if he has managed to stem the raids by men like Alain of Auxerre."

Henry of Almain said, "But he has sent them."

"Then let us see what lies he tells. I want the man discomfited. For too long he has had free rein here. We have to buy Robert time to get to your father and for him to act. It will be more dangerous for us but this castle is now stronger than it was when we came. However, there is the possibility that they may well try to extract you from here and use you as some sort of hostage, Prince Edward, and from now on our vigilance must increase. My plan is a dangerous one for you do not poke a man like Simon de Montfort and think he will ignore it. Your father sent me for a reason and while I may not like it, I will do as I was commanded."

Chapter 8

Henry Samuel

Bearding the beast

This time I made sure that my hair was well-groomed and I had shaved. Dick had curried and groomed my horse and my helmet, whilst it just hung from my cantle, gleamed as did the mail which he had put into a sack with sand and then hand polished until it looked almost gleaming white. Wearing the gryphon and blue livery of the Warlord we rode to the castle. As luck would have it the sentries were the same ones who had turned me away. One of them looked at me curiously as though he recognised me but then decided he had not and we were waved through to the outer ward. Dismounting, Dick and Edward took the horses to the water trough. Just Kurt and Godfrey accompanied the two royal cousins and we headed through the gate into the inner ward. One of the sentries must have signalled for a liveried servant approached us at the gate to the keep.

"My lord, this is unexpected. Do you wish to speak to the Lord Lieutenant?"

I smiled and gestured at Prince Edward, "I believe that he will wish to speak to the future Duke of Aquitaine, The Lord Edward."

Realisation dawned and he said, "If you would wait here then…"

Prince Edward took charge, and his voice was firm with authority,

"You would leave a member of the royal family out here in the sun? I think not. Lead on and take us to the man whom my father asked to watch over my Gascon interests."

The man might have argued with a mere knight and future baron but Prince Edward was a different matter and, defeated, he led us into the castle. As we passed into the gloomy interior I said, quietly, "Well done, my lord."

There were enough men in the castle to give warning to the Earl of Leicester so that by the time we reached the Great Hall he and his lieutenants were ready. I recognised his brother Amaury. I realised that whilst they had seen me and knew me to be of the Warlord's family, they did not know my name. There was no reason why they should. When we had met at Westminster I had been in the background and it was the king and the prince that held their attention.

Simon de Montfort rose from his seat that was on a dais. It looked to me to be a throne. He descended and gave the slightest of bows, "Prince Edward. I did not know that you had arrived in Bordeaux." The look on his face told me that it was a lie and besides we knew from the men sent to abduct him that he knew the prince was in the Duchy.

For one so relatively young, Prince Edward seemed to have an intuitive sense of what to do and to say. Perhaps it was the Plantagenet blood in his veins. "My lord, my companions and I have been in Gascony for some time, not openly of course, so that I might meet and speak to the people that one day I shall rule. I confess that thus far I am disappointed in what I have seen."

De Montfort affected a puzzled look, "Disappointed, Prince Edward? How so?"

"I have heard stories of bands of knights and men roaming the land and ravaging both the people and the countryside."

"You do not want to believe all that you hear, my lord. There are Seigneurs who deliberately flout my law and spread scurrilous stories about me. This land is peaceful and the only danger comes from the handful of rebels who defy me." He smiled.

I spoke for the first time, "And we were attacked when we left Auch. One of the men told us that the orders came from Bordeaux." It was an arrow sent into the dark and was patently untrue. I had not been told that. It struck home, however, and the earl's eyes became large and his face contorted with rage. He seemed to see me for the first time. "And who are you to thus accuse me? I know you are of the blood of the bishop killer but which of the brood are you?"

His careful choice of words was a deliberate insult but I kept my calm because I knew I had been right, "I apologise, my lord. I should have introduced myself. I am Sir Henry Samuel of Elton, the nephew of the Earl of Cleveland."

If anything his face grew redder. "Samuel! Is that not a Jewish name? How does a Jew gain his spurs?"

The insults were mounting and I knew that I had to say something. "My lord, this may be your castle, but I will not suffer insults. I will happily meet you in single combat to decide the matter, but you should know that my great-great-grandmother was a Jew and a great lady."

I felt the tension in the room. If swords were drawn, then there would be blood. It suddenly came to me that King Henry had known the reaction of the earl to my name. The Earl of Leicester had famously thrown all the Jews from his lands and was known to hate them with a passion.

King Henry's son was calm and he spoke firmly, "Sir Henry Samuel, it is not the Earl of Leicester's castle but mine and I would have you, Sir Simon, apologise for the insult."

Things had come to a head far faster than I could have expected. I had not even had the chance to bring up the name of Alain of Auxerre. We were outnumbered in the castle and even with Godfrey and the other bodyguards, we would be overpowered. In one fell swoop, Simon de Montfort could take the piece on the chessboard that was The Lord Edward.

It was his brother who poured oil in the troubled waters. He put his hand on Simon de Montfort's arm and said, silkily, "My brother meant no harm, Sir Henry. We all want what is best for The Lord Edward, do we not?" He looked pointedly at his brother whilst squeezing his arm. "Brother?"

Simon de Montfort began breathing more slowly and, finally, nodded, "I meant no harm and if any offence was caused by my innocent comments, Sir Henry, then I am sorry."

As apologies go it was not the best, but I was here to serve the king and I nodded, "Apology accepted and if it helps, my lord, I can give the name of the man who said the orders came from Bordeaux; it was Alain of Auxerre. Have you heard of him?"

The widening of the eyes told me that he had but his voice and shake of the head denied it, "I have never heard of him. Are you going to believe the word of a hired sword or the word of the Earl of Leicester?" The question hung in the air and we said nothing. I saw that Simon de Montfort was thinking on his feet and concocting a believable story. "He may be one of the men who came to me offering his sword. I reject any who are untrustworthy. This sounds like just such a scoundrel. Do you know where he is now?"

I shook my head, "At this moment no. The conversation I had about him was in a low tavern. I wished to speak to you before I did more about it and now that you have denied any knowledge of him then I know how to deal with him should I see him again."

The earl, his brother and his lieutenants were silenced by my words. If they had used Alain of Auxerre as their go-between then he had to be silenced before he could speak to Prince Edward. I had also spread doubt in their minds. They had to have known of the incident at the inn but as I had said I was seeking their man they would have to wonder where he was. Doubt is like a fog in the mind and stops a man from seeing clearly. Such a man makes mistakes.

It was the prince who broke the silence, "So, my lord, what do we do about these bands of men who ravage the countryside?"

"I have few men to effectively control them and they are just rabble. I will do all that I can but I fear that without more men and they cost gold, then I can do little." He was lying and it was clear to all that he was doing so.

Prince Edward showed his increasing skill for he handled the earl with dexterity. "Ah, so if I could send to my father…"

"For more money? A good idea, my lord."

"No, earl, I was about to say if I could send to my father for men then perhaps the men he sends and those that I have brought with me could deal with these, what did you call them, scoundrels? It seems to me that if what you say is true then they will not stand up to knights, men at arms and, of course, English archers." He turned to his cousin, "Come, Henry, we will not delay the earl any longer."

Simon de Montfort was now thoroughly confused, "Delay, my lord?"

"Of course, I assume that you will take however few men you have and begin to do something. It will take time for my father to be informed of the problem and even longer for him to reach us. Every day we procrastinate exacerbates the problem. Let us go."

We left a stunned Great Hall but I knew that we had merely created more problems for ourselves. De Montfort would now be forced to do something about us. He would make an excuse to be far from our castle and any direct involvement but we would be in danger.

We mounted our horses but did not speak until we had crossed the drawbridge, "My lord, that was well done but we should ride to the port. The earl has to be told that you have sent a missive to your father or all that we said might sound like a bluff."

"I am glad you are on my side, Sir Henry, of course. Let us find a church. They will have parchment and I will write to my father."

It was late afternoon by the time the letter was ready and sealed. Fate smiled on us for we found an English cog that was about to depart on the evening tide. For a gold piece, the captain was quite happy to see that the letter reached the Tower. The fact that we hoped the king was already on the move was immaterial. We were still deceiving Simon de Montfort.

There was little point in trying to lose our followers. There were simply too many of us. However, the Earl of Leicester still had no idea how many men we had. He might suspect where we were staying but he could not know how many defenders we had. Godfrey and the bodyguards had barely moved a handspan from the sides of their charges whilst in Bordeaux and as we headed down the river road, they maintained that closeness. I rode with Alfred.

"Well, brother, we know now who is behind the unrest in the duchy."

"We always knew but we have had confirmation. It is as though we have pulled off the mask of Simon de Montfort and now, we shall see what he will do."

"Attack us?"

I shook my head, "Not directly but I expect that he will try to get men inside the castle. Not today and not, I believe, tomorrow. He will want to put a distance between himself and any deed like that. That suits us for the defences still need improvement. We cannot stop them from gaining access to the outer ward but we can make the inner wall and ward a veritable fortress. I will be reliant on you."

"What about Geoffrey and Thomas?"

"They have skills but you and I, brother share the same thoughts. Back there, when I thought there would be bloodshed in the castle I knew, without turning, that your hand was ready to draw your sword and that I would have my back protected. The other two are good knights and I doubt neither their courage nor their skill but we share our father's blood. When we reach the castle you and I will walk the walls and decide our strategy."

As we approached the castle, I viewed it as an attacker might. It was not a large castle. With a simple ditch that sometimes flooded when there was heavy rain, the small curtain wall was there to slow down an attacker. A man could easily be boosted over it. Its purpose was to stop horses and rams. The flat ground meant that the original builders had been forced to use cunning in their design. The inner wall was much higher and had a fighting platform. Although they had neither hoardings nor embrasures there were two good towers at the northeast and southwest corners. The other two towers, whilst smaller, each had a roof and archers could easily use them. The keep was a square one; with three floors it rose above the inner wall and archers on the top had a clear sight of both walls. The two gatehouses were also different. The outer gatehouse was a simple affair with a drawbridge and portcullis. The two towers were small and would only accommodate a handful of men. It was the second one that would hold up an attacker trying to gain entry for it had two strong towers. There was another ditch and drawbridge but this time there were two portcullises as well as murder holes and a sally port. As we crossed the ditch to enter the inner ward, I knew that when the attack came it would not be a direct attack. They would sneak in and try to take us unawares. That meant a night attack.

As we dismounted Thomas and Geoffrey emerged from the keep. I saw that they were eager for news but the inner ward was not the place for it. I held up my hand. "It is time for a council of war. Have food and wine brought to the Great Hall and have the castellan replace any of our men on the outer wall with his own. From now on our men remain hidden. Then the castellan can join us."

Our squires took our horses and we ascended the stairs to the Great Hall. The castellan had given up his chambers on the top floor of the keep and slept with us in the now cramped warrior hall. It meant that the prince and his cousin were in the safest place in the castle. I glanced at the steps that led to the subterranean cellars. I would let Alain of Auxerre sweat a little longer but I would have the knights and squires move into the larger rooms of the keep. It might not be as comfortable but we would be on hand to help the prince and prevent any harm coming to him. The smell of bread reminded me that we would have to ensure that the bread ovens were doused sooner rather than later. If we left fire for an attacker, then we might all die and the fire that caused our death put down to an accident.

I took off my coif and my sword belt and hung both from the chair at the head of the table. I waited until the food and drink had been placed on the table before I spoke. Jack and Henry, as well as the bodyguards, made to leave us but I shook my head, "Sit and join us. We are all in this together now. It matters not if you are a knight, a spearman or an archer, a knife in the night can end a life just as easily."

Prince Edward asked, "You think it will come to that, Sir Henry?"

I shrugged, "It may not and if that is the case, I will spend a night on my knees in the chapel thanking God for watching over us. I cannot read the mind of Simon de Montfort but I think, when he lost his temper this day, that I had the measure of the man." I sipped some of the wine. It was, as was all the wine in this part of Aquitaine, good. I would eat later. "The man is ambitious. He sat on a dais and his seat was like a throne. He is also clever and masks his intention by using men like Alain of Auxerre. Did you notice that he did not even hint that the men who had spoken to me were nobles or knights? Had we not rattled his mind he might have named some Seigneur who might be behind it. It was a mistake and showed me his thoughts."

The castellan said, "My lord, it is well known that the Earl of Leicester has many hired swords who enter the castle of Bordeaux, but they rarely leave in daylight. It is rumoured that he has an army in the hundreds, but none have seen them gathered. If they were to attack this castle, we would be hard-pressed to defend against that kind of number."

I nodded, "We have time. Not much but just enough. He will have to distance himself from the deed and that gives us two or three days. We subtly make the castle more defensible. I have no intention of defending the outer wall. Therein lies failure and as the keep is offset in the centre, we will make a second defence between the stables and the warrior hall although if we lose the north wall then we have lost the battle. I hope it will not come to that. I want them hurt before they reach the inner ward. During the day there will be men watching but Henry son of Harry, I want some of your archers, dressed in plain clothes and without bows, hidden in the woods and villages watching for the watchers."

"You would have our men take them?"

"If they can but the important thing is that we keep them in the dark. If they run when our men approach then let them."

Prince Edward asked, "Why do they not need bows?"

"They might need them, my lord, but if bows are seen then the enemy might suspect a trap. Knowing that there are archers in the castle might change their plans. They know that we have two archers in the castle but not that we have enough archers to rain death upon a direct attack."

Godfrey had listened to all my words and he coughed before speaking, "My lord, we are too few to guard all the walls. How do you plan to ensure that The Lord Edward is safe?" He gave a sad smile, "As you know, my lord, protecting the prince is my sole priority and whilst I would be happy to fight on the walls with you, I cannot."

"Nor would I expect you to. You and the other bodyguards are essential to my plans. With you guarding the two cousins we can defend the castle more confidently. One advantage we have is that they do not know our true numbers. The handful of men we took to his castle might make him believe that we have half a dozen retainers. That will be confirmed by the survivors of the attack close to Auch. They saw four knights, the bodyguards and a handful of men." I let silence fill the hall so that I could look at each of them in the eyes. My grandfather had done so and my training had not been wasted. "They will come at night and you are right, Godfrey, we cannot guard the outer wall. It is too low. Castellan, you will man just the gatehouse at night but we will rig traps to alert us to men climbing the walls. We use oil and grease on the top. We put sharpened spikes disguised by the rubbish in the ditch. As soon as the night guards hear a noise then they abandon the outer gate and come here to the main defence, the inner ward and the keep. Jack, from now on the spearmen will sleep during the day. The rest of us will toil to improve the defences. They will be the night watch on the walls. As soon as the men on the outer gate give a warning then we will be roused, silently, to repel the enemy. Henry, the archers will be used at the top of the keep and in the towers. I know that nighttime is a difficult time for archers and so each night we will light three braziers in the outer ward. It is a risk, I know, for it gives our enemies fire but that light will enable the archers to make a killing ground of the outer ward."

The castellan said, "We have throwing spears and darts in the armoury." He gave a sad smile. "In times past this castle had a mighty garrison and would have laughed away a siege. There are weapons aplenty."

"Good. All that I wish to do is to discourage these hired swords. As we saw on the road from Auch they are used to easy victories. If I have learned nothing else from the conversations with villagers, churchmen and lords alike it is that these raids have not been against men who can defend themselves but weak almost defenceless villagers."

Prince Edward asked, "And if they do not come or we repel their attacks, what then, Sir Henry?"

"We hope and pray that your father comes and arrives with an army. If he does not then Simon de Montfort might change his strategy. If an army does not come to end his reign, he may try to take the duchy and from what I have seen, he could do that for it is riven with factions and old feuds. A man like de Montfort could exploit those weaknesses."

"That is a depressing thought, Sir Henry. Then there is no hope?"

He was showing his lack of confidence in a father whom Simon de Montfort had said was such a bad leader that, like Charles the Mad of France, he should be locked in a tower. I smiled, "Of course, there is hope, my lord and it is in this room." The prince looked around and I shook my head, "It is you, my lord, that is the hope. You are the one who can repair the rifts and heal the hurts in this land. You are too young yet but with God's help and the blood of the Warlord, then we will prevail and when the snake is scotched and you have come of age then the blood of the Plantagenets will make this land that was theirs, safe once more."

It was a rousing speech and the smiles on their faces told me that it had given them confidence. I knew that we needed more than a small measure of luck as well. A leader used any weapon he had in his armoury.

Chapter 9

Henry Samuel
Bloody blades in the night

We had to work as surreptitiously as we could to plant the stakes. The archers who would watch in the woods were sent out before dawn, and it was only when Henry son of Harry was able to report that there were no watchers that we were able to work in the outer ditch. It was the garrison, the knights and the squires who did the work. The archers were our sentries and the spearmen slept. As we took our noon break and food I saw the prince, his cousin and the bodyguards come to join us.

"Sir Henry, we squat like toads in the castle while you toil. That is not right for the work is for our benefit. We will join you." He held up a hand, "And I will brook no argument."

"And you shall have none although if you end up with bloody hands I will expect to be chastised by your father."

He nodded and said, sadly, "Perhaps if my father had done as I intend to do he might have been a better warrior for he would know what warriors have to do to keep their lands safe."

I knew, from the conversations I had enjoyed with the two cousins, that the king's poor performance in the one war he had fought rankled with not only them but also the king's brother, Richard of Cornwall.

It was during the night that watchers were sent to view the castle. The castellan took his duties seriously and it was he who commanded the first watch that night on the outer gatehouse. I had not expected an attack so soon and I had not ordered the braziers to be lit but he spied men scouting out the defences. They did not try to cross the ditch but I was summoned and watched the half dozen shadows walking around the outside of the defences. They might see some of the sharpened stakes as we had not had time to disguise them all but there was no way that they would be able to see the traps on the walls and fighting platform of the curtain wall.

I nodded to the castellan as the last of the shadows left just before dawn, "We now know that they might come any time now. Tomorrow night or soon after will be the time they will come. Tomorrow night we light the braziers."

As we worked the next day to finish the traps and to disguise the stakes, we heard that Simon de Montfort had left his castle and taken with him more than half the garrison. He had let it be known that he intended to ride to Barbezieux to deal with the rebellious Seigneur there. It was a march of some days north of Bordeaux and I knew that he was giving himself deniability from any involvement in a nighttime attack. When we had no attack that first night, Thomas and Geoffrey began to doubt that we would suffer any attack. Thomas questioned the need to lose sleep. The prince smiled at them, "Sir Henry has the right of it. I saw de Montfort's face. I know that I am safe for I have bodyguards but I think that the man appointed by my father to watch over my interests wishes Sir Henry dead for he sees him as the threat. I am viewed as a boy. The Earl of Leicester will learn that this cub has grown teeth and his memory is long."

He was right, of course. My prisoner ensured that they would come and that they would try to rid de Montfort of the man that linked him to the unrest. They would try to kill me and then eliminate Alain of Auxerre. It was the main reason I had not questioned him again. I wanted him kept in the dark, quite literally. The passage of time was the regular meals and the emptying of his pot. He expected torture and when none came that, in itself, would be a torture too. I wanted him confused and more willing to speak but I wanted him alive.

Alfred and I slept in our mail for the next two nights. It was uncomfortable but the most comfortable sleep a warrior could have was death itself and the mail might keep me alive a little longer. With the prince and his bodyguards in the chambers above the Great Hall in the keep, we slept close to the most vulnerable part of the castle, close by the north wall. The defences we had erected between the walls, the stables and the warrior hall were simple enough. We had hewn stakes from the woods and built a small palisade. It would only slow an enemy who could simply hack through it, but it would take minutes to do so and minutes could be the difference between life and death.

Sleeping in mail meant that I never slept for long and when my bladder demanded that I rise I did so. Alfred rose as well. We said nothing as Thomas, Geoffrey and the others were soundly asleep although as was our habit we picked up our sword belts and donned arming caps. It was cold at night. We went outside to the large pot and made water. I nodded to the wall. My spearmen were there but, as they had been ordered, they were not moving around. Alfred knew what I wished of him and while I headed for the river wall he went to the ladder at the north wall.

Jack was on duty at the northern gate tower, "All quiet?"

He spoke even more quietly than I had, "Aye, my lord, too quiet."

His words reeked of worry, "Too quiet?"

He put his hand around his ear, "Can you hear owls, my lord? Where are the noises of the animals moving by the river? All is silent in nature's world and it should not be. If there are no animals then it means that there are men there."

I nodded at the gatehouse of the outer wall where four of the garrison watched, "They have seen nothing?"

He shrugged, "I know not. Our men are there but I have not seen them move."

Sometimes you have to trust your instincts. Something was wrong and Jack was too good a soldier to be nervous about nothing. I turned to Hob, one of the spearmen, "Go to the warrior hall and rouse the others but do so silently. Tell Egbert to wake Godfrey and the others in the keep."

"Yes, my lord."

I pulled my coif over my arming cap and turned so that I could see the other men on the inner wall. I waved to attract their attention. It was Alfred who turned. I mimed danger and he nodded. He, too, pulled up his coif. That done I slipped my sword in and out of its scabbard in case the night air had made it stick and I peered at the outer gatehouse. There were shadows there, but they were not moving. That, in itself, was not worrying for we had told all the sentries to remain still. Jack was quite right, there was no noise and there should have been. I glanced over to the warrior hall when I heard movement and saw my archers, knights and squires heading for their allotted positions then I knew my commands had been obeyed. Thomas would be in command of the northeast tower, Alfred the south-west tower and Geoffrey the north-west tower.

It was as Paul and Rafe climbed up to join us that the crossbow bolt flew from the outer gatehouse. Had Paul not ducked to string his bow then he would be a dead man. The bolt slammed into the wood of the hoarding above our heads.

I shouted, "Stand to!"

Paul murmured, "Bastard crossbowman." He pulled a war arrow from his warbag and nocked it. He used one of the uprights of the hoarding for cover as he peered into the dark. More bolts flew from the gatehouse and then I saw first one shadow and then a second flit across the outer ward. The braziers gave the shadows form. Paul said, without turning, "Yours, Egbert." He was pulling back to aim at the crossbowman on the outer gatehouse. I saw the shadow of his head as he rose and knew that he would rise, rest his crossbow on the wood at the back of the outer gatehouse and then release it. He would be an incredibly small target. It was night and the outer gatehouse was more than a hundred feet from us. Paul's arrow flew a heartbeat before Egbert's. They say that arrows are silent but they are not. The thrum of the bowstring and the noise of the flights as air passes over them gives a sound but they are invisible. The man who ran across the outer ward knew not what hit him. The crossbowman, in contrast, saw death as the white goose fletch raced at him. He would have been concentrating on putting the bolt in the crossbow and then lining up on one of us. I saw his head slammed back.

More bolts came in our direction. We had spread out archers out as we were uncertain which direction they would choose for their attack. Henry son of Harry was in the keep with half of the archers and the others were in pairs. Their use of crossbows had fooled us. They were the greater threat and so only three archers were able to send their arrows at the flitting shadows. There were too many of them and most of the thirty men I saw pouring across the outer ward almost made the wall. It was then that my spearmen, knights and squires were able to add missiles to the attack. I picked up a throwing spear and hurled it at the man who was just forty feet from me. I was aided by the height of the gatehouse and by the brazier's light but it was still a difficult strike. I hit him in the thigh and he stumbled. He took his sword and hacked off the haft of the spear. He was a veteran and knew that the spearhead embedded in the leg would slow down the bleeding. I picked up a dart and as he lurched to reach the safety of the ditch I sent it in his direction. It hit his upper shoulder. He wore mail but a dart has a head which is bodkin shaped and I knew that I had hurt him.

Jack said, "How did they manage to avoid our traps, my lord?"

I shook my head, "I have no idea. Perhaps they had more watchers than we knew, or it may be that one in the village gave them information. It is too late to worry about that now."

Half a dozen men had been hit crossing the outer ward but there were only two bodies. These were tough men. Then I saw the gates open. Egbert and Paul switched targets and the two men who had opened them were hit in the back but they managed to pull them open before collapsing. The men who entered had ladders and, more alarmingly, large shields held before them. They would stop the arrows from doing them harm.

I turned and shouted, "Abandon the east towers and wall. We need you here! The gatehouse is our fort."

It was now clear that their attack would come through the main gate. I should have realised that. The attack across the ward had been to divert our attention as had the crossbows in the outer wall. Henry and the archers on the top of the keep now had better targets. They were able to use the height of the keep to send arrows up into the sky and fall vertically negating the effect of the shields. The ladder men had no such protection. The lack of numbers came back to haunt us.

The arrows that fell managed to strike two times out of every five but the column of men moved inexorably towards the survivors of the first attack who were now sheltered and protected by our wall. They would be able to use the ladders as bridges over the ditch. This was a well-planned attack.

Dick had joined me unscathed, and he had brought my helmet, "I will not need it, Dick, and I have a better line of sight without it."

"There are more of them than I expected, cuz."

"Aye and me. I thought a handful of assassins would come but this is a full-blown attack. De Montfort must be desperate." I turned to look at the keep. The castellan was there with the rest of the garrison as well as half of my archers and the four bodyguards. If our gate and walls were breached, then they would have to hold. It was then I heard the axes on the gates. "Egbert, I leave you in command here. Dick, come with me." I spied Geoffrey, "Geoffrey, with me."

Grabbing spears and darts we headed down the stairs to the chamber above the entrance. There were murder holes there. I had wanted boiling water and oil but the smoke from the fires to keep them hot would have given away the trap. I had to hope that we would use the murder holes to thin their numbers before using the tiny sally port to attack them. If it came to that then it would be a desperate time for in the confined space of a gatehouse luck would play just as big a part as skill. We moved the wood to reveal the holes. Geoffrey and his squire joined us. The noise from the axes was regular.

"How goes it, Geoffrey?"

"We are holding them but the shields make the bows less effective. By my reckoning, we slew less than one in five and the rest are the ones battering at the gates."

"We use the darts and the spears and when they learn where they can avoid them then we use the sally port. Edgar and Dick, your task is to guard the sally port and, if we fall, to close and bar it."

"Aye, Sir Henry."

The shouts and screams from without told me that we were still causing casualties but the noise of splintering wood that the gate would soon be breached. The portcullis would hold them up but not for long. I idly wondered if daylight might deter them. I suspected that they would have expected to have made more progress than they had. Had Jack not been so observant then the crossbows they had used might have reaped a greater harvest. The sound of the axes on the portcullis was different from that of blades on the gate and I knew that the first gate had been breached. I readied a dart. The advantage of a murder hole was that you could simply drop a dart or a spear. The open portcullis did hold them up but not for long and I saw men passing beneath us. I dropped a dart which struck a man on the neck. His coif was mail but luck favoured me and the bodkin head penetrated the mail and his neck. Blood spurted. The other three also had varying degrees of success. I grabbed a javelin and as a face looked up to see whence came the missiles I threw it. It struck his skull.

I heard a voice shout, "Murder holes! Get to the side!"

I rose and took my last throwing spear. I would have to use it as a normal spear. I entered the narrow spiral staircase that led to the tiny chamber and door. The space was just big enough for one man and I stood there with Geoffrey behind me. I slid back the bolt. One of the measures we had taken was to grease all the bolts on the gates to make it easier for us to egress. It slid silently. The gate did not open directly onto the gatehouse but was recessed and to any in the almost black gatehouse at night it would look like a garderobe. I waited until I heard the axes on the second gate before I opened the sally port and stepped into the recess. I was hidden by the dark and I felt Geoffrey slip in behind me. I risked peering around the gatehouse and saw that there were fewer men than I had expected. Then it struck me, they would be using their ladders on the wall. Whoever commanded these men knew we had fewer men than he and was spreading his attack around to find our weak spot. I stepped out and thrust the spear into the back of the first man I came across. The axes drowned out his shout and withdrawing it I rammed it into the back of another. Geoffrey did the same and I was about to do the same to a third when the man turned.

"Ware behind!" I pushed the throwing spear into his chest but his mailed hand grabbed it and wrenched it from my grip. I drew my sword and dagger and, while he tried to pull the spear from his body, I slashed across his eyes. I barely managed to block a blow from an axe with my sword. The axeman had used two hands and the axe's blade caught my coif. I stabbed my dagger through his mail coif and into his ear and then his brain. He slumped to the ground.

Dick and Edgar had disobeyed us, and I was glad for as they joined the confused fight their weapons brought us victory. The ones hewing at the gate were either slain or wounded so severely that they were effectively out of the battle.

"Dick, go to the wall and bring my brother, cousin and their squires. Use the sally port and join us. Let us take the battle to them!"

"Aye, but be careful, cuz. You still have much to teach me."

I nodded and led the other two to the shattered gate. The three braziers still illuminated the outer ward and I peered around the side. They had not risked ladders on the gatehouse which was higher and more strongly defended than the walls. They had also avoided the two towers but four ladders, two on each side, now rested on the walls and men with shields were ascending. I ran at the nearest ladder and hoped that my archers on the walls would recognise me. When a bolt flew from the outer gatehouse, I knew that not all the crossbows had been silenced. I heard Paul's triumphant cry as he sent an arrow to hit the man.

Two men flanked the bottom of the ladder holding it steady and Geoffrey and I simply ran at the one on our side. My sword sliced into his side, but it was our combined weight that knocked him, the ladder, and his companion to the ground. The weight of the men on the ladder did the rest and the ladder crashed to the ground.

Egbert's voice shouted, "It is Sir Henry! Kill the attackers, let none escape!"

He was right. There was no honour in these men who had come at night to end our lives and we slew helpless men who squirmed on the ground. I heard a cheer from behind me as my brother led help, "The Warlord!"

Dick was with them and the eight of us ran at the second ladder on this side of the wall. This time the men at the bottom were ready for us but as goose fletched flowers sprang from their chests they fell and died. The ladder was, once again, knocked to the ground and the men despatched. I turned to look at the other ladders but they had been abandoned and the men ran. A third fell before they reached the safety of the outer gate for my archers on both the keep and the walls were ruthless. We kept running until we reached the gate and I saw the last of the men disappearing into the small copse that bordered the river. I heard horses neighing.

"On, let us rid ourselves of these snakes in the night!"

I suppose that they outnumbered us, but a fleeing man thinks of one thing; his own safety and it was every man for himself. I instinctively brought up my sword to hack at the rider who neared me. He had two hands on the reins, and I drew blood but he escaped me. Four horsemen risked the river and forced their mounts into the water. Others managed to evade our blades and make the road. When Egbert and Jack led the defenders from the walls to join us it was to gather the horses and question the three dying men who were left. These were not like the warrior on the road and they died silently having refused to answer our questions. As dawn broke and the villagers peered from their homes, we led the horses back into the castle. We had won the battle and now it was time to count the cost.

We found the first that we had lost in the outer gatehouse. The men there had their throats cut. It was now clear that they had died far earlier than I had thought and that the attackers had used the time to gain entry to the gatehouse. The burning braziers must have upset their plans and they had adapted them. When we reached the second gatehouse, I saw that I had lost one archer, Peter, and three of my spearmen were dead. In the scheme of things, it was a small price we had paid for we had counted twenty-three bodies but any price was still too high a price. Once again it was my family and Sir Geoffrey that had saved the day. Had my brother and my cousin not joined me, then the battle might have hung in the balance. Thomas had not faltered, and his early lack of confidence had disappeared since he had been wounded.

    We brought the enemy dead into the outer ward and searched their bodies. It was not for treasure, although my men found plenty, but for clues as to their identity. They had been clever and none had either coins or clothes that gave a clue to their master although we all knew who it was. The only evidence we found came from an unexpected source, the horses. Three of them bore the mark of the castle of Bordeaux. Of course, the castellan might argue that the horses had been stolen but we now had the first link between the attack and Bordeaux Castle. As we headed to the keep to speak with The Lord Edward, I decided that it was now time to speak to Alain of Auxerre once more.

Chapter 10

Henry Samuel
The cleansing of the castle

Before I went to the cellar to speak with the man we had captured we first set about repairing the gates. Prince Edward ordered his bodyguards to help my men and they did so. I think Godfrey felt some sort of guilt that while he had done his duty men had died while he watched on. He was too good a soldier for that to sit well with him. While our men did that I washed the blood from my body and changed to a clean surcoat. The two royal cousins waited patiently while I did so. Once that was done, I was assailed by questions.

"Do we have the evidence we need, my lord?"

"Who were these men?"

"Should we ride directly to the castle at Bordeaux?"

I held up my hands to stop them, "My lords, we have evidence but not enough. The men may well have been some of the Earl of Leicester's retinue for they were well led but most, from their weapons and clothes, were swords for hire. And, yes, we should ride to Bordeaux Castle and it should be sooner rather than later but the garrison lost too many men and we cannot leave the castle in such a parlous state. I know that some of the rats may flee and report to de Montfort, but we can do little about that. I intend to have the prisoner brought up. We will make a pyre of the dead and use their crossbows as kindling. I want him to see the faces of the dead. We will watch his reaction. He is still our best chance of catching de Montfort in a lie. Now, no more questions, my lords. We have much to do."

It was noon by the time that the inner gate was repaired enough to give us security. The outer gate was unharmed. The broken timbers, ladders and crossbows made an effective pyre for the bodies. I had Alain of Auxerre fetched from the cellar. It gave me great satisfaction as, with his hands tied behind him, he stumbled into the light which must have been as painful for him as the blow that had felled him outside the inn. I said nothing but waited until his eyes adjusted to the light and he saw the pyre.

I nodded to my men who, as I had ordered, brought each bloody and battered body to the wood and threw it onto the pile. Their mail had been taken from them and some were just dressed in tunic and hose. I saw the grim look on Alain of Auxerre's face. When they were all piled, and our prisoner had seen each face my men threw oil and pig fat onto the pyre. Dick handed me a burning brand and I went to Prince Edward, "Would you like to do the honours, Prince Edward?"

I did so for two reasons. I wanted Alain of Auxerre to have confirmed that the heir to the English throne was here and I wanted Prince Edward to have a lesson. Kings ordered others to do such things. I wanted the young prince to experience the lighting of flames that would melt flesh and set alight hair. I wanted him to have the smell of burning flesh in his nostrils. It would make him stronger.

"Of course. This," he looked pointedly at the prisoner, "is the price all traitors pay. There will be no absolution nor a grave in a churchyard. Their spirits will wander the land until the end of time and then they will rot in hell with all others who seek to take what is not theirs." He hurled the brand. There was no sudden flaring but as the dried, fat-soaked wood caught alight and spread it seemed to ignite in a circle that suddenly whooshed into the air. I watched Alain of Auxerre's face. I saw the fear that he might be hurled alive into the flames. His eyes flickered as he sought an escape. My two archers held him so tightly that he could not move.

I waited until the bodies were on fire and then turned to the mercenary, "Do you know who this is, Alain of Auxerre?" I pointed at Prince Edward.

He looked at the prince and while he might have guessed his identity, he was not going to speak it. He was going to feign ignorance. This was a clever man. He shook his head.

"This is The Lord Edward, and we are now in his duchy. The Earl of Leicester acts for him at the moment but that could change at any time. It is he who will decide if you will live or die. I asked you when you were first brought here if you would tell me the name of your master and you declined to do so. I wonder if your time in the dark has done anything to loosen your tongue." He remained stubbornly silent. "Perhaps you were hoping that rescue would come, after all, you have done all that you were asked to ensure that there was dissension and disorder in the duchy." I swept a hand at the burning bodies on the fire. The smell of burning hair and melting flesh was nauseous. "This was not a rescue but an attempt on our lives and the life of the heir to the English crown. Such an act is treasonous. Hanging is the punishment."

He stared defiantly at me, "Then hang me and be done but do not taunt me or try to loosen my tongue."

I turned to Prince Edward, "Shall we hang him, my lord?"

It was a measure of his increasing maturity that he shook his head and said, "Put him back in his cell until I have made my decision. Now that the Earl of Leicester has left Bordeaux, I have a mind to stay in my castle."

I saw fear fly across Alain of Auxerre's face. Had he counted on his paymaster brazening it out? The more I thought about it the better the prince's idea sounded. The Earl of Leicester might have been careful but who knew what evidence he might have left behind.

"Take the prisoner back to his cell. Alain of Auxerre, look upon the sun for who knows when you shall see it again?"

After he had been returned to his cell I sat with the castellan and The Lord Edward, "Before we leave this castle, we shall ensure that it is fully defensible."

The castellan shook his head, "But we have not enough men to keep watch. I fear the attack means the demise of the castle."

It was Prince Edward who shook his head and said, forcefully, "You shall hire more men and I will make the funds available." We both looked at him and he smiled, "Unless the Earl of Leicester has managed to empty the treasury then I can use money from there. I want a garrison of forty men. Hire archers too, castellan. I was more than impressed by the skill of Sir Henry's men."

The castellan nodded.

It was my turn to be forceful, "I will go, Prince Edward, to the castle of Bordeaux and take my knights. It is to let them know that we were attacked."

"But Sir Henry, that will alert the Earl of Leicester."

I nodded, "He will know that soon enough. The men who fled will lick their wounds and then ride to their paymaster. Not all for some will not wish to face his wrath at their failure but he will hear, in a day or so, that his men failed, and I am still alive. By that time we should be in the castle, and he will have the added news that Alain of Auxerre is our prisoner and that he is talking."

"But he is not, Sir Henry."

"Prince Edward, only we know that. All that we are doing is buying the time for your father to come and bring men with him. Meanwhile, whilst in the castle, we can discover just how much trouble the earl has caused."

"And how will you do that, Sir Henry?"

"You will be safe in the castle at Bordeaux, and I will take my men and ride abroad."

"It is a risk, Sir Henry."

"Life is a risk, but we will take our chances."

With help from the villagers, I knew that we could have the defences repaired in two days. The next morning I led my conroi to Bordeaux. I saw, as we neared the gates and the walls, that while the gates were open there were far fewer men on the walls and watching for strangers. I had half expected opposition but the sergeant at arms, whom I did not recognise, bowed, "Welcome, my lord, neither the Earl of Leicester nor his castellan are here to greet you."

I nodded and dismounting, led my horse into the outer ward, "Then who commands?"

He looked embarrassed, "I suppose it is me although the Archbishop of Bordeaux, Géraud de Malemort has taken up residence in the absence of the earl."

"Then take me to him." I turned, "Dick, come with me. Alfred, see the state of the garrison and the defences; use our men to man the key points of the castle. Thomas, find the treasury and guard it. Geoffrey, return to the gate and admit no one."

The archbishop was not in the Great Hall but an antechamber I had seen when we had visited the earl. I had not been in the room but now I saw that it was an office of some kind. There were parchments strewn upon the desk and the archbishop and four of his priests were searching through them. "Your Grace? What is it that you seek?"

The five of them started and three of the priests made the sign of the cross. The archbishop recovered first and said, "And who are you to question me thus?"

I smiled and gave a low bow, "I am Sir Henry Samuel of Elton, and I am here with the future Duke of Aquitaine, The Lord Edward."

"He is here, already?" Fear filled his face.

Shaking my head I said, "I am his messenger only. He will be here ere long and he sent me to ensure that all was well. I ask again, Your Grace, what is it that you seek?"

He was most definitely embarrassed, "The earl has gone to quell rebellion and I seek a missive I sent to him. A trifle but I would have it returned to me."

I nodded, "Then when we have sorted all the papers, we will send it to you."

He smiled, "It is not a problem."

"But it is, Your Grace, for this castle does not belong to the archdiocese but Prince Edward and I must ask you to quit the castle so that I can ensure it is safe for him to occupy."

"Safe?"

"Did you not know? Men tried to scale the walls of our home and they slew some of the garrison. There is treason and treachery abroad." I shrugged, "My hands are tied for whilst it may offend you, I have a greater duty to the son of my king." I opened the door and waved them through. They were defeated and they left but I knew that this was more than the trifle the archbishop had said. "Dick, stay within and guard these parchments. Admit no one except they come from me."

He pulled out his sword and laid it on the table, on top of the parchments, "And no one shall."

My plans had, once again, been upset. There was evidence, somewhere in the castle, of wrongdoing and I could not do as I had intended, ride in, sow the seeds of doubt so that Simon de Montfort might be forced to act. The sergeant at arms had waited outside the chamber and obviously heard all. He was shifting uncomfortably from foot to foot.

"Come with me."

"Yes, my lord."

I went to the Great Hall where I saw Alfred approaching. I sat and waved Alfred to sit next to me. The sergeant I made stand.

Alfred said, "The archbishop, what did he want?"

"Evidence." Alfred threw me a curious look and I gave a slight shake of the head. I looked up at the sergeant, "How many men are there in the castle garrison now?"

He smiled a weak smile for he was on safe ground, "Ten men at arms and eight crossbowmen."

"Servants?"

"The cook and ten who help him. There are the horse master and two ostlers. The weaponsmith and his two apprentices are in the workshop." He rubbed his chin, "Then there are another five who perform the rest of the tasks."

"That does not seem many for such a large castle. Where is the steward?"

The sergeant looked confused rather than furtive, "He left with the Earl of Leicester. The earl took many of the staff with him. He did not tell me why."

A disturbing picture filled my mind, "Sergeant, how long have you been here in the castle?"

He was growing more confident as my easy questions came at him, "Why fifteen years, my lord. I came with my father to serve as a spearman. Through diligence, loyalty and hard work, I rose to be a man at arms and then, sergeant at arms."

"Obviously you were here before Lord de Montfort."

He nodded, "Yes, my lord, and I thought that I had lost my post for he brought many of his own men and I was relegated to sergeant of the night watch. The men at arms who remain are my night watch. I have risen in my lord's estimation for when he departed, he let me command the castle."

"The eight crossbowmen who remain, were they here before the earl arrived?"

"Why yes, my lord. Like me and the night watch, we are the older men. Perhaps, that is why he did not take us with him, eh my lord?"

"Before the earl left a large number of men left the castle, did they not?" He nodded, "Including crossbowmen."

"Yes lord. I thought that they were the advance guard, but…" he hesitated.

"But?"

"They did not head north but east."

"Who led them?"

"Gaspar de Louche, one of the earl's men."

Thomas came into the hall with Ralph close behind and I raised my hand so that my cousin would not blurt out whatever his eager face told me he was going to. "What is your name, sergeant?"

"Jean de Margaux, my lord." Worry filled his face for my voice had been heavy with threat.

"Jean, I believe you have answered me honestly and I see no treachery on your face but there was treason in this castle. I will take over the castle in the name of The Lord Edward and I will command. Your men will obey all of my commands. Understand?"

"Yes, my lord."

"The castle, until I say otherwise, is in a state of siege. None of those in the castle shall leave and my men will procure the supplies and food that we need. My men are watching the walls. Go now and tell all that which I have said." He nodded, "And Jean, if any complain or behave strangely then I would know their names."

He looked as though he was going to ask another question but one look at my face made him change his mind, "Yes, my lord."

When he had gone, I said, "Ralph, make sure that none are close by and then close the doors. Join us at the table."

"Yes, my lord."

"This is worse than I thought. Thomas, your face tells me that you have news."

"Aye, cuz, the treasury has almost been emptied. I believe that it was intended to be completely scoured of coins but we found a small door and behind it were four small chests filled with silver but the marks on the floor told us that the larger boxes had been shifted."

"It was not guarded?"

I saw his face as he realised the implications, "Why no and, to speak truly, the door was not even locked."

Ralph had secured the doors and joined us. I turned to Alfred, "Brother?"

"The sergeant was telling the truth about the garrison. It is like the one at Stockton but more so. The men are all old. The sergeant looks to me to be the youngest of them. If we had to defend the castle with those alone then we would fall. There are too few to defend it."

"It is as I thought. The earl planned well. I believe he thought he would succeed but, in case he failed, he left the castle without coin and defenders. I fear that when he learns his killers failed then he might return here. We have no time to lose. Ralph, ride to our castle. I want the prince, his cousin, the bodyguards and the prisoner brought here. Take half a dozen of our best men."

He nodded, "I will, my lord." He hesitated.

"Speak, man. You should know me by now."

He smiled, "Aye, Sir Henry, it is like your grandfather is here in the hall. I should have mentioned something earlier but so much has happened…" I waved a hand to hurry him on and he nodded, "When we fought the other night one of the men we fought was dying and I gave him a warrior's death. Before he died he said. '*You shall not enjoy this long. The two-tailed lion will come back to devour you.*' I thought it a dying man's bravado but from what you say it might have been prophetic."

I saw that Sir Thomas looked confused and I said, "De Montfort's livery is a rampant lion with two tails on a red background. Thank you, Ralph, now choose your men well."

"I will my lord."

"Let us find Geoffrey and inform him of what we know and then we have some reading to do."

"Reading, brother? I would have thought that the sharpening of swords was the order of the day."

I shook my head, "Even if a rider took the news of their failure directly to the earl, he could not yet have received it. Even now he might be hearing the news that his first plan has failed. The Seneschal of Gascony might well wish to return and take back this castle but he cannot be here for another three days at least."

"And when can King Henry be here?"

"Robert may have reached England by now if the winds were fair but he has to find the king. I pray that he is in London and, preferably at the Tower to enable him to get here sooner."

Alfred looked downcast, "I cannot see that we will be so lucky and we know there will not be a large number of men in London who are available to him. We should add a month."

I nodded, "At the very least."

Thomas spread his arm around and beamed. This was almost a reborn Thomas, "At least we have better accommodation and an easier castle to defend. If what you say is true, Henry Samuel, then even if Simon de Montfort chose to return immediately to Bordeaux, we have a week."

"Well said, Thomas, and you are right. Let us look at this goblet as half full rather than half empty. We have survived two attacks and we must have eliminated some of the better men who were available to the earl."

We were all of better heart when Prince Edward arrived. The prisoner was taken to a purpose-built gaol cell close to the wine and beer store. His guards had ensured that he had spoken to none and had no chance to escape. I dare say that the brief journey in daylight gave him hope but when he reached the castle the hope was dashed and, once more, he descended into darkness. We held a council of war in the Great Hall to tell the prince what we had learned and our thoughts.

His face clouded over when we told him of the ransacked treasury. "That was not his to use! It is treason!"

I shook my head, "Your father made him Seneschal, Lord Lieutenant, while you are a minor. It is his to use as he sees fit. You may be right in that it might be considered immoral to do so but legally he has yet to act in a way which might be deemed illegal."

Henry of Almain said, "But we have been attacked twice. Is that not illegal?"

"And the only connection we have to the Earl of Leicester is conjecture. The evidence is not yet damning." I stood, "That reminds me, Prince Edward, if you and your cousin will come with me we might find some evidence." I turned to Alfred and the others, "You know what you need to do. We will be in the small chamber down the corridor, sifting through parchments."

Dick was alert as we opened the door and I smiled, "Go and have some food and drink. You have done your duty. The castle is under our control. Find us a chamber and we three will search these papers for evidence."

The archbishop and his priests had done us a partial favour. There were a number of parchments that had been opened already and, I presumed, read. I gathered those and placed them to one side. I needed the evidence the archbishop was trying to find first. I pointed to the racks on the walls. "We need to read those. The archbishop was attempting to find one that, I assume he wished he had not written. This will be tedious work and may well be fruitless but if we are to find evidence that will stand up to scrutiny it must be written."

I sat in the seat the archbishop had occupied and took a handful of the parchments. The first four that I read were all mundane in that they recorded the taxes received from the port at various times. The next two were similar in that they contained the details of taxes that had been taken from manors. I was about to discard them to the pile of read ones when a thought struck me. I took a wax tablet and stylus left by one of the priests and wrote down the amount of taxes that had been gathered. Although I had only read four documents, the amount taken was high. Simon de Montfort was overtaxing the city. The pile of discards grew and I began to fear we would fail when my eyes lit on one that had the seal of the archbishop hanging from the ribbon that bound it.

My body language was such that Prince Edward was alerted, "What is it, my lord? Why do you start, and your eyes grow large?"

"I have found the first missive from the archbishop. It may be nothing but…"

The two youths stopped searching and came behind me to read over my shoulder. I read carefully while the two youths let their eyes race across the dancing figures on the page. The Lord Edward snorted, "It is nothing, my lord. It is about indulgences."

I held up my hand for silence. They had read ahead and now that I knew the matter I was able to anticipate the words. The two youths resumed their reading. When I reached the bottom I knew that I had evidence that would damn the archbishop and, hopefully, the seneschal.

"You may stop reading, my lords. I have some proof of wrongdoing."

"How? It speaks of indulgences and the selling of indulgences is not a crime."

"Had you read on further, Prince Edward then you would have seen that this was not just one or two indulgences but a hundred and the men were not named, just the price."

"That is wrong. An indulgence is for a sin committed and to lessen time in Purgatory."

"Aye, and the letter is addressed specifically to the Earl of Leicester. It is a chink only but one that gives me hope. Tomorrow we visit the archbishop, Prince Edward and we take this evidence with us. It might be used to bargain for more substantial evidence against the Earl of Leicester."

Chapter 11

Henry Samuel

The ridding of the rats

The cathedral lay close to the castle walls and the town hall. With my brother, our squires and their bodyguards, Prince Edward and I walked to the hall of the archbishop. The priest who was at the door had obviously been forewarned. They would have seen us leaving the castle and heading towards the church.

"I am sorry, my lord, but the archbishop is indisposed. If you could call back in a day or two?"

I nodded, having expected this. I held up the parchment and I watched the priest's eyes widen when he saw the seal, "I have found that which the archbishop sought and I thought he might need it." I turned.

"No, my lord. I will take it from you."

Shaking my head I said, "It is for the archbishop's eyes, I think."

The priests used by the archbishop were clever men and they were able to join together things unsaid with words that were spoken. "You have read the parchment, my lord?"

I smiled, "Oh yes, as has Prince Edward."

The priest seemed to see the two royal cousins for the first time. "You had better come in." He saw the bodyguards, "I cannot allow armed men within the archbishop's chambers."

Godfrey's grin made me shiver, "And do you think that you can stop us? We are charged with the protection of The Lord Edward and where he goes so do we."

Defeated he led us, not to a bed chamber where a sick archbishop reposed but to a large chamber where scribes were busily writing. Géraud de Malemort looked up when we entered and I saw his shoulders droop in defeat when he saw the parchment. He waved a hand, "Leave us alone, Gilbert fetch us wine."

The priests scurried out like mice at the approach of a cat and we sat. I kept hold of the parchment. When the door closed, I said, softly, "I believe you sought this?"

He nodded and then said, defiantly, "There is nothing wrong with payment for indulgences."

I nodded, "But the amounts you charged and for unnamed sinners in such numbers does raise questions. For whom were these indulgences intended?"

The door opened and Gilbert and two more priests brought in wine and goblets. They poured and left us. The time had allowed the archbishop to think. As he spoke, I did as my grandfather had taught me and I stared into his eyes. "The Seneschal of Aquitaine and Gascony asked me for indulgences for some of his men who had committed sins whilst on his service. I asked for their names and he told me that he just needed one hundred of them and that I would be well paid." He hung his head, "The money of which he spoke was not trivial." He stared at me, "The money was not used for my pleasure but for the poor. The sale of indulgences helps those who are needy and there are many who cannot afford to live well in Bordeaux."

I nodded, "Because the earl taxed them so much. Ironic, really, Your Grace. The help you gave to the poor was only necessary because Simon de Montfort taxed them so much."

He drank some wine and laughed, "The money for the indulgences was as a drop in the ocean. The bulk of the taxes was intended to hire warriors. Have you not noticed, Sir Henry, that Bordeaux teems with warriors for hire? I admit that what I did was not good but the seneschal did far worse."

I looked at Prince Edward. We had spoken before we left the castle and he knew what to say, "I am the future Duke of Aquitaine, and I would have what you say recorded so that Simon de Montfort can be held to account."

The archbishop laughed, "And I have learned the folly of committing such matters to parchment. When you have the seneschal in custody and secure then I will give spoken testimony."

That was as good as we could expect and I nodded and rose, "Until then we will hold on to this testimony."

Defeated Géraud de Malemort nodded, "The Seneschal is powerful. You will need a bigger rat trap to catch him, I fear."

On the way back to the castle I said, "One thing is sure, the archbishop is right about the danger of swords for hire in Bordeaux and while they remain are a threat. The Earl of Leicester may be far to the north and his sword cannot strike us yet but he has left a dagger that can strike at our back."

"What do you intend, brother?"

"We know of one rat trap, *'The White Cockerel'*. We will go after dark and surround it. I will use your authority, Prince Edward, to apprehend all those within and question them."

Surprisingly he nodded, "Aye, except for one thing. My cousin and I will be with you. If nothing else it will give four more swords that can aid you."

There was no dissuading him. The king had given me his son to learn about his inheritance. He had learned more than that. Prince Edward was not only better informed, but he had also grown as a person. He was no longer the youth who had left England. He was now almost a man and making the decisions that men make.

Sir Geoffrey asked, "Why do we go at night? Surely there is more chance of them fleeing in the dark for, as you said, the entrance is well hidden."

Dick answered for me, "When Sir Henry and I visited at lunchtime there were few men within. The nighttime was different. The place was filled with scoundrels of all types."

It was Alfred who came up with a suggestion that would keep us safer and within the law, "Prince Edward, you should announce that all hired swords and mercenaries should present themselves to the castle by noon tomorrow."

The young prince said, "But that means we will not be going today."

"My brother is acting a little hastily, I think. Sorry, Henry Samuel, leaving a day will make little difference to us and this way we may find honest men who seek work, and they will present themselves in the morning. We need more warriors both for here and Château de La Brède. I doubt that any of Simon de Montfort's men or those who would work for him will come. That way when we raid the inn, and apprehend the others that we discover, we do so within the letter of the law."

I nodded, "You are right to reprimand me, brother. I was acting hastily. My fear is that the seneschal will return but we still have days to go before that can happen."

We sought the help of the archbishop who was only too glad to oblige. He provided two scribes and they not only made the notices that were displayed at the castle entrance but also promised to be there the next day to take names. I sent the sergeant at arms and four men to make the announcement at the market, the quay and all other public places. Pointedly they went to *'The White Cockerel'* first.

I asked Kurt and Walter to adopt plain clothes and wander the streets to gauge the mood. When they returned it was with the news that, as we might have expected, the villains of the town were both worried and angry while the general populace was happy for the gangs of warriors roaming the streets were a danger. The next day the prince and his cousin watched the proceedings from the gatehouse of the inner ward. Men were admitted to the outer ward and the two scribes waited with wax tablets. I stood with my knights to study faces. Men were waiting to give us their names from before the gates were opened. I studied each man and I saw that most studied us.

I was close enough to hear them as they spoke. The first man was clearly an archer. I could see that from his build. As with all good archers he was slightly misshapen. He had no bow and his gardyvyan was clearly almost empty. He wore a hat and I knew that he would have bowstrings beneath. His dagger was a short one, but I knew that it would be razor-sharp.

"John of Parr. Archer."

"And where do you live?"

He gave a wry smile, "Anywhere I can."

The scribe made a note and then waved him to the side. There were eight men waiting. John of Parr looked at me and I waved him closer, "John of Parr, come so that I may speak with you." He did so and I saw that while he was not quite as tall as me he was almost half as broad again. He was a powerful man. "Let me see your hat." He gave a small smile and as he handed me his hat I saw that his knuckles had been bloodied recently. As I had expected there were three bowstrings within. I handed it back to him. "Tell me, John of Parr, how does it come to pass that an archer who has a gardyvyan and three bowstrings has no bow and has been fighting in the last few days?"

He smiled, "Very perceptive my lord. I came to Bordeaux some months ago for I heard that there was work to be had. I stayed at an inn and was approached by a man whom I did not like. I did not approve of the work he wished me to undertake for it seemed more like banditry than the work of an archer. I confess that it was a mistake. I should have taken the coins and then run at the first opportunity I had. When I refused my bow was hacked in two and I was given a beating and thrown from the inn."

"*'The White Cockerel?'*"

"As I said, my lord, you are perceptive. I slept rough and did some work at the docks. Two days since a weasel-faced man came to the merchant who employed me and I was told I no longer had any work. I believe that the merchant was threatened. I found the weasel-faced man and he will be eating broth for a few days. It was a small victory and I have been hungry since."

I turned to Dick, "Stand close by." I turned back to the archer, "We can offer you employment."

"But I have no bow, my lord."

"I brought English archers with me, and they have spare bows," I smiled, "until you make your own. What say you?"

He dropped to his knee, "I thank you, my lord, and pray that God watches over you and your family."

"Dick, take him to Henry son of Harry."

I listened to the other stories and five of the men, another archer and three men at arms impressed me enough for me to offer them work. The others were not the villains I sought but I needed more time to be convinced of their loyalty. We had the places where they slept or lodged and as none of them came from *'The White Cockerel?'*, I was content. A second inn's name came up, *'The Pichet of Wine'* and I made a note to visit that one once we had made our first raid. The scribes took away the wax tablets to make a fair copy for us and I went to visit the new men. Prince Edward used some of the money we had found in the ransacked treasure to pay them. They were given better weapons and helmets from the armoury but we made it clear to the sergeant at arms that they were to be my men. I anticipated employing the rest of the men we had interviewed for the castle's garrison, but not yet.

"Tonight you will come with us for your first night's work. You all have unique knowledge for you know the men we seek, those who hire brigands and bandits. I wish to take prisoners but I do not want you to risk your lives."

We divided up into four groups of equal size. Two would approach from the rear and two from the front. One group would watch the front while a second watched the rear and the other two groups would enter. I anticipated some violence and my spearmen and new men at arms were ordered to wear mail. The archers had leather brigandines studded with metal. Godfrey and the other bodyguards would be at the front with Alfred and me. We headed towards the tavern when we thought it might be at its fullest. Thomas and Geoffrey, at the rear, were already in position. Unless there was access to the two adjacent buildings then we should be able to trap them. There was an upper floor and it was close enough to the ground for a man to risk a leap.

I nodded to the prince and then stepped up to the door. Taking out my sword, I opened it and stepped inside knowing that Jack was at my heels along with my new archer, John of Parr. Dick was relegated to the middle of the men who would follow me. As had happened the first time I had entered, all speech ceased and I was able to roar, "I am here with Prince Edward, the future Duke of Aquitaine. We have come to apprehend all those warriors who did not attend the castle this morning." I held up a copy of the parchment. "If your name is not on this list then you will be taken a..." I got no further for men drew weapons and while some lunged at us, others tried to flee. When I heard a collective wail, I knew that some had discovered the presence of Thomas and his men in the rear of the building. By then, however, the three of us who had entered were fighting for our lives. The stocky and pungent-smelling Frenchman who lunged at me with a short sword almost caught me by surprise but he made the mistake of using the tip of his sword. My mail held and whilst I would have a bruise on my hip, he had an eternal sleep as I brought my sword across his neck. Jack and John easily dealt with their men and we were able to step into the room, which was a confusion of bodies, chairs that had been knocked aside and fallen half barrels. Wooden beakers were hurled as those within tried all that they could to hurt us.

I made my way to the bar where I saw the owner, cudgel in hand trying to make his way out. I used my mail mitten to punch in the side of the head of a man who came at me with the broken leg of a chair. Something hit my head. The arming cap and coif did their job but it was a warning. I heard a shout from behind but it seemed distant and I guessed that someone had leapt from the upper floor.

"Dick and John come with me!"

The owner disappeared. I clambered over the bar and saw a barred door leading to the back, but the man had vanished. He had not used the back door for the bar was still across it. There were half a dozen firkins of wine, the barrels wine merchants sold to smaller establishments. They made a barrier and when I looked beyond it, I spied a square in the floor. It was a trap door. I put my sword in the gap and prised it open. It was pitch black.

John of Parr said, "It is dangerous to go down a rat hole, my lord."

"Aye, but we need this one." I spied a full pichet of wine that had somehow survived the mayhem. I picked it up and hurled it down and towards the back. I heard it smash, and I jumped down. Once again, a blade came at me and I used my left hand to deflect it. There was more than one man for a second blade came at my head, but Dick had jumped down behind me and his quick reactions flicked it up to stick in the wooden beam above us. While Dick skewered the killer, I punched at the man who had thrust at me. My eyes had become a little more accustomed to the dark and I spied a chink of light in the distance. The hilt of my sword connected, and I must have been lucky for the man whom I hit screamed when I hit his eye. He turned and ran. I saw two more shapes running. I had followed just one man down here but there were others. We needed these men.

I hurried, crouching for the tunnel we used was not high enough to stand upright and I heard Dick and John's feet as they followed me. The light drew me but it also warned me of danger. I saw that there was a wall ahead and that meant the passage went either left or right or both. I spied a broken piece of wood and picking it up, held it out as I neared the passage. A hatchet came down to hack into the wood. I pulled and thrust with my sword at the same time. A man I did not recognise fell across the opening and my sword entered the side of his head. I cursed myself. I needed prisoners. It did, however, tell me that they had gone to the left. The tavern owner was not one of those we had slain and so I had hopes of information.

We moved down the tunnel awkwardly using a crouched motion. It was not made for mailed men and so I slipped my sword into my scabbard and took off my mail mittens. I would be able to feel my way down the underground escape tunnel. The light had been taken by one of those we followed and I saw the light ahead as they moved down the passage. I was glad that I was wearing my coif and arming cap as I banged my head a number of times. When the light suddenly disappeared after a loud thud I knew that they had left the passage by some sort of trapdoor and I discovered where when I banged into a stone wall. It was the foundations of a more substantial building. I put my hands above my head and felt around. I found a beam and then what felt like narrow planks of wood. I pushed and it gave a little.

"Are you two still with me?"

John of Parr's voice came from behind me, "Aye, lord, but I wish I was not. This feels like a grave and I am finding it hard to breathe."

Dick's thin voice came from further down the tunnel, "And I am here too, cousin. I am also struggling to breathe."

"I think I have found the way out. Follow me."

I pushed up with my hands and the hatch above me rose. My nose was assaulted by the smell of wine. I knew where we were. There were wine merchants situated on the street and we had to be in the cellar of one of them. There was little light and what there was just showed me row upon row of firkins. I feared our prey had fled. I pushed the wooden hatch up and used my arms to pull myself up. Suddenly there was a light, almost as though something had been blocking it.

Above me, a voice snarled, "Now I will end your interfering life!"

Even as something smacked into the side of my head, I recognised the voice. It was the tavern owner. I think that my life was saved because he had not realised I was wearing my coif and arming cap. He hit me from behind and I was knocked forward, clearing the hatch which, I hoped, would allow John of Parr to follow me. I was stunned and I saw stars but I did not fall into unconsciousness. I spied the two figures, the tavern owner wielding the huge mallet they used to drive taps into barrels and the weasel-faced man who, now almost toothless lurched towards me grinning and holding a wicked-looking dagger. My hands did not seem to want to move and I groped for either my dagger or my sword. Even as the tavern owner raised the mallet to smash into my face John of Parr's sword drove up into his body. The weasel-faced man whipped his dagger around to slash at John of Parr's throat, but I saw that Dick had half of his body out of the hatch and his sword was driven up through the groin and into the weasel's vital organs.

John of Parr hurried to my side, "My lord! Are you hurt?"

"I know not. Thank you, John of Parr, although I hoped that we might have taken this pair alive. Come, there must be a way out of this cellar or else they would not have used it.

Fetch the light. Then search them. They must have a way of getting out of here."

The two men had been using a brand and I saw now that it had been placed in a sconce. No doubt the wine merchant used the sconce to illuminate the cellar. John of Parr found the homemade key in the purse of the tavern owner, and he held it up triumphantly. He handed it to me.

Dick took it from me and said, "And I will lead, cuz. That was a mighty mallet, and you need a healer to look at you."

I obeyed for he was right, and I did feel dizzy. Dick found some stone stairs and we headed up them. I saw that there was a hoist next to me confirming how the merchant moved the barrels. The door was not barred and after opening it, we found ourselves in what must have been the room the merchant used to sell his wine. Dick took the key and, after jiggling it around, found that it opened the door. We heard the noise from lower down the narrow street as my men continued to gather those from the inn. I felt dizzy and I sat on one of the half barrels which stood on either side of the door.

"Are you alright, cousin?"

"Just dizzy." I pointed at the key, still in Dick's hand. "You had better lock the door." As he did so I said, "I am guessing that the tavern owner used the tunnel he dug for two purposes, to steal wine and to have an escape route. We could have watched the inn for an age and not seen the real leaders of this subversive activity."

"It is locked, Henry."

I tried to stand but first my legs gave way and then all went black.

Chapter 12

Henry Samuel
Rebellion

When I opened my eyes, I was in a well-lit chamber and a physician hovered over me. I saw the hint of a smile on his face, "Praise be to God. He lives." He made the sign of the cross. "You have been as the dead for a whole day, my lord. Your brother and The Lord Edward will be delighted to hear you have recovered."

Dick appeared and the relief on his face was clear, "We thought you dead, cousin. John of Parr carried you back here and the physician sewed the wound on your scalp. I was sure the stitching would bring you around but it did not. We all prayed for an hour in the chapel and God answered our prayers."

"What happened? Did we get the evidence we needed?"

Dick shook his head, "I am sorry, cousin. We found those who were leaders. John of Parr identified the bodies of those who interviewed him. They fought too hard and were slain in the confusion. The ones we captured were little fishes who were of no consequence."

"Did we lose any?"

Shaking his head he said, "Bruises and cuts only."

I lay back on the pillow and closed my eyes. I had so hoped to have some palpable evidence to share with the king if and when he arrived but there was none.

"The Lord Edward has taken charge. He and the other knights are, even now, searching the other inn. It was Alfred's idea. He said that it was better to strike sooner rather than later. The Lord Edward has ordered *'The White Cockerel'* to be pulled down. The wine merchant is happy about that. He had punished his cellarman for the losses of barrels. All is now explained."

My grandfather's words came back to me. I would make the best of a bad job. We had not fully succeeded but we had made Bordeaux a safer place. "All becomes clear to me now. It was no wonder that the inn could charge such low prices and yet still remain open and the tunnel, whilst it would have taken some time to dig, was a perfect escape from the rat's nest."

"Aye and but for the new archer, you might be dead. The physician said that the skull had a crack in it but a second blow might have shattered it."

Almost as though he had been listening the doctor returned, "Squire, you can feed your lord some broth and then he must sleep. I have a draught for him to take. Sleep is the best medicine."

Ignoring the doctor I asked Dick, "What o'clock is it?"

"Just after nones."

"Then I will take the drink after Prince Edward and the others have returned." I added, "I will sleep easier with knowledge rather than having a fitful slumber riddled by doubts."

Dick fed me the broth which was most welcome and I drank sparingly of the wine sent by a grateful wine merchant. My cousin gave me his thoughts. "The mood of the town is more positive, cousin. As we brought you back to the castle people cheered for word spread of what we had done. The inn was like a spider's web and the owner Henri de Marin was at the centre."

"De Marin, the same name as the man we killed?"

"His brother. One of the wenches we questioned told us that."

"And what of the ones who survived our attack?"

"Your brother divided them into the men who might have been swords for hire and those who worked in the inn. He let the latter go with the warning that if there was any more wrongdoing and they were involved then they would be branded. I believe it was the right thing to do." He looked at me for approval and I nodded. It was what I would have done. "The others were shackled and are in a cell." He saw my look and shook his head, "Alain of Auxerre is still isolated and knows nothing."

We heard the sound of men returning to the castle long before the door opened and Alfred, Thomas and the royal cousins entered. The looks on their faces were of relief.

"Sir Henry, God has answered our prayers and the treacherous men of *'The White Cockerel'* did not end your life." Prince Edward wagged a finger at me, "You should let others put themselves in danger and not you. My father charged you with ridding this land of the pestilence that is Simon De Montfort."

"It is not the way in our family. Are the lives of the men we lead any less valuable than our own? Besides, what is done is done and I survive. How went the raid?"

Alfred spoke, "We found fewer men and there was less fighting. We managed to take prisoners but, it seems, the Marin brothers and Alain of Auxerre were the ones who reported to their leader. Once the men accepted the coins, they were taken by one of the three to…we know not who." he shrugged. "We have cut off the head of the Hydra and the tentacles will wither and die but we have no evidence."

"Not yet but I spy hope. Prince Edward, what are your plans?"

"We have ordered the demolition of the second inn and we have the prisoners here." I saw him chew his lip and then he said, tentatively, "I thought to take their weapons and coins from them and have them taken beyond the town walls. We cannot afford to feed them and I am reluctant to order their execution." He was seeking my approval.

"I think it is the right thing to do. True, they can make their way to join the Earl of Leicester but they are obviously men of poor quality and without weapons not a real threat. Of course, you may be storing up problems for the future for they may become bandits but until your father comes then we have limited choices."

I lay back for the talk had wearied me.

"My cousin needs rest and I have a draught here prepared by the physician."

I heard Alfred's voice, "Dick is right, let us go." He leaned in and spoke in my ear, "Get well, brother, for we need you."

"Before you go take the list of men who came to the castle. We need to hire them. John of Parr seems a good man, brother, use him to sift out the bad apples."

"Aye, now take the drink. I have broad shoulders and I share the same blood as you, Henry Samuel."

I woke refreshed and rose whilst it was still dark. Dick had a pallet close by me and he protested when I stood, "The doctor has not yet said you can rise, my lord."

I knew when Dick gave me a title that he was concerned, "Dick, I know my own body and while I was hurt my head feels clear and we have much to do. Help me to dress and then we can have breakfast. The sleep has given me the appetite of a wolf and, I feel, I must be a wolf if I am to counter the evil that plagues this land."

By the time we had eaten, it was daylight and the others had risen. I had managed a longer sleep than they and it had sharpened my mind. As they ate I spoke my thoughts. "We need to find where the Earl of Leicester and his men are to be found. Alfred, have Henry son of Harry send out two good archers to find him. Prince Edward, thanks to the earl the town is not in a state to be defended. I could do it but you are the lawful master of this realm. Order the muster of your people in this town. Put them under arms so that we can call upon them to defend the walls if we need them. We need to ensure that there are enough supplies to feed us should we suffer a siege."

"But we have scoured the city of the danger from within, Sir Henry."

"And what of the danger of without? The men we have fought well the other day but are they enough to defend the city from an army?"

He nodded and as soon as they had eaten the proclamation was read out. It did not mean that we had the burghers of Bordeaux on the walls but that they had their arms close by and if the cathedral bell sounded then they would assemble and await orders. Egbert and Paul were chosen to ride forth and find the earl.

Even before the two archers returned, two days later, word reached the city that Gascony had rebelled. Simon de

Montfort's attack in the north, taking the Château de Barbezieux, had incensed many of the seigneurs who had had enough and they revolted.

I advised Prince Edward to keep the gates of the city closed and he agreed. Our better men were at the gates. Honest visitors and those who had good reason to enter were admitted as were real refugees. Those who might seek to cause trouble were soon spotted. Three were killed by my men when they were discovered for they used swords to try to escape. It was a valuable lesson to all. The prince also sent another letter to his father. He might be on his way but, equally, he could still be debating if his son and I had overreacted. It was too early to expect a fleet of ships to appear on the horizon and until they did, we would be on our own.

When Egbert and Paul returned it was with the news that the Earl of Leicester was ransacking the lands around Barbezieux and that, whilst unwelcome in many ways, was also a relief. He was not marching back to take Bordeaux but there was also bad news. The Seigneur of Périgueux had endured enough for his lands lay close enough to Bordeaux to have suffered at the hands of de Montfort's roving bands of brigands. He had assembled an army and was heading for Bordeaux. Other men, noble and farmer alike were joining him. We would have to defend Bordeaux and de Montfort had succeeded. There was a rebellion against English rule. Despite the fact that I was not totally recovered I had to take charge. I wondered how many of those we had allowed to go free would join this ragtag army heading for Bordeaux? It was too late to reverse that decision and, in any case, it was better to have those men outside the walls than in.

I held a council of war. This time we included the archbishop as well as the mayor and the leaders of the merchants and the guilds. They all had a vested interest in the defence. Prince Edward asked me to lead the meeting. He had grown but not enough to be able to confidently lead such a meeting. While we met, I had the castellan, Henry and Jack ensuring that the ditch that ran around the west side of the town was clear of rubbish. They would not do the work but the men of Bordeaux would have to put aside their own trade and become warriors for the working day. Already supplies were being rationed. We were not under siege and it was unlikely that we would be any time soon but a wise commander was cautious.

I stood to speak for the table was full. The archbishop had a scribe noting the salient points. He was no fool and if the worst came and the city fell, he wanted evidence that he had done all that he could. The matter of the indulgences still hung over him.

"We know not how many men the Seigner of Périgueux brings but it will not have to be many to outnumber our professional soldiers. He is taking advantage, I believe, of the absence of the Seneschal and the bulk of the defenders." I looked at Prince Edward, "It will be a bargaining piece to enable him to pay fewer taxes and have greater power."

The prince looked grim and determined, "Even if he managed to take the city, I have a good memory and will remember such deeds."

"I believe that he will cross the river upstream from here and march up the river road. I have sent a messenger to the castellan at the Château de La Brède. Thanks to our efforts it is more defensible and rather than bring his men here he will act as a bastion for us to make the approach of the men of Périgueux that much more difficult. The Seigneur will be denied the river road." I looked at my knights, "This time we cannot afford to abandon the outer walls but these are substantial ones. They might not be the mighty walls of Carcassonne but they cannot be scaled without ladders or towers. Even now we have men making sure that the outer ditches are an obstacle." I looked at the mayor, "If this teaches us nothing it is that the men of Bordeaux have a duty, even in times of peace, to ensure that the city can be defended. As I have discovered there are many in the city who ferment mischief but throwing rubbish in the ditches merely enables an enemy to succeed."

The mayor and the civilians from the town looked suitably shamefaced.

Prince Edward smiled, "Sir Henry, I am sure I speak for all of us when I say that we have the utmost confidence in your ability to safely guide us through these troubles."

I shook my head, "The attack from Périgueux is not my main worry, my lord, but the effect it will have on the rest of Gascony. If we fail and by that I mean do not defeat this army, then others will seek to take advantage of what they see as weakness. Remember what we heard in Auch."

I saw him colour and he said, "If you have no more words for the mayor and the others then I am sure that they could be better employed looking to our defences."

They took the hint and left.

When they had gone, I said, "I had no intention of mentioning Castile, my lord, but we both know that the King of Castile has cast a covetous eye upon this duchy. I got the impression that Auch might welcome the king. I fear that when your father does finally reach us then it will be too late."

Alfred, who was normally positive said, "If he comes at all."

We all looked at him and I said, "This is not like you, brother, why the pessimism?"

He waved a hand around the room, "Are we the sacrificial lamb, brother? Why did the king send so few of us? It seems to me that we were sent here to light a fire in the duchy that would flush out Simon de Montfort. We have done that." he looked at Prince Edward, "No offence, Prince Edward, but your father is not known for his military strategy. Will he come to be defeated as he was the last time?"

I feared my brother had gone too far but the future King of England nodded, "No offence taken, Alfred, and you may be right except that when he comes, and I believe he will, then this time he will have Sir Henry as a counsellor as well as knights in whose veins runs the blood of the Warlord. Sir Henry is right, we cannot afford to lose."

That effectively ended the meeting and I went with my knights to walk the walls of the castle from where we could see the outer defences of the city. We said little that was not to do with the walls and the towers. Alfred and I had the most experience of fighting within and without castles. Thomas and Geoffrey listened more than they spoke.

"This will not be like Château de La Brède. The walls cover a greater area but I would have each of us take charge of one section. The castellan, bodyguards and Prince Edward can guard the keep and the inner wall." I pointed to the northwest wall. "Geoffrey, I would have you command that wall. Take one-fifth of the warriors we now have. Thomas, you will take one fifth and guard the main gate and the west wall. Alfred, you will take a fifth of the men and yours will be the hardest task for you will have the south-western wall. As that is the direction they will take when they come you will be the one who will face them first."

"And you, brother? You have no doubt given yourself the hardest of tasks but tell us what it is."

"I will take the two-fifths of the men who remain and we will be the cork that plugs any gap that appears. We cannot let them breach the outer wall. The castle might be safe but if the property of the citizens was destroyed then the flames of revolt would be fanned and even if we defeated the men of Périgueux then the hope that the English could be defeated would be planted in their minds. I want each of you to have a horn. One blast tells me that Geoffrey has been attacked and needs my help. Two, Thomas and three, Alfred." I smiled, "I will choose my men first."

We kept the gates closely watched and the refugees who arrived spoke of an army of almost fifteen hundred. The only advantage we had was that they were largely on foot and were moving slowly. Each hour of delay meant our defences were improved. We had sand and braziers ready for heated sand that could be used to cause wicked injuries on enemy warriors not to mention igniting wooden rams and ladders. River stones were fetched and stacked on the fighting platform. Every boy who could wield a sling was ordered to collect as many stones as they could. There were enough of them to have missiles ready on every wall. We also ordered all the ships in the river to head for the sea. The river was narrow enough for an enemy to use stone-throwers to hurl flaming missiles and set them alight. Such a fire could easily spread to the city and that we did not want. Each night we collapsed into our beds long after Vespers.

The villagers from La Brède took shelter in the castle there when the men from Périgueux arrived but one young man was sent to bring the news to us. He would join our ranks for the fight. I was not worried about La Brède and its castle. If the Seigneur tried to assault it, he would lose men and it would make it less likely that he could succeed against the sturdier walls of Bordeaux. The circumnavigation of the castle gave us a precious few hours to man the walls. The women, children and the old were brought to the outer ward of the castle. The move made the men on the walls more determined to fight. Their families were in the safest part of the town.

Leaving my men in the two towers at the main gate I toured the walls with Dick. My knights had done as I had commanded. Our archers and spearmen, though few in number were sprinkled around the walls to give strength to the less well-armed and experienced citizens. They wore a variety of helmets, mail and carried all kinds of weapons. The slingers were also spread around the walls to give us a steady shower of stones at an advancing enemy. The fires had been lit and the sand was being heated. It would be some hours before it was hot enough to be effective but the enemy warriors were not even in sight. I ended my tour on the southwest wall and I stood with my brother. His squire, Edward, had a long hauberk and a good helmet. His preferred weapon was a thrusting spear and while I spoke to Alfred, he and Dick ensured that the men on the walls were spread out evenly.

"The longer we keep them from gaining the top of the wall the greater the chance that we defeat them. Our archers are our greatest weapon."

Alfred nodded and pointed to the stack of pitchforks he had gathered, "We can use those to push the ladders away and we have plenty of rocks to dislodge them."

"My hope is that they have underestimated our defence and that might dishearten them but if they examine the men on the walls they will see that we have perilously few soldiers."

Just then one of the sharp-eyed boys shouted, "My lord, I see banners!"

There were houses that had grown beyond the walls of the city. They were empty now but they disguised the numbers that approached. We saw, however, their banners. Led by knights they emerged from the houses and halted. The road swept around the city walls to the main gate. There was a gate below us but it would not accommodate a horse. Hammered and nailed shut it was almost as secure as the stone walls in which it was set. The man I guessed was the Seigneur had his leaders around him and I saw them pointing and gesticulating. When he waved them to the west, I knew that he was heading for the other side of the city.

"I will join Thomas. Remember, brother, use your horn if you need me." We clasped arms and I added, "That means if one man reaches the fighting platform!"

He laughed, "I hear you brother and fear not, this knight will not let the family down."

I hurried along the fighting platform. It was only wide enough for three men and that was reassuring. Unlike the castle, there were no hoardings to protect the men on the walls but Gascons favoured the crossbow and not the bow. I did not think it would be a problem. I reached the main gate before the enemy. The Seigneur had taken his men beyond the suburbs. We could see their banners but that was all.

Thomas nodded at the banners' tops, "They come."

"Aye, and it looks like they have chosen the main gate for the attack. I wonder why?" One problem I had was that, like my grandfather, I always planned to defend against an attacker like myself. If they were not as skilled as I was that created a problem.

When the army arrived, they set about demolishing the houses that lay beyond the walls. I think it was for two reasons: to test our defences and reactions whilst giving themselves room to mount a solid attack. I would have left the buildings whole and used them for cover. It did not take them long to destroy the houses. They were made of wood, lath and simply constructed. By the time they were done, it was night and I took the decision to send two men in every three to eat and have some rest. Had we had more men I might have risked a sortie to upset their camp. As it was, we would have to endure a night of broken sleep. I did not think that they would risk a night attack but we had to plan in case they did. I was amongst the last to go for food and when I returned it was to the sound of hammering from the dark.

Thomas pointed to the campfires that they had lit, "They are using the wrecked houses to make ladders and I think that they have brought wheels for Ralph here thinks that they are building a ram."

The veteran squire nodded and pointed, "My eyes are old, my lord, but one of the slingers said he saw six wheels being carried. They will need to fill the ditch first."

At least we knew the point of the attack. My hidden men had relieved the ones on the walls but if the enemy counted the men they faced then my small command would not be in that number. When they attacked the appearance of my men, though few, would have an alarming effect on them.

I slept but an hour and I was up before dawn. The citizens on the walls showed the effects of a night with broken sleep. They would not be as well prepared as they might have been had the enemy attacked the previous day. The only good thing that I could see was that the enemy might be just as tired. They had marched to Bordeaux and had been building all night. When I viewed the ground before the city walls I saw that they had used the night to clear every obstacle from before the town walls and the ditch. Ralph had been correct and they had a ram showing that the Seigneur had been prepared. Covered with hides and filled with men it waited menacingly three hundred paces from the walls. Arrows would be wasted on it for they had thick hides covering the top. The rest of the enemy army was lined up with shields to the fore and I could see the ladders they had both built and brought behind them. How would they cross the ditch? I knew that the Seigneur was tempting us to waste arrows but I was not so foolish as to fall for that trick. The shields would easily protect the men and we would wait.

Suddenly the horn sounded and the attack began. Twenty men with huge shields, pavises, stepped forward and began to move towards the ditch. This seemed to me a strange attack. When they ran, a risky thing to do at the best of times, I wondered why. Egbert was the archer commanding the archers on this wall and he raised his bow to send an arrow at the target he saw. One of the pavise men had not kept his heavy shield high and the arrow slammed into his head and made him fall. I saw then their plan. There was a cart behind the men with the huge shields being propelled by men protected by the pavise. They were going to use it to fill the ditch. They would be able to use their ram!

Chapter 13

Henry Samuel

Blood on the walls

Egbert shouted, "Loose!" This was the time for arrows before the pavise could close up. Two more men fell, including one of those pushing the cart but it had momentum. "Pick your targets and do not waste arrows."

The closer they came to the ditch the nearer they were to our arrows and even the citizens who had bows would be able to strike flesh. They lost men when the pavise men who had led them had to move out of the way to allow the cart to be pushed into the ditch. Eight of their men fell and while a few crawled away wounded, the brave men had paid a heavy price. The Seigneur or whoever's idea it was, had been clever. The cart was filled with rocks and as the two pieces of wood at the front dropped so the cart turned upside down. The wheels smashed off leaving the relatively smooth bottom of the cart as an improvised bridge. It filled the ditch where our bridge would have been and whilst it was not as smooth as they might have liked, it would enable the ram to be pushed across and there was enough road close to the gate to give them purchase when they pushed.

"Thomas, make sure that the sand is hot."

"Aye, cuz." The advantage of heated sand was that men could use metal spades to drop it onto an enemy. Pouring oil or fat could often splash onto the fighting platform and a fire there was the last thing we needed.

The pavise men and the pushers walked backwards and made their own lines without further loss. They were cheered by the waiting men. A horn sounded and was answered by two others, one to the north and one to the south. They were attacking at three points. The presence of the ram meant I had to stay here. Geoffrey and Alfred would have to do the best they could. I would wait for our own horns to sound.

"Well done, Egbert. We have the sand for the ram. Keep the arrows and stones for those with the ladders. They can protect them until they reach the ditch but they cannot hold a shield while descending into the ditch."

That there were not enough traps in the ditch was clear. The stakes we had embedded could be avoided. Of course, if stones and arrows were hurled then a moment of carelessness might bring a reward. The ram led the attack. Ralph said, "I reckon, my lord, that they have more than a dozen men in the ram and there are another dozen with shields ready to push it across the ditch."

The men of Périgueux had brought their own crossbows. Egbert was wise to them for the crossbows were preceded by the pavise men. Before they could send their bolts at the walls the pavise had to be removed. My archers hated crossbows. Every crossbowman was struck by an arrow sent with deadly intent. Their missile attack was halted while our slingers happily sent stones to clatter into shields and helmets. When one warrior was struck in the head and fell it heartened our boys and they all cheered and renewed their efforts. We had plenty of stones and soon it sounded like a hailstorm. The ram kept coming and I saw it reach the cart. The cart was not completely flat but the rocks beneath it gave a more solid foundation than I might have wished. Although it lurched alarmingly the men behind added their strength to help propel it to the more solid ground beyond. It cost them three men to do so but the men of Périgueux cheered as they pushed it to begin to smash the gate.

At the same time, the enemy used their ladder men to cross the ditch. Protected by shields some men fell but enough made it so that ladders struck the walls. "Dick, go and ready our men."

I could see the knights gathered around the Seigneur. They were counting the men on the walls. The helmets marked those that were a danger and more than half of our men had no helmets.

Thomas turned to his squire, "Ralph, I think it is time for the sand."

I was pleased that my cousin had given the command. This was his post.

"Aye, my lord. Right my lovely lads, go carefully with the sand. We want no fires here."

The four men under Ralph's command each took a shovel of the sand that had been heating all night. I saw the metal of the spade as it began to glow and even though I was five paces from it I could feel the heat. They walked to the battlements and each poured it over. It would take time for it to ignite and more shovels would be needed. Ralph picked up one of the bundles of kindling we had prepared and dropped it over. I risked peering over the top and saw a shield protected warrior run forward to try to kick the kindling away. An arrow slammed into his arm and he retreated. I saw that the second bundle thrown by Ralph had landed and stuck on the roof. It began to smoke and when the next spadeful of sand was thrown it burst into flames. Encouraged by their success my men threw more kindling and more sand. The kindling crackled as it burst into flames. There was so much heated sand that the fire was impossible to contain. Soon the ram was afire and the men within had to flee or be burned to death. Less than half made their own lines as stones and arrows took their toll.

The ladders, however, had yielded results and Thomas shouted, "Ware left!"

I turned and saw that one ladder had managed to make the fighting platform. A slinger and two men of the city lay wounded. "Dick!"

Drawing my sword and a dagger I ran down the fighting platform. Even as I did so another two men were slain as more men poured over the top of the crenulations. I heard Dick shout, "We are coming, Sir Henry."

I ran with more confidence and managed to catch one of those who had made the wall as he was about to finish off a wounded man. My sword hacked down and sliced through his right arm. He tumbled to the road beneath and, as I hurried forward to the next man, slashed almost blindly at another warrior who was clawing his way over the stone battlements. I knew that I could leave the ones on the ladder to my men and I tried to get to the other three who had made the fighting platform. The three were mailed.

I shouted to attract their attention for another citizen was about to be butchered. "Rebellious snakes, turn and face a warrior."

Two turned but the third could not. A goose feather fletched arrow sprouted from his head as Paul ended his life. I blocked the sword of one with my dagger and the axe with my sword. I saw them both reach for a dagger and knew that they would defeat me. Paul's next arrow came so far through the body of the axeman that it almost struck my chest. I rammed my dagger into the side of the swordsman's head and he too died. I heard a crash and a cry as Jack and Dick pushed the ladder to the ground. As it fell, it crashed into another ladder and I heard the enemy horn as it signalled a retreat. The ram was a burning pyre and the falling ladder meant the other attack faltered. It was then I heard our horn sound three times. Alfred needed help.

"My men, with me. Thomas, see to your wounded."

The main wall would be weaker as men had died but as the central attack had ended I could deal with that later on. We ran along the wall and I saw that we had suffered casualties. Most were just wounds but they were costly. I spied the bridgehead the enemy had made on Alfred's wall. This time one of my archers and a spearman lay hurt and a third was spreadeagled on the ground below. Alfred, his squire, Edward, and the rest of his men were backing towards the corner tower. On the top of the tower, my archers were doing their best to thin out the enemy but the men who had made the wall were mailed and had shields. I could not do this alone. I shouted over my shoulder, "Dick, have the archers with us help those in the tower. Henry, I want you and four men with me. The rest get rid of the ladder."

There was a chorus that told me my orders would be obeyed. Henry and Matty joined me and three others formed up behind us. We all wore mail and we ploughed into the back of those who were hacking and chopping at Alfred and his men. This time more than ten men had made the wall and

I wondered why Alfred had delayed so long in asking for help. The inquest would have to wait. Our pounding feet on the fighting platform and a shout from the next man up the ladder made the ones at the rear of the enemy turn. The man at the top of the ladder paid for his cry when an arrow knocked him from the ladder. I hacked down at the knight in the centre of their line and he blocked my sword with his shield. His companions hampered his own sword strike and when it struck my helmet it did no harm for it was a weak blow. The men pressing from behind enabled us to push forward and slightly unbalanced the three knights we faced. It allowed me to drive my dagger up under the armpit of the knight I faced as he raised his sword to slash at my neck. I saw his eyes widen as the blade tore through flesh and sinew. His sword dropped as I severed something vital and I pushed harder, even as he shouted for mercy. When the bright blood spurted, showering both me and Matty, I knew he was dead. The blood enabled Matty to kill his opponent and an arrow from the tower killed Henry's. We stepped over the bodies and the remaining men at arms and squires were hewn down where they stood. As the enemy horn sounded the withdrawal, I knew that we had won. As our archers sent arrow after arrow into the backs of the fleeing men, I hoped that we had hurt them enough to end the attack and that they would return to Périgueux.

Alfred came to greet me, "I am sorry that we did not send for help sooner. Edward and I were ridding ourselves of one ladder and they were upon us before we knew. I am sorry, brother."

"We survived and," I waved my bloody dagger at the corpses, "and they did not." I turned to Henry son of Harry, "Have the wounded taken to the healers and after you have stripped the bodies throw them beyond the ditch."

He nodded and then said, "Naked?"

I said, grimly, "Such an act will not affect the knights but the Seigneur has farmers and labourers with them. Let them see the fate of those who fall."

"Aye, my lord, you are right."

"Alfred, I will return to the castle and report to Prince Edward. Keep a good watch but allow half the men to eat."

He nodded, "And do not forget to eat as well, brother."

As I passed along the streets to the castle, I found myself amongst some of those who had been wounded. Surprisingly they seemed in good heart, "We showed them, my lord!"

"They will not risk a ram again, eh, Sir Henry?"

"If they come again, we will send them hence in the same manner we just did."

It had just been the opening of what might be a long siege but it heartened me. The women in the outer ward had lit fires and were cooking food. They would try to make their lives as normal as possible. The gates to the inner ward were closed. The castellan and Godfrey had less than twenty to defend the castle and the safety of the prince was paramount. I was admitted and the sergeant at arms questioned me, "Went the day well, my lord?"

"Aye, Jean. They used a ram, which we burned and eliminated their crossbows. They made the walls but paid a price for doing so. They now lick their wounds and wonder what to do next."

"We are all happy to fight, my lord."

"I know, Jean and none doubt your courage but if we fail then you and your men will have to keep the gates safe until we are all within."

"Will it come to that, Sir Henry?"

"I hope not."

The two royal cousins and their bodyguards were eagerly awaiting news in the Great Hall. Godfrey showed that he was a veteran for even as Prince Edward began to question me, he placed food and wine before me. Between bites and swallows of wine, I told them how the battle had gone. I told them how we had burned the ram and used my mobile men to repel those who had made the walls.

"Then they will leave, Sir Henry?"

I wiped my mouth with my cloth and shook my head, "I do not think so. They will have to try again and this time it may be a night attack for that way they will hope to minimise the effect of the archers. If we can survive this night and they do not gain the walls then there will be hope."

"You do not sound as optimistic as I would have expected, Sir Henry."

I shrugged, "I will not sweeten the medicine with honey, my lord. That is not my way. I have given you the truth and if it does not sit well then so be it. With the paltry numbers of men I have at my disposal then this is the best that we can do."

Henry of Almain was his usual thoughtful self, "And when you came you left more knights and men at arms in your valley than you brought, is that not so?"

"I did but they defend our homes and that brings me comfort. Your father had other men he could have sent with us, my lord. The more I think about it the more I believe that we were bait. A tasty morsel to tempt Simon de Montfort and he has taken the bait. I do not think your father envisaged a siege but when you throw a stone into a pond you know not how many ripples will result." I stood, "And now I return to the walls."

Rather than being refreshed by the food and the wine, I felt weary as I headed back to the wall. There was simply too much to consider and I now began to understand the weight my grandfather had borne on his shoulders. Even more, was the burden that the Warlord had carried. Empress Matilda and her son Henry had been an even greater prize and he had kept them safe. I would have to do the same.

I climbed up to the fighting platform on the north side and spoke with Geoffrey. He and his men had been subjected to weaker attacks than the rest of us. That was largely down to the marshy ground that lay before the walls he defended. I told him what I anticipated happening. "It will be tiring but I want our men to watch this night. Half watch while the other sleeps and they change at Lauds. Let the citizens sleep."

"Aye, Sir Henry. I wish we had more men from the valley."

I nodded, "That is what Henry of Almain said. I would have more men but not from the valley. I sleep easier here knowing that my family is safe. Why I may even have another child born now."

He smiled, "I had forgotten that, my lord."

"I had not and each night I pray to God that Eirwen is healthy and safe."

I said the same to Thomas and finally, when I reached Alfred, I told him not only what I had told the others but my plans for the next night. As I turned to leave, he said, "You need sleep, brother. Remember your wound."

"I have not been bothered by that except that it itches. They say such itching is a good sign. I hope so."

Before I went to sleep, I had Henry son of Harry gather bundles of kindling. The ram still glowed in the dark. We hurled a couple of bundles onto the ram and they flared into light. It showed that the naked bodies of the dead had been removed. "Throw a bundle every hour. It may discourage them."

He nodded and said, "Or, more likely, send them to attack another section of the wall."

He was right but at least the main gate would be safe.

Dick had made a bed for me in the gate tower. The others who were enjoying their sleep first were close by me. Here there was no distinction between lord and archer. After ensuring that I would be woken well before Lauds I rolled into my cloak and slept. I was woken not by a hand on my shoulder but by the distant clash of metal on metal. I stood immediately and was gratified that the rest of the sleepers had been similarly roused. I donned my arming cap and slipped the coif over it. Drawing my sword I left the gatehouse.

Egbert pointed to the north wall, "There is fighting yonder, lord."

"Take command here until Sir Thomas rises. My men, with me."

There were far fewer men on the fighting platform. Most of the men of Bordeaux were in the outer ward, enjoying sleep and comfort there. It made it easier for us to get along the wooden walkway. The burning ram had worked and forced the Seigneur of Périgueux to change his plans. I heard

Sir Geoffrey exhorting his men. He had Edgar on one end of his wall and he was on the other. Jack son of Oswald was in the centre. Even as we approached, I saw one of my spearmen struck by a crossbow bolt and tumble over the wall. That meant there was a gap. As we passed Edgar, I saw him and two others pushing a ladder away from the wall. By the time Dick and I reached the place the spearman had fallen three men had made the platform. John of Parr seemed to be my shadow these days and he carried an axe he had taken from a dead warrior as well as his bow. The three of us hit those who had made the wall as Paul and two other men hurled rocks at the ones ascending the ladder. His strong archer arms added power to the throw and even as I blocked a sword blow and stabbed upwards with my dagger, I heard a scream as a man fell to his death. John of Parr's axe smashed through the helmet and into the skull of one man while Dick tripped his man to fall to his death on the cobbles of the street below. Paul and my archers now unslung their bows and began to pick off the men ascending the ladders. I had five archers with me and they soon cleared those attempting to attack. They sent arrows at the fleeing men until they disappeared into the dark.

"Pull up the ladders. We will burn them on the ram. This way they will have to make new ones."

Geoffrey came over to me, "We had no time to sound the horn. The first men must have crept close and had their crossbows ready. We lost three men."

"And that is three more than I wished." I turned to Paul. "You and the other archers stay here until dawn. You can sleep but be ready to repel any further attacks."

We took the three ladders we recovered and hurled them onto the ram. By the time they burned there would be nothing left of the ram, cart and ladders. We would not be able to use the fire the next night. I wondered what the dawn would bring.

I did not manage any more sleep and I watched with my cousin as the fire burned. I saw the enemy at their fires. It seemed to me that while most slept, they still kept watchers. Behind us, the sky became lighter as the sun appeared on a grey and cloudy day. The rain began to fall soon after dawn. Within a short time, the last flames from our fire died. My men donned their oiled cloaks and pulled their hoods over their heads. As the first of the men of Bordeaux arrived, I took a decision. "The night watch will return to the castle for hot food and some rest. Dick, tell the others what I have commanded." The mayor, who wore a mail hauberk and a good helmet joined me, "We have watched and fought this night." I gestured at the rain. "I cannot see them attacking yet. We will use this respite for the rest of our own. If you see them massing for an attack then sound the horn three times." He nodded, "Do not be foolhardy. You and the others have done a good job but it is my warriors who have borne the brunt of the battle."

"I know and we are no heroes. It was good to wield my sword yesterday but I know that I am no knight. This mail hauberk is for protection and is not a measure of my skill. If nothing else, my lord, this siege has shown me that no matter what taxes we pay to keep a garrison here it is money well spent. There will be no carping in the future."

By the time Dick and I reached the Great Hall the majority of my men were enjoying hot food. I frowned when I saw Prince Edward and Henry of Almain dressed for war.

"My lord?"

Godfrey stepped forward. "I tried to dissuade him, Sir Henry, but Prince Edward would show himself on the wall."

"I can speak for myself, Godfrey! I wish to show the men of Bordeaux that while I am young, I am not afraid of rebels. You must think that there will be no attack, Sir Henry, why else would you bring your men from the walls?"

He was right of course. I nodded to Godfrey, "At the first sign of an enemy attack then you will return."

"Of course."

I did not enjoy my food as much as I might have liked for I worried about the young prince. I was going to head back to the walls when my brother restrained me. "You need rest and Godfrey will not risk his charge. You cannot do everything. Trust others."

I did as he advised and I slept. It was not long before noon when I woke although, as Dick and I left the castle to head back to the walls, it was hard to tell what time of day it was. The rain had stopped but a wall of cloud hung over the land and I could see that it threatened more rain. As I left the gatehouse tower to step onto the fighting platform the mayor and the other men cheered me. I was more embarrassed by the gesture than anything.

Prince Edward looked animated, "I have spoken to the men of Bordeaux and find that they are men of good heart. I am now angrier that my Seneschal abused my people so." He pointed at the enemy who appeared to be making moves, "I think that I understand why these have revolted. I cannot condone the deaths they have caused but I see the reasons behind it."

The young man was learning.

I looked at the enemy and saw that five men had detached themselves from the warriors and were riding towards the ditch. They wore no helmets and carried not only the standard of the Seigneur of Périgueux but also a religious banner and I saw that one of the men was a bishop. Their hands were not mailed and they approached slowly.

Prince Edward said, "Do we have the archers prepare to loose, Sir Henry?"

I smiled, "They come to talk and not to fight. Come, Prince Edward, let us go to the wall." I turned, "Dick, have the archbishop join us. He may be needed."

"Aye, cuz."

If the Seigneur brought a bishop, we might need his superior.

"Come mayor, Sir Thomas, you may be needed too."

The five men stopped by the now burnt-out remains of the ram. I said, quietly, "They have initiated the talks and so we let them speak. Besides, it might be better if they know not to whom they speak."

"I am in your hands, Sir Henry."

The Seigneur spoke and his voice oozed confidence, "I am Geoffrey of Périgueux, who is it that commands the city and can speak of surrender?"

"I am Sir Henry Samuel of Elton and I command here. Do you wish to surrender?"

The knight wore a coif that covered his mouth and I could not tell if he was smiling but there was a laugh as he said, "I like your confidence, Sir Henry. No, we do not wish to surrender but you have fought well and we are willing to end the siege if the city of Bordeaux pays us reparations for the damage we suffered at the hands of the Seneschal of Aquitaine and Gascony."

I glanced at Prince Edward who nodded and, after clearing his throat spoke. He was learning how to be a leader and that day I heard him use his voice as a weapon, "I am The Lord Edward, Seigneur, and the future Duke of Aquitaine. Know that the Seneschal has fled this city and no longer speaks for me. You may address your concerns to me and I will try to answer those that I can and then I will deal with the question of rebellion."

The Seigneur was in a quandary and he turned to speak to his bishop. I heard huffing and puffing behind me and saw the archbishop struggling out of the door. The stairs and ladders had almost defeated him.

I smiled, "Get your breath archbishop. You may be needed soon."

The Seigneur said, "You may or may not be who you say you are but I have never met you and you could be an imposter. Sir Henry might be playing a trick on me to play for time."

Prince Edward stepped aside and waved forward the archbishop who had managed to get his breathing partly under control, "You know me, Bishop Martel." The bishop nodded. "I can confirm that this is The Lord Edward, the son of King Henry of England."

The Seigneur bowed, it always looked amusing when done from the back of a horse but no one laughed, "I am sorry, my lord, but I had to be sure. As for rebellion, I can say that there was no rebellion in our hearts but we had endured intolerable raids by the man you appointed as your seneschal."

"My father made a mistake and I will now rectify that mistake. Put down your weapons and dismount. We will lower the drawbridge and we can speak in the Great Hall and not shout to each other like costermongers in the Cheap."

I doubted that the Seigneur knew either what a costermonger was or the Cheap but he got the drift and said, "We come in peace and before I agree, I need to know that we can leave at any time we wish."

This time I answered for the prince, "Of course and I am a man of my word."

"Then under those conditions, we shall enter."

"Sir Thomas, you may have the gate opened."

And with that, the siege ended. It came as a shock to all of us and showed what the future King of England was capable of. His words saved lives and, more importantly, stopped one part of the rebellion. A remarkable achievement in one so young.

Chapter 14

Henry Samuel

The maturation of a prince

The archbishop was mindful of the parchment I still held that linked him to corruption. He did all that he could to make the negotiations go smoothly. For his part, the Seigneur and his men wished to return home for they had been handled roughly in their failed attacks. Godfrey knew one of the knights who accompanied the men of Périgueux and when we took a break for food and wine he learned that they had lost far more men in the attack than they had expected. They had heard that the earl had taken the majority of the garrison and they expected the city to yield as soon as they arrived. Surprisingly they did not know of the presence of The Lord Edward. As the day went on so the focus shifted from the archbishop and me to Prince Edward. He used his tongue well and was persuasive. He kept the veiled threat of retribution and the imminent arrival of his father to gradually weaken the resolve of the Seigneur. When Prince Edward said that he would forgive the rebellion if the army outside the walls dispersed and returned home, the Seigneur and his bishop were delighted to accept and there was no further talk of reparations. It was, I think, the promise that Simon de Montfort would be brought to book that made the difference. When a day later and the army had left us I walked with the prince around the town and the suburbs to assess the damage, it was not as great as it might have been.

"Your words were powerful, Prince Edward, but there is a world of difference between saying them and achieving their intent. How do you intend to curb the excesses of Simon de Montfort?"

We had reached the abandoned Périgueux camp. It was clear that there would need to be a great deal of work and the householders whose houses had been destroyed would need compensation. I had the scribe who was with us make a note on the wax tablet and as we turned to walk back Prince Edward, who had not simply blurted out an answer gave me a more thoughtful response.

"We can do nothing until my father comes and when he does, I will ask him to make you the commander of the army we use to retake the duchy."

"And if he brings no army?"

He stopped and stared at me. He had not even thought of that as a possibility. "But he must."

"Simon de Montfort has stirred up a wasps' nest. The task of bringing peace back to this land will not be easy. You did well, my lord, and negotiated peace skilfully. What about Auch? They may well welcome Castile. Simon de Montfort holds Barbezieux. While Périgueux might be back in the fold there are other Seigneurs who will seek to withhold taxes and to dispute English overlordship."

We had reached the ditch. The remains of the ram, cart and the stones had been removed and the drawbridge was in place once more. The damage to the gate was slight but men were working on it. Prince Edward smiled and spoke to the workmen and we re-entered the city, "You know, when I walked the walls, while you slept that day, I learned much about the Gascons. They do not wish to be French and yet they wish not to be English. They are independent and I must be mindful of that. I must cease to be the heir to the English throne while I am here. The Lord Edward is a better title for there is no hint of a royal title within it. I must be the Duke of Aquitaine when I attain my inheritance. If my father does not bring an army large enough to retake the duchy then I will seek Gascons who want rid of Simon de Montfort. I will use the general hatred of the man to enlist help."

I was silent for it was as sound a plan as my grandfather could have concocted.

"What say you, Sir Henry?"

"I think it has much to recommend it. Let us hope that the retreat of the men of Périgueux makes other potential rebels think again. We could not withstand another siege and we are now dependent upon the arrival of your father."

It was a week or so later and the city was back to normal and shipping was once more moving barrels of wine to England when King Henry and a fleet of ten ships arrived. As an army, it was not as large as we might have hoped but as the knights, archers and spearmen disembarked I saw that it was, at least, an army. Perhaps Prince Edward's plan to enlist loyal Gascons might be the answer.

As we escorted the king to the castle, I saw his eyes taking in the damage the city had suffered. We had repaired it but the fresh mortar and wood were as clear an indication of what we had suffered as the actual damage. I was not offended when the king took his son and nephew to speak with them alone. I was able to speak to Robert who had much to tell me.

"England is not yet ready to finance a large army to retake Gascony. There are many lords who feel that the taxes they pay are too high. The king has called in favours and dipped into his own treasure to finance this. He also fears war with Castile and so he has been forced to come."

"How many men did you bring?"

"Two hundred knights with their squires. Three hundred archers and two hundred spearmen and men at arms."

"It is not enough."

"No."

"De Montfort alone has more than that and I think that the earl will be eager to face King Henry in battle and prove that he is his superior."

He said quietly, "I have to tell you, Sir Henry, that our speedy return was due to the fact that the men we brought were already at Winchelsea and the king awaited word in the Tower. I think he will rely on the loyalty of Gascons and their hatred of Simon de Montfort to bring peace to the duchy."

I nodded, "Then he and his son are in accord and I now have a little more hope than I did."

Our conversation was ended when Sir Percival Mandeville, one of King Henry's household knights, fetched us. The king and Prince Edward were in the Great Hall and the king now sat on the dais once used by de Montfort. "My son, The Lord Edward, has told me of your valiant efforts, Sir Henry Samuel, and we are grateful. When we return to England, I shall find another manor to give you an income but first, we have this disturbed duchy to calm. My son has told me all and I believe there is a prisoner you hold?"

"Aye, my lord, Alain of Auxerre. He is a tough man but I believe that he might be ready to speak."

"Then let us repair to his cell. Sir Percival shall accompany us, for the rest take food for on the morrow we go to retake my son's inheritance."

When we entered the cell with lighted brands Alain of Auxerre retreated to the corner. It had been some time since he had seen bright lights. I spoke and I used gentle words, "Alain of Auxerre, you have had time to reflect upon your crimes. I have brought King Henry of England to speak to you as I promised. Your fate is now in the king's hands. I implore you to reconsider your decision to protect the man who has abandoned you. Simon de Montfort is ensconced in Barbezieux and he could have paid a ransom to have you released but he has not. What say you?"

The mercenary's eyes had adjusted to the light and his gaunt face looked up at me. He glanced to the king. We had fed him and given him drink but living in a cell with no hope of release saps life from a man. He smiled, "Sir Henry, you do not know Simon de Montfort. I knew that there would be no ransom for me. I was paid as a mercenary and as a mercenary, I could expect no loyalty from my employer. I was a sword for hire."

Prince Edward pounced on the words just as a cat would on a mouse, "Then you admit that Simon de Montfort paid you and others like you to cause mischief and mayhem in the duchy?"

"In here, aye, my lord. Outside? I would deny it. I am a warrior and if I become a turncoat then who will hire me? I am sorry, my lord."

"Then what if I hire you?"

Both his father and I turned to look at the prince. Only Henry of Almain looked unsurprised by the words. The two were close and this idea must have been discussed in the hours they had been closeted together.

"You, my lord? Hire me as what?"

In answer, he turned to me, "Sir Henry, what do you think of Alain of Auxerre as a warrior?"

"I think he is a doughty fighter and had we not taken him as we did then we might have had wounded men to contend with."

"Then, Alain of Auxerre, I would have you join my bodyguards and protect me." I saw the mercenary's mouth open and close like a fish. None of us had expected this when we had walked into the cell. I saw his father's face with a wry smile playing upon his lips. "Of course, I would expect an oath from you. So, what is it to be? The axe or employment?"

His incarceration had affected the man. I could see, from his eyes, that he yearned for daylight, a sword in his hand and some sort of normality. "Then I will so swear and serve you, Prince Edward."

"The Lord Edward."

"The Lord Edward."

"And you confirm that Simon de Montfort hired men to cause trouble?" The king was keen for evidence.

"I do, I was asked to find men who had no master. I sought those who would do all that was required of them without question. We used the inn to find the best that we could. The Earl of Leicester found landless knights like Sir Guy de La Réole to lead these bands of men." It was as though a thought suddenly struck him, "King Henry, it seems to me that if you could turn one of those knights then their word might carry more weight than a sword for hire. I will happily give testament against this man but he can deny it and who would believe me?" He shrugged, "I know this means, my lord, that I may no longer be useful to you but I must now speak the truth. I am a man of my word and I swore an oath."

Prince Edward nodded and smiled, "And you are right but I am also a man of my word and I will not retract my offer.

Come, this cell stinks and you need to bathe. My father and I have much to say and this is not the place for such words."

As I expected Godfrey was not happy about the arrangement. I knew that there would be words, and perhaps blows between the two men. Those words and blows would be in private and the two warriors would settle matters between them. I knew from my own men that was their way. For my part, I was happy as I had a few days without the pressure of command. The king and his son spent hours behind closed doors with Sir Percival and the other knights the king had brought with him. I was not offended that I was not included. Indeed I hoped that Prince Edward had forgotten that he wished me to command. Part of me hoped that the king would allow me to sail back to England. I knew that was unlikely as my men and knights were a vital part of the army. We knew the land and we had fought the rebels.

It was the king himself who addressed us in the Great Hall when their decisions were made. "We have decided that it is time to retake the duchy. On the morrow, we march north to Barbezieux where we will seek the Seneschal of Gascony and bring him to account for his actions and misdeeds. We will have Sir Henry Samuel and his valiant knights as the van for our progress. They will lead the men of England but I hope that the men of Gascony will join us for The Lord Edward wishes to unite his duchy."

That was the moment that I knew Prince Edward would be a great king. The words that had come from the king's mouth had been formed in The Lord Edward's mind.

Our task necessitated new orders and a different formation. With the extra men we had hired we were now a larger force than the one that arrived in Bordeaux. Robert Williams was no longer needed as a pursuivant and he was attached to my conroi. He was as self-deprecating as ever, "I know I am not the equal of any of your men but, mayhap, my languages and knowledge of the land may prove useful."

I laughed, "Robert, I am just grateful for your company but I thought you were promised a manor?"

He gave a cockeyed smile, "As were you and, like you, I have to wait until we return to England and that may be some time." He lowered his voice, "The king has plans to wed his son to the sister of the King of Castile."

"How do you know?"

"I travelled on the ship from England and the king and his brother spoke of such matters while we crossed. The alternative, it seems, is war and there is no money for it. That is the reason Richard of Cornwall did not land, he went to Castile to begin negotiations."

"But the sister of the King of Castile might not be the one Prince Edward wishes to marry."

He laughed, "Ah, Sir Henry, you married for love?" I nodded. "Princes do not have that luxury. If he does not find her attractive then there are pretty wenches who will give the prince the company he needs. However, it is early days and Richard of Cornwall is a good negotiator. The king believes that his brother will secure a good arrangement."

I suddenly realised that I had not seen the king's brother. The ship that landed the king had left the same day to head for the sea. King Henry might not be a great general but he had a mind that could conceive complicated plans and plots. He was his father's son.

We had much to do. Fortunately, our horses had enjoyed much rest. We had not needed them since our ride to Auch. My archers had managed to not only recover many spent arrows but had also been able to make new ones. When we left for the eighty-mile ride we had ahead of us there was some relief, at least for me. I was no longer The Lord Edward's protector. My retinue just had ourselves to watch out for; and, of course, the enemy. The problem we would face was discriminating between friend and foe. While the Earl of Leicester's men were, in theory, our friends, we knew that they would fight us if we neared them and we would have to be cautious when we neared the snake's nest. Then there were rebels. Until we reached a town or village, we had no idea if they had rebelled or not. The Seigneur of Barbezieux would be in no mood to talk to us for, as far as he knew, the Seneschal was acting under royal orders. It was complicated but we knew our task. The army was not a mounted one and we would be able to move faster than the main battle for I had managed to procure horses for the men we had hired. Some had been taken after the failed night attack on the castle but I used some of the king's coin to buy others.

We had to head east before we could ride north. The two rivers, the Garonne and the Dordogne had few bridges and we would use the one close to the Château de Vayres. The Seigneur there was neutral and by that I mean he waited until King Henry and The Lord Edward arrived before he showed his colours. For my part it was easy. Either they let us pass through the manor or they did not. While we were not welcomed, we were not hindered either and after sending a rider back to the main column to let the king know what had happened we pushed on to the village of Libourne where I secured the ferries to transport the army across the river. We had a rough camp but as we had brought plenty of supplies from the grateful burghers of Bordeaux and as it did not rain, we enjoyed a happy camp.

It was close to the large village of Sauvignac that we found trouble. I had forgotten about the men Prince Edward had released from Bordeaux. Luckily the men we had hired knew them and as we neared the village and passed what looked like an abandoned farm where some men were, apparently working, John of Parr nudged his horse next to mine, "Sir Henry, the man we passed at the ruined house. I knew him. He was one of those from the inn."

I did not stop but slowed my horse a little, "It may be innocent."

"It might have been if he had not hidden when he recognised me. He was armed."

I had learned that pride could sometimes get in the way of wise decisions. This was no time for bravado. "Arm yourselves!"

In the case of my knights and spearmen that meant pulling up our shields. In some cases men donned helmets. For my archers, it meant dismounting and stringing a bow. They used the horses for protection while they did so. It was an ambush but by halting and preparing our defences then the danger was slightly mitigated. I was in the act of raising my shield when I heard the distinctive crack of a crossbow. Only a fool did not take precautions. I raised my shield and the bolt slammed into it. As it had come from ahead then I knew the ambush was there but John of Parr had seen a man to the right and behind us.

"Sir Geoffrey, take four men and see if any hide close to the abandoned farm. Work your way around the village."

"Aye, Sir Henry."

No more bolts came our way and that led me to believe that they just had one crossbow.

Henry son of Harry shouted, "Ready, my lord," and that told me the archers were ready.

"Knights and spearmen, follow me." Spurring my mount I galloped towards the village. The crossbow had been reloaded but sending a bolt at a fast-moving target was not easy and I made it harder by jinking my horse from side to side while I scanned the houses, trees and hedges for danger. I caught the glint of metal by a mean, one-storied dwelling and I drew my sword to head for it. I had the best horse and even Alfred struggled to keep up with me. The metal I had spied was a pike and I saw the wicked blade appear when I was just ten paces from the dwelling. It was on my right and I would have no protection from my shield but as the man had not appeared he would have to gauge my position through sound until he actually looked. I rode as close to the house as I could and when he heard my hooves almost upon him, he stepped out and swung the long, spiked pike. I jerked my reins to the right and leaning from my saddle hacked through the wooden haft of the lethal weapon. The head fell and I was past the man. As I looked, I saw that there were five men there and I wheeled my horse to the right to put myself amongst them. The move took the pikeman by surprise and my slash caught the top of his shoulder. My move had not fooled my brother and cousin who had followed me closely so that the three of us filled the passage. Our horses terrified the men and when we slashed and stabbed, there was but one outcome, they died. I heard shouts from the centre of the village and also the distinctive sound of war bows releasing white-feathered death. Ahead I saw Sir Geoffrey as he led his men around the back of the village.

Wheeling my horse I said, "The trap is sprung. Let us take as many as we can."

When we reached the centre of the village it was all over. Sir Geoffrey's move down the flank had effectively trapped them and when eight were slain by arrows the rest surrendered. John of Parr recognised three men from the inn in Bordeaux. All the prisoners were bound and guarded. We released the villagers who had been held in a large barn. The headman was all for stringing the men up but I shook my head, "We will wait for King Henry and Prince Edward. There were will punishment but it will be a legal one."

We searched the dead and found that some wore the livery of Barbezieux but not enough to suggest that these were all local men. They had a variety of weapons and were all warriors. These were not the citizens who had defended the walls of Bordeaux. There were bodkin blades, axes, falchions, and clubs. These were killers. We had been lucky that they had just had one crossbow.

One of the farmer's wives brought us out some ale she had made as well as fresh bread and cheese. I sat on the low wall of one house and spoke with my knights.

Thomas was buoyant. Since his wound, he had become a different man and now oozed confidence, "If this is all the opposition we can expect, cousin, then the war will be over in a month and we can return home."

I shook my head. Thomas was far more confident and optimistic these days but he also needed to be realistic. "These may just be a band of men who seek to take advantage of the situation. There will be stiffer tests ahead."

Alfred said, "I think you are wrong about these men, brother. This ambush was aimed to take us. Who would attempt to attack knights and English archers?"

He was right. "Dick fetch me one who lives and wears the livery of Barbezieux."

The soldier Dick brought was an older man and John of Parr shook his head as he passed him. He had not been in Bordeaux. I decided to be direct with him, "You were one of the garrison at Barbezieux." He nodded, "Then why were you sent here to ambush us?"

He hung his head, "We were told that you had good horses and would not be expecting an attack." He gave a sardonic laugh, "The money we were paid was to encourage us to attack. We thought it better than gaol."

It made sense now, "You were sent by the Seneschal of Aquitaine."

"No, lord, his brother, Amaury."

Thomas said, "I would like to run the brothers through with my sword. They are both as treacherous as the other."

"Fear not, cousin. When the king reaches us, we will soon get to Barbezieux and there they will be brought to justice."

The man shook his head, "They are not at Barbezieux, my lord. The brothers left for Paris. They are visiting with the French King."

Was this more treachery? Why were the de Montforts in Paris?

"Then the men who remain in Barbezieux…?"

"They are the ones who followed him from Bordeaux and the others who joined him last week."

The Lord Edward had been lenient and now that mercy had come back to haunt us.

The news we had meant we had to speak to the king for this changed much. We waited until the middle of the afternoon when the king, his son and their bodyguards arrived. Our presence told them that we had potent news. We held the meeting beneath a large tree whose canopy offered shade. I told him all that I knew. "I can bring over the man so that you can question him."

The king smiled, "You have many good qualities, Sir Henry, and one of them is that you speak the truth. I believe you but the question remains, what do we do about this?"

Prince Edward had grown but he was still sometimes naïve about military matters, "We just ride to Barbezieux and demand their surrender. If they refuse then we besiege them."

The king shook his head, "It is not that simple, my son. It is one thing to risk a siege to curb the ambitions of a man like de Montfort but if the men who hold it are just hired swords, then we risk much with little to gain. The rest of the duchy watches Barbezieux and our actions will determine the success or failure of this campaign."

I agreed with the king who had a clever mind, "Your father is right, my lord. We have relatively few men and a siege can be costly both in time and men. We need some other way to get into the town. The castle may not be a fortress but the town wall might be a bit too much for us." Thomas coughed and I looked at him, "You remember my cousin, sire, Sir Thomas. Either he has the coughing sickness or he wishes to speak."

Prince Edward smiled and his father said, "Speak for any idea you have would be a welcome one."

"I remember a tale told to me by my mother about grandfather. I was young and the details are hazy but she said that he and his men pretended to be enemies; they dressed in different livery and others pursued them. The castle opened the gates to grandfather and they took it easily." He pointed to the disconsolate prisoners and the pile of bodies we had gathered ready for burning. "We would dress in their clothes and have you, King Henry, chase us. If we leave a suitable gap so that the men who guard Barbezieux feel safe, they might open the gates and allow us in. We could take the gate."

Prince Edward beamed, "A wonderful ruse and I like it. It is like the tale Master Bartholomew Pecche told me of the Greeks, the Trojans and the wooden horse."

"Let us take it one step at a time, my son, first we need to know who commands in the town. Fetch me the one to whom you spoke, Sir Henry." I sent Dick to bring the man. He abased himself before the king. He feared for his life.

"What is your name?"

"Jacques de Nimes, King Henry."

"Then you know who I am?"

"I recognised your livery and I fought against you when last you came to France."

The reminder of his failure made the king scowl, "Who is it that commands in the town of Barbezieux?"

"Sir Guy de Poitiers."

The king frowned and said, "But Poitiers is still loyal is it not?"

Robert was close by and he nodded, "Aye, lord. When I took ship to bring you the news there were some merchants from Poitiers aboard and they said that the town was loyal."

"Then here is a mystery." The king was trying to cut through the layers of treachery in his mind and could not get to the heart of it.

"Prince Edward, the new bodyguard, Alain of Auxerre, may have knowledge that can help us."

The prince waved over the bodyguard who, having been fed well, dressed, shaved and washed looked a different man. Even his manner as he confidently strode over made him look reborn.

"Alain, Sir Guy de Poitiers, what do you know of him?"

The mercenary nodded, eager to be of service now that he had changed tunics, "He and his father fell out. He is the second son and his father thought him dissolute and cut him off. He went to Italy to fight as a mercenary and there he met the Earl of Leicester. He commanded the bodyguard of the Seneschal. Why, my lord?"

"He commands Barbezieux."

"Then we will have a hard fight to take it for he learned the art of defending and taking castles when he fought for the Normans in Naples."

"Thank you, you may go." The king rubbed his neatly trimmed beard. "Then perhaps your idea, Sir Thomas, has merit. Sir Henry, what did you promise the men you captured?"

"Justice, King Henry."

"Good. Then have the clothes taken from them and choose your men."

I looked at the pile of bodies and the prisoners, "If we are to make them believe that they managed to ambush us and take their horses then we have to have a number smaller than the total. I will take twenty men with me. Twenty-one seems to be a lucky number. If we are to convince them of our identity then we need to ride quickly. If we leave before dawn, King Henry, and you have your horsemen just half a mile behind us then we might be able to pull this off. However, as a precaution, I will send my archers this night to cut off Barbezieux from the north."

"A good plan. See to it and now we will eat and rest. I like not this campaigning with its hard floors and early mornings. The sooner that the fire of rebellion is snuffed out the better and we can make plans to make Gascony safe once more."

While the squires collected the tunics from the dead and the prisoners, I gathered my men around me. "Henry son of Harry, you will command the archers and the spearmen I do not need. Leave immediately and get around the far side of the town. Stop any who try to leave in the morning."

"Aye, lord."

"I will need John of Parr."

My captain of archers frowned, "Why my lord?"

"Because he has shown himself to be handy with a sword and he looks like the men we replace." Nodding his understanding he left and I chose my men. The ones I did not take were disappointed as I knew they would be.

We had to appear to be the men we had taken and that meant removing spurs and chausse. Some of the ones we had taken wore mail hauberks and the surcoats and tunics we wore would mask the fact that almost all of us would wear mail. We left our good helmets and, like the men we had taken, wore either a coif or a simple conical helmet. As we ate, in the open, I told them of my plan. I had heard the same story as Thomas and I knew that the risk lay in discovery before we had entered the walls.

"We wear cowled cloaks to hide our heads and faces. When we ride, we keep turning to view our pursuers. We have to feign fear and ride as though it is the devil himself who pursues us. If it does not work then we will have to turn around and ride away as quickly as we can." I waited for that to sink in. "If we fail then it will be likely that we will die with a bolt in our backs."

After we had eaten, I went to the disconsolate leader of the ambushers, "Jacques, is there a password you use when you return to the castle?"

His face became a mask and I knew that he was now working out how to use this to his advantage, "Password, my lord, I do not understand?"

I put my face close to his. I was trying to intimidate him but also to see how I could look like him, "I think you do. Your life hangs in the balance, my friend, I know not if the king plans to hang you or treat you as a traitor and have you hung drawn and quartered but you need a friend and if you cooperate then who knows, you might just lose your right hand."

His eyes went to his hand and I saw, in his eyes, that he was calculating what to do. He nodded, "Golgotha, lord. We use the name of the place Christ was crucified by the Jews."

I nodded. That made sense for it sounded like de Montfort, "I will speak to the king but I promise you nothing."

Chapter 15

Henry Samuel

Quenching the flames

It was well before dawn that we walked our horses to close with Barbezieux. Other prisoners had given us information so that we knew the castle keep rose above the town and had a good view of the road. The farms and villages that lay before it were small and a party of horsemen would be seen from some distance. We found a wood where we could wait just a mile from the castle. The road twisted and turned which meant that the defenders of the town would glimpse us as we approached. Sir Percival Mandeville commanded the forty knights who would chase us and I waited until he reached us before we left. The sky to the east was becoming lighter and would help our disguise as sentries peered to identify us.

"Do not come closer than half a mile, Sir Percival, but if your knights could hurl curses and abuse at us then it will add to the illusion."

He laughed, "Aye, we will play the mummer for you." His face became serious, "I like the plan, Sir Henry, but you know that it might well fail?"

I nodded, "But if it succeeds then lives will be saved and the reputation of our king made."

"Aye, and we need that. God speed my lord and know that we will follow you inside if this succeeds and if not, we will fetch your bodies so that they are not despoiled."

I rode with John of Parr next to me, Thomas, Alfred and Geoffrey just behind me and I had the squires at the rear. If this gamble failed then they might survive. We walked our horses until we were half a mile from the woods. The sun had just risen and we might be seen from the walls but we were behaving exactly as Jacques and his men would. We would be conserving our horses. The noise from behind surprised me as Sir Percival and his men left the wood and shouted like huntsmen following a deer.

I dug my heels into my horse's flanks and he took off like a startled stag. As soon as we began to gallop then the hooves on the stones thundered. Even a sentry who was half asleep would hear us. As if to confirm that, I heard the bell tolling in the town ahead as we were spotted. We leaned over the necks of our horses as men trying to get more speed from a horse might do. It also disguised us. Glancing up I saw that men were now manning the walls and I knew that crossbowmen would be winding back the string and readying a bolt. We would have to ride up to the gates if we were to pull off the trick and at forty paces my mail would do me little good. At that range, a bolt could give me a speedy death even if they aimed at my head. It was a chilling thought and I found myself wishing, not for the first time, that I was back in Elton with my wife and family.

I heard the guards shouting something but I could not make it out. I glanced over my shoulder, as someone fleeing might do and saw the men led by Sir Percival. Turning back I stood in the stirrups so that the sentries could see my surcoat and I shouted, "Golgotha! Golgotha! It is I, Jacques of Nimes! Open the gate for the love of God."

Perhaps it was the use of the name that did it but by the time we were fifty paces from the gates they had not loosed their crossbows and the gates were looming open."

"Get inside before the English come!"

Thanks to our prisoners we had a good idea of what lay beyond the turreted gatehouse. There was an open square with a water trough and some of the poorer houses and then a short road led to the castle which just had an outer wall and a large square keep. As soon as I was inside the walls, I wheeled my horse to head for the far corner of the square. Alfred took the other corner while Geoffrey and Thomas took the last corner and as we turned, we drew our swords. Henry and John of Parr leapt from the backs of their horses and they ran back to the gate with others who had quickly dismounted. The squires who had been the last to enter effectively blocked the two men with the bar and while

Henry and my other men began to hack and slash at the confused soldiers standing there the squires slew the two men and then dismounted to lift the bar.

We four knights then wheeled our horses for we heard the cries of alarm. The crossbowmen who had been on the walls to loose at us as we advanced now turned to send their bolts at us. In the time it took to turn, lift their bows and aim, John of Parr and four other men had raced up the stairs to the fighting platform. They simply ran at the crossbowmen who were either slain or thrown to fall onto the cobbles. A man at arms led a dozen men from the direction of the castle to charge us. I turned my horse and galloped at them. Alone and with just a sword I confused them. My horse knocked aside two men as I hacked into the skull of the man at arms. A spear raked along my unprotected leg and I felt the pain as it tore through flesh. Then Alfred was beside me and we kept riding towards the barbican and the castle wall. Behind me, I heard a roar as Sir Percival and his knights galloped into the town.

"Cleveland! On me!"

As we ripped through the dozen men who had been led by the man at arms, the others who were leaving the castle turned as they realised the walls had been breached. They ran back to the castle. A horse, especially one that is on the move, will always travel faster than a man on foot. As Alfred and I, now joined by Geoffrey, Thomas and our squires, caught up with the fleeing men we used the flat of our swords to fell them for who knew when we would need an edge to fight men with swords. The warriors at the gate had a dilemma. Did they close the gates while their men were still outside or risk losing the castle? They only hesitated for a moment or two but it was enough. Although the gates managed to close as we reached them, they had not put the bar in place and Alfred and I made our horses rear. Their hooves did the job for us and the gates cracked asunder. We had done all that was necessary and so I shouted, "Wheel and form a defensive circle. We must keep the gates open."

The four of us faced outwards with our back to the gates. I knew that Henry would lead our men to come to our aid as soon as he could although as he had dismounted, he and the others would take time to reach us. From the keep I heard a French voice, "Crossbowmen, kill them."

Without shields we were vulnerable. "Dismount and use your horses for shelter. They will not attack on foot until they have used their bolts."

As I stepped from the saddle a bolt slammed into the cantle while a second passed through the air I had just occupied. Ralph's horse had a bolt scrape along its rump and the animal reared. Ralph was too experienced for it to make him panic and he began to calm the animal. Another bolt ricocheted off Alfred's saddle and I wondered just how many crossbows they had.

At that moment I heard hooves and a dozen of Sir Percival's knights joined us. Behind them, I saw my men labouring towards us encumbered by mail.

"Leave your horses and let us get to the keep."

Enough of the enemy warriors were still outside the keep for them to hold the door open. I guessed that at least half of the warriors had been outside the castle and they would need every man that they could get. As we ran up the staircase leading to the gate in the wall Dick shouted, "Sir Henry, you are wounded."

I had forgotten the spear thrust but I felt the blood sloshing in my buskin.

"We keep going. To falter is to lose."

This time there was no one there to close the gate and we simply followed in the last of their men. As he turned to close the door Alfred ran him through. We were within the walls. The danger now lay in the narrow passages and doors that led to the next floors above us.

Alfred said, "I will lead, brother, for you are wounded."

"And it is time that I did my share of the work. I will follow my cousin." Thomas had come of age.

Now that my attention had been drawn to it, I felt my wound and I acceded to their demands. While our squires dealt with the four men who were still in the same chamber as us, I followed Thomas up the wooden stairs. Alfred had wisely picked up a shield and when the spear was thrown through the open door of the first floor, he deflected it away. He took the last steps in three strides and I heard a cry as he slew the man who had hurled the spear.

There were ten men waiting for us and until our men joined us, we would be outnumbered. I saw that one was a knight by his spurs and I took a guess at his identity. "Sir Guy, surrender for you cannot hold out. Your walls are breached and the king comes."

Laughing he said, "So you know who I am; then you know that there is nothing for me other than this castle. I was left to hold it and hold it I shall. My father will realise when he hears of my death, that I am the true knight in the family and my brother is worthless."

His words built to a crescendo and so I was not surprised when he launched himself at me holding his sword in two hands. My right leg was weak and so I did the only thing I could. Planting my left leg I pirouetted around to swipe his sword to my right. His blow was so powerful that it unbalanced him and he had to readjust his feet. Every moment I gained made it more likely that we would be reinforced. I just had to hold on and I knew that was what I must do. A man who has decided that he can die fights with abandon. I had a family and I wanted to live. He held the advantage. I also held my sword with two hands. I saw his eyes go to my foot and the trail of blood I was leaving. He lifted his blade on high and swept it down to my unprotected knee. Had I enjoyed the full use of both legs I would simply have moved but the wound was now hurting. I just managed to block the blow with my own sword and the edge came perilously close to adding to my wound.

Just then there was a roar from the floor below as Henry son of Harry led my men into the keep. It was only a slight distraction but it was enough for Sir Guy's eyes to flicker to the door. It was not a move I had used before but as I had deflected the knight's sword there was nothing to stop me from back slashing at his knee. He wore chausse but it was a powerful blow and I hurt him. He reeled and it gave me breathing space.

Henry was the first man up and I saw him block the blow that would have felled Dick who was fighting a man at arms. My squire was in danger and that drove all thoughts of self-preservation from my head. Ignoring the pain and blood I lunged with my sword. There is a rhythm to sword fighting and hitherto we had been using the same blows. My lunge confused him and he did not manage to completely block the strike. The tip and the edge sliced through the surcoat and ripped some of the mail and gambeson. I was not sure if I had drawn blood but he stepped back and, in doing so slipped, ironically on a patch of my blood. I swung hard at him as his body fell across me. I hit his right arm and this time I did draw blood. I was not in any state to consider either mercy or giving my opponent a chance. I lunged at his open face and the sword drove through to the back of his skull. Even as he died, my right leg gave way and I dropped to one knee. In an instant Dick, Henry and John of Parr were at my side. The two spearmen who tried to take advantage of my condition and avenge their lord lasted but three or four strokes.

Alfred shouted, above the clash and din of battle, "Your lord is dead! Surrender or die!"

It was the right moment and swords were hurled to the ground. We had won.

Dick said, "Lean on me, cousin, and is it not time that you let another lead? You now have two wounds and I fear that Lady Eirwen will not forgive me easily!"

I laughed and, as John of Parr took my sword, leaned on Dick, "She will forgive you anything, Dick, for you beguile all the ladies of the family. I will be the one to bear the tongue lashing, but, you know, I would happily endure it for it would mean I was home and my war was over."

I was taken to the healers and the rest of the clearing of the town was left to others. I needed five stitches and such was the loss of blood that I passed out while he was repairing the wound. When I woke, I was in bed and Dick and Prince Edward were at my side. The prince looked serious, "When I am king, Sir Henry, I will need men of your quality to be at my side as I fight for my land. Do not be so reckless with your life. Others could have fought Sir Guy."

I nodded, "I am the leader of this conroi and it is my duty to be the one that takes the most risks. Is your father happy?"

"That we have taken the town with so little loss and so quickly?" I nodded. "Aye, and now he questions the survivors to try to gain an insight into what the others will do. It seems that there are now bands of men formerly hired by the Earl of Leicester and they roam this land taking towns and milking them dry of all treasure. Once we have recovered, he intends to use his army to sweep in a large circle and defeat them all, one by one."

I smiled and laid back in the soft bed. He was a clever king and whilst not the best of generals he had learned ways to help him win. His knights would outnumber any enemy he found and Sir Percival would be able to defeat them. This way he would end the rebellion without having to fight the seigneurs of Gascony.

"And you, cousin, are forbidden to rise for a week. We will remain here whilst the king completes his victory. We will have a month without risk of further hurt."

"And did we lose any men?"

"Yours was the worst injury."

"What of the men who tried to ambush us?"

Prince Edward said, "Like me my father is lenient. They have all lost their left hands."

It struck me that it was draconian but men like Jacques of Nimes knew the risks they took when they raised the standard of rebellion. They had been treated better than they might have expected.

The king stayed a week. I thought that was a mistake for in that week much harm could have been inflicted on his people. However, he was king and what he said was law. His son went with him and, as I was now allowed by the doctors to walk, I left the bedchamber I had used and walked the walls with Dick and my knights. The citizens were just happy to be free from war. The ones who had held the town were little more than brigands. We treated them well and the Seigneur, now released from his incarceration, regretted his rebellion. He entertained my knights and me four days after the departure of the king.

"Had I known that the Seneschal was acting for his own foul purposes then I might not have provided him with such an opportunity. He emptied my treasury of the taxes due to The Lord Edward and as my castle and town had not been prepared for war he took it all without much loss. Now we have to rebuild. Your Prince Edward seems to be a young man who has a clever mind. I hope so."

Alfred was enjoying the wine, "And once the last of the rebels is hunted then we go back to England, eh, brother?"

Robert who had been reunited with us following the victory shook his head, "Have you not heard? We sail for Castile. The Earl of Cornwall has finished his preliminary discussions with King Alfonso and Prince Edward, it seems, may have a Spanish bride. The Lord Edward wishes us to be with him."

My heart sank. I had thought that, while the king's plan might not be the quickest, it would be effective and we would be able to travel home. I resigned myself to at least four more weeks in Gascony for I could not see the campaign ending before then.

We used the time while we waited to practise, as we had in England. We had lost some men and gained new ones. Whilst we had fought together we had not enjoyed the formations and commands we had when in England. The men who had defended the castle had been mercenaries and brigands. The mail, helmets and weapons we took enabled us to fit out more of my men. We had left England with spearmen but they had all become men at arms. We used the area before the castle to simulate the sort of action we might encounter when next we fought. We practised being ambushed where the archers dismounted and the others held their horses. We formed shield walls and wedges, protected by archers. We used lances so that we could practise a charge. It occupied us and it made us a closer conroi.

I had been the one to suffer wounds and once the stitches were out the only result would be a slight stiffness in my leg. The skin would eventually change, I knew that, but the doctor also warned me that the wound might, back in England, react to the cold clime. Such problems were minor but as my grandfather had told me they had to be borne in mind when fighting. I knew that the young knight who had followed his grandfather to war was long gone. If I could have looked back in time I would have seen a youth who fought well but differently from me. I was just glad that the wound had not been a deep one and was a discomfort rather than disabling.

I also noticed the changes in Geoffrey and Thomas. Geoffrey had grown into a knight. He still behaved largely as a squire would do when first we came but commanding a number of my men in the two castles had forced changes in him. He was now more confident. It was Thomas who was the revelation. The diffident and nervous man had changed into a confident and skilled leader. Ralph had not wasted his time and he had spent every spare moment teaching my cousin all that he had learned in a lifetime of fighting. When I rode at the head of my knights, I was supremely confident that they would protect my back and that we would fight as one. Our squires too had changed. Dick was always keen, eager and diligent but having been forced to fight in situations that he should not have been had made him a skilled warrior who knew how to fight. My father and grandfather had both taught me that simply having skills with a sword were not good enough. To be a true knight a man had to know how to fight. I was not a tournament knight and I doubted that I would be any good at it. The ones who watched tournaments wanted grand gestures and clean strokes of a sword. I knew that Dick had learned to use every part of his sword and shield as a weapon.

The messages came to us as the king progressed in a wide circle that took him north and east, then east and now we heard that he was approaching Auch. When he reached Bordeaux, his campaign would be over. We estimated that was a week away.

The training of my men was soon to be tested for, one afternoon the sentry on the town gate summoned the Seigneur and we joined him. The sentry pointed to a youth who was at the woods we had used for cover. "Seigneur, the youth is hiding. See how he is not using the road but running from bush to bush, almost as though he is pursued."

The Seigneur had learned to be cautious. "Have the walls manned and send two men out to fetch him within these walls. Whatever this portends, I like it not."

Chapter 16

Henry Samuel
Hostages to fortune

We stayed with the Seigneur on the walls and as the youth neared the castle the Gascon said, "I know him! It is Louis of Saint Severin. He turned to me, "Come we shall descend and speak to him. He was the one who brought us news last year when his father's farm was attacked. That attack was beaten off that time but the return of the youth does not bode well. I fear that King Henry's route has taken him in too great a circle. Saint Severin lies close to here. The youth's movements make me fear that trouble has returned."

The youth was little more than fourteen summers old and his clothes looked as though he had been forced to hide in thickets that had torn them and given his hair the look of a scarecrow. He dropped to his knees, "Seigneur, the wolves have descended once more upon our home and village. Men came in the night fourteen nights since. They took my mother and sisters as hostages and disarmed the men. They hanged the smith and they have imprisoned my father in our cellar."

He gabbled it all out so quickly that he was out of breath by the time he had finished. The Seigneur put his arm around the youth, "Peace, Louis, come, you need food and ale. Speak to me as we go to my hall."

"But time passes and who knows what the devils will do." I could hear the terror in his voice.

"Be calm. I promise that we shall act and your family and village will be rescued but we need to know all." The Seigneur's voice had an effect and when the youth spoke once more it was steadier and clearer. The men, he estimated them to be more than thirty in number had arrived in the night. The men of the night watch had been slain. Even as he told us I realised that the attack had taken place not long after we had retaken Barbezieux and the king left for the northeast. This band must have decided to find somewhere to hole up. The youth and his brothers had been put to work with the rest of the village. The leader of the band was not a knight but, from Louis' words, a man at arms, Charles of Dijon. They were ruthless and seemed intent on stripping all that they could from the village before winter. The youth and his brothers had hatched the plan for him to escape for he was the smallest and the only one that could fit through the opening of the wind hole in the castle. He had managed to evade the sentries and make it beyond the village. The hunt had started the next day and had he not been such a clever youth might have been captured. He was not helped by the fact that they knew where he would go. The two-day journey had exhausted him but he was still willing to return directly.

"No, Louis, you will rest and then I can plan how to rescue your family." The Seigneur would brook no argument. Once he had eaten the youth was put forcefully to bed where nature took over.

I sat with my knights and the Seigneur as we discussed the problem. "How far away is this village?"

"Forty miles or so. It is almost as close to Périgueux as it is to here. In times past our ancestors often fought over the land but not for at least a generation."

"Then horses will be needed."

He shook his head, "And I have none save mine and my squire. My knights were taken as hostages by the Earl of Leicester and I think some were suborned. The others…" he shrugged, "When the Seneschal left he took most of the horses with him." He looked at me meaningfully, "Yours are the only horses and, if I am to be honest, Sir Henry, you and your men are the only hope for this family."

"What do you mean?"

"I listened beneath the words he said, I know Lord Guillaume. He is a hard man and the only way he would cooperate with brigands was if he felt his family's lives were at stake. There are two daughters…"

He left the words unsaid but I knew what he meant. Men with nothing to lose could and would behave badly and the normal rules and conventions of warfare would not apply.

With the present confusion, they could easily disappear and what better way than to make sure there were as few witnesses as possible?

"And there is something else, Sir Henry. I know my own limitations. When the Earl of Leicester attacked, he found it too easy to defeat us. I am a knight who is not afraid of danger but if I went to rescue them then I might blunder in and get not only myself killed but also the very people I am trying to save." He shrugged, "You and your men are the only hope for the village. Unless, of course, King Henry returns early."

I knew that would not happen and I thought of Elton. We were a small village and if the same happened then the people would be safe because my uncle would come to their aid. Here it was different and I saw, not for the first time, the legacy of the Warlord. We had his blood in our veins and I knew that we had to do this.

"Very well. We will need a horse for Louis and a mail shirt. What we have to do is dangerous enough without risking the youth who brought us the news."

"Do not worry, Sir Henry, he will be fitted out and armed." He smiled, "And you will ever be our friend. I swear that we will never turn against The Lord Edward so long as you serve him." Once more the king and the royal family would benefit from the shedding of our blood and I knew that it would come to that. These would be desperate men.

I gathered my knights and captains. It was a pity that we did not have Alain of Auxerre with us. He might have given us the names of some of those who were with Charles of Dijon. As I recalled Dijon and Auxerre were not too far apart.

The Seigneur asked if he could be present when we planned and I saw no reason to refuse. There were no secrets. I told them what had been asked of us. To their credit, none of them even hinted that they might not wish to be part of the rescue attempt. "So, the question is, how do we eliminate the brigands whilst saving the family? There is little point in charging in and risking their deaths. Their lives are paramount."

Jack rubbed his beard, "Use the night, my lord. I doubt that they will keep a large number of men on watch. These appear to be men who think only of themselves." He looked at the Seigneur, "Does the village have a wall, my lord?"

"No. There is a ditch and a bridge. Before you ask the castle is a simple one. The small keep has but two stories above ground level and the curtain wall was a herisson, a palisade, but it needs work and should not impede you. Lord Guillaume had plans to improve his defences but…"

"Then where will they keep the prisoners? Louis said his father was in a cell. It does not seem to me that the castle is big enough for a cell."

"There is a lower floor, Sir Henry, which is below ground level. They use it to store their barrels and it acts as a cold store. They can also bring their horses there. As for the family? I am guessing in the family quarters above their hall." His face darkened. "And I fear that the presence of three attractive women may prove too great a temptation for men such as these."

I had a plan beginning to form in my head, "Then there are two objectives. The men will be housed, I suppose, in the stable or the barn."

The Seigneur said, "Probably. We will ask Louis when he wakes."

"Then we use three groups. One takes the sentries on the wall. Henry, they will be archers."

"Aye, my lord. It will be knife work but we are ready for that."

"Alfred and Thomas, you will take half the men at arms and make your way into the keep. I think that there will be few men there."

Thomas was curious more than challenging when he asked, "What makes you say that, cuz?"

"Simple. The family chambers will not be large and this Charles of Dijon will like his comfort. He will have just enough men with him for protection and the majority will be elsewhere." Thomas, satisfied, nodded. "The archers can join me when the sentries are eliminated." I looked at their faces, "Any refinements to the plan?"

Alfred said, "Only that as you have suffered two wounds I will be the one to rescue the family. That seems like the more difficult option."

I grinned, "Climbing the steps might prove too hard. I will stay at ground level and I will lead the men to take the warrior hall. I will make sure that I have the majority of the men. Do not fear, little brother, I have led enough."

Louis woke in the late afternoon and he was fed once more and my knights and I joined the Seigneur to wait patiently for him to finish. He wolfed down the food. From the initial conversation, we gathered that the journey had taken two days.

"So, Louis, we will go back with you to help rescue your family."

He looked from me to the Seigneur, "Not the Seigneur?"

The Seigneur sighed, "Louis, Sir Henry here is a puissant knight who serves the future duke. He and his men will succeed where there is a chance that I might fail. That is what you wish, is it not? Success." The youth nodded. "Then trust in this man. He and his men won me back my castle. They are good warriors."

Louis nodded and turned his attention back to me, "Louis, we need to know as much as we can about the men who hold your family. We will be attacking at night and your words will be invaluable. It is your words that will save your family."

"At night they have eight men on guard. They did not remove the bridge over the ditch. They are lazy men and two of them watch the bridge. Two are at the top of the tower and two watch the barn where the men are kept at night. They patrol around it constantly. Simon the Baker tried to escape and he was caught. They hanged him and left his body for the crows. The other two wander the village. My father is kept in the cellar beneath the castle. I fear that my escape means that my two brothers will have joined him. The man who commands, Charles of Dijon, sleeps in my parents' chamber. He had five men with him. My mother and sisters sleep in the room my sisters used. Until I escaped, we were also kept with them. A man sleeps outside the door so that escape that way is impossible. Three of the men sleep in the chamber my brothers and I occupied and one is on the ground floor guarding the door to my father's cell."

I saw a chink of light, "Do any guard the door to the castle?"

He shook his head, "That is how I was able to make my escape. They keep it barred so that none may enter and no one watches within the keep."

I looked at Alfred, "I make that eight men in the castle. Two on watch. Can you manage that?"

"Aye, brother."

"And the other men, where are they?"

"We have a hall. It was once used for warriors but since I was a child, we have had few warriors and the hall is now used to house those who work for my father. They also have some men who sleep in the stable. We have a dozen horses."

"Dick, fetch a wax tablet." As my squire hurried off, I smiled at the young Gascon, "You are doing well and I believe that we have the chance to effect a rescue."

"I will come."

"Of course and we shall arm and protect you but Dick, my squire will command you and you will obey all of his orders. I want none of your family to be hurt. Understand?"

"Aye, but I want vengeance."

"And you may well have it but you need to trust us. We know our business and while these mercenaries may feel confident, we have met their type before." Dick returned. I took the scribe and drew a circle. I had two marks for the bridge over the ditch and then a square for the castle. "Does this look roughly where the castle and bridge are? The circle is the ditch."

He nodded, "The castle is a little more to the right, but that is about it."

"Mark for me the hall, stables, houses and any other buildings."

"There is a kitchen between the stables, hall and the castle."

"Then mark them."

I watched as he did so. I saw that the village was largely to the west of the castle and the other buildings to the east. There was a bakehouse close to the ditch and a couple of houses too. When he had finished, I nodded my approval, "And the women of the village, where are they?"

"Their men are in the barn and they are allowed to sleep in their own homes. When they came, the brigands killed four men as an example. The women and children are too afeard to do anything."

I sat back and looked at the wax tablet. The plan I had made could now be modified. I used the scribe to point as I did so. The others nodded their understanding. "Dick, fetch Henry and Jack."

When we were alone, he asked, "Sir Henry, when do we attack?"

"We leave early in the morning so that we can be there before dark. It always helps to have the lie of the land in daylight." I turned to the Seigneur, "I know that you have not the men to help us in this but four or five to watch the horses would be useful."

"Of course, it shall be so."

When my archer and man at arms arrived, we went through the plan again. The two had refinements I had not thought of and by the time we had finished I was more confident. "We rise at Terces. All of you get a good night of sleep. I shall spend an hour in the chapel to pray for success and I shall confess."

My brother gave me a shocked look, "You do not think you shall need absolution, do you?"

I smiled, "No but we all know that in a battle at night anything can happen. I will sleep happier knowing that I am shriven."

Robert said, "And in all of this you have not mentioned me."

"That is because I want you to help Dick to watch Louis. He is a brave youth but who knows he may be reckless. One of the spearmen, Tam, can help you. Your task is to keep him out of trouble."

In the end, we all spent some time on our knees and then made our confessions to the priest. It helped and I slept soundly knowing that I had a clear conscience.

I had Dick and Ralph flank Louis as we headed towards Saint Severin. We rode in silence, not through any fear that there were enemies but because each of us was reflecting on what we did. Those were not our people but what we did was right. My grandfather had gone to the Baltic to help the people there. My great grandfather had died at Arsuf trying to protect Christians. I had fought alongside my grandfather for people like my wife Eirwen. It was what we did. There would be no financial gain for us and the combat would not even merit a mention but it was important and we did it knowing that some of us might die. Once more I was happy that I had brought single men. I was the only one with a wife and there would be no grieving children if any died, except, of course for mine. They would be too young to know. I thought of my father who had been treacherously slain. I had been barely a toddler when he had died and it terrified me that I could hardly remember his face. My children were even younger than I had been, others would have to tell them about me.

As dawn broke so my archers loped ahead of us to scout out the road. From what Louis had told us Charles of Dijon kept his men close to Saint Severin. I knew, from what he had said, that the mercenary leader was aware of the approach of winter and was working the villagers as hard as he could. That meant he could not afford to have men watching beyond the village. The Seigneur had told us that this was the time of year, now that the rebellion in the area was over when villagers would work every moment of whatever daylight there was to gather as much as they could for the winter. While winter was not as harsh here as in the north of England there were still few crops that would grow in winter. No one ever had enough food. We passed men, women and children in the fields who barely acknowledged our passing for they were working to gather food that might help them to survive. Our livery was unknown to them but as we did not approach them then they felt safer but warriors, even those on their side, were rarely welcomed. We did not stop except to water our horses at the streams we crossed.

The road passed through a wood and we halted just a mile from the village and dismounted. There were woods within half a mile of the village and we would use those for cover but we walked our horses to them and did not use the road where the hooves of our horses might alert a sentry. We filtered through the woods and game skittered away. Sir Guillaume might have hunted but Charles of Dijon had no time for such an activity. From what I deduced he was a man who let others do his work for him. Henry, Egbert and Paul left us and their horses. They headed through the woods. They were all three masters of evasion and were able to hide almost in plain sight. They would circumnavigate the village. Louis had told us of the village he knew. I wanted new eyes to see obvious things he might have either forgotten about or not even seen. Such familiarity could make one blind.

We tethered the horses fifty paces from the edge of the woods. The men assigned to us by the Seigneur were keen to do all that they could. I think it embarrassed them that their own lord had not been able to do what Englishmen were happy to attempt. We then prepared for the night attack. We took off our spurs. We would be afoot and they might trip us. We all fastened a cloth about our coifs to keep them in place. The cloth would also act as protection and would not impair our view for it would be dark when we entered the village. I had Dick and Ralph help to fit out Louis. He was the son of a noble and would know how to use a sword, even the short one we gave him but he had never tried to move in a hauberk, no matter that it came just to his waist. I doubted that he had worn an arming cap and coif. The two squires, one young and one a veteran treated him as gently as they could. Ralph, especially, knew that this could end badly and while we would try to save all his family there might be losses. The task was not an easy one.

The three archers returned just before dark. Jack and his men were watching the walls and they saw the change of watch. We would speak with them later but we had to pick the brains of our three archers first.

Henry shook his head, "These are cruel and heartless men. We saw the carrion ravaged corpse of a villager but … It was all we could do not to intervene when a child of fewer than ten summers was beaten because he dropped a sack that was clearly too heavy for him."

My men had hearts but I needed cold men and I said, "Henry."

"Sorry, my lord. We managed to spy the ditch and there are no traps in it. My archers can use it and even with two men at the top of the tower the buildings help to provide cover. The herisson has been pulled down to use for firewood and to help the men in the tower have a better line of sight." He smiled and turned to Louis, "When this is over, have your father build a palisade."

"I will."

"I will choose the places the men will enter, my lord." It was not a request. Henry son of Harry knew his business and I trusted him. I nodded. "When the sentries are dead, I will come to the bridge and wave."

Thomas asked, "Will the men in the tower not see you?"

He smiled, "My lord, I did not say that I would wave towards the woods but that I would wave. I am guessing that the other sentries who walk around the village will both wave and talk to each other. Both sets of men can use the ditch to the east of the castle, my lord."

He sounded certain but I wondered why, "What makes that the safest?"

"It stands to reason my lord. There are men watching the men in the barn and the majority of their men are in the hall. As we passed, we heard their noise. They are carousing and enjoying themselves. The sentries in the tower are more likely to watch the houses with the women and the children within. After all, this young man managed to escape, did he not?"

I nodded but I worried about the cost to those within the village for his brave deed. "Thank you, Henry. Let us get into position. We are in your hands now."

Dick and I stayed close to the woods while Alfred led the rest to the east of the castle. I would give the command to move myself for timing was all. Henry left two archers with me when he and his archers disappeared to make their way towards the ditch. It was not for my protection. They would carry the bows for the archers. The knife work they would need to get into the village meant that they needed both hands free but archers preferred using their bows and the two sentries on the tower would have to be silenced before they could raise the alarm.

    I hid behind a tree and Dick another. We watched Henry, Egbert, and Paul, as my three most experienced archers moved closer and closer to the ditch. There was no cover but they had cloaks and they were able to judge when to move as the two sentries sometimes turned to speak to each other or did as Henry had predicted and wave to the two wandering sentries. I saw white faces on the tower but Henry was correct. They looked to the houses where the women and the children were kept. I saw the two wandering sentries wave at the men on the bridge and shout something before heading to the houses to inspect them. That was the moment when my three archers raced to the ditch. Another three would be to the east and they would take out the two watching the men while the third group of three would be to the west and secreting themselves in the ditch.

    It seemed an age before Henry, Egbert and Paul struck. I knew why it had taken time. They had to wait until the two men on the tower were looking elsewhere and the two men on the bridge looking away from the ditch. The three rose so quickly that it startled me. Egbert and Paul rose on one side and Henry on the other. The two sentries died without a murmur. We were close enough to be able to see and when the bodies were dropped into the ditch, Henry and Egbert donned the two cloaks of the dead sentries and stood where they had. Paul's task was now to get around the ditch to the archers at the west and see if they had succeeded. When they had then the archers would head for the bridge over the ditch. Paul would then have to retrace his steps and get to the east and the last two sentries. Henry would only wave once Paul returned.

Waiting was much harder than acting. I heard all sorts of sounds; the badger snuffling, the hunting owl as it swept down to take a mouse. Even, deep in the woods, the sound of deer moving and munching as they grazed in the dark. I did not see Paul return but I saw Henry wave to an imaginary sentry and I left the two archers to take the bows to their comrades. Dick and I ran to the place at the east where the rest waited. We had with us Louis, who would stay with me. I wanted him to reassure the men of the village that we were friends. Tam and Robert would watch over him.

When we reached it, I saw that Alfred had already divided the men into two groups. He merely nodded when I arrived and then led his smaller group over the ditch. I gave him a start for he had further to go and then I led my men towards the ditch. I felt naked and exposed until we dropped into the ditch and then clambered up on the other side. Already Alfred and Thomas along with their men had disappeared. I waved Geoffrey to lead half of the men to the rear door of the hall while I went to the front. Paul and Egbert appeared as we neared the barn. They would release the prisoners but only when the alarm was given. Robert tapped Louis on the shoulder and led him towards the archers. We could not rely on the men of Saint Severin remaining silent and until Alfred was at the gate to the castle that was what we needed.

Chapter 17

Alfred

The blood of the warlord.

I confess that I was nervous as I headed for the tower. In theory, we had the easier task but while I knew that my brother, Henry Samuel, would succeed I still felt inadequate next to him and I was determined to do as well as he would. We passed the bodies of the dead sentries. The archers had hidden them from the tower but passing close to the kitchen meant that we saw them. The archers had slit their throats cleanly. I shuddered as we passed for that could have been me if the men of Périgueux had sent such killers at night. As we neared the keep and the two watchers on top of the tower, I held up my hand, halted and looked up. I saw a white face peering west. There were still two sentries there. I waited until the face disappeared and then waved my hand to advance. Louis had said that the wooden steps leading up to the door creaked. If the sentries were not eliminated then that might cause a problem. I put my hand on the wooden rail and placed my foot as close to the stone wall as I could. When I put my weight on it the step did not creak. Then I heard the thrum of bowstrings. Had my ear not been attuned to expect it then I doubt I would have known it for what it was. I had just stepped on to the second step when I heard what might have been a thud and then a groan but it was over in an instant. The archers had waited until the two sentries were in the right place before silencing them. I hurried up the stairs. The creak as one of my men stepped onto the third step sounded loud but I knew that was an illusion.

Thomas and I drew our swords when we reached the gate to the small keep. This was the trickiest part. Louis had told us that the door had been put in by his great grandfather when the castle was built. It was very old and had shrunk. Standing on either side we found the gap and slid our swords in. There was no resistance to my blade. I glanced at Thomas and saw the smile that told me he had found no hindrance. As Louis had told us that the door opened outwards all we needed to do was to lift the bar. Ralph would then pull the door back and my squire, Edward, would stop the bar from falling. We both lifted and although the bar was heavy I felt it rise. We lifted until it was clear and then disaster struck. The bar fell from our swords and crashed to the floor of the keep.

There was no point bemoaning the situation and Ralph pulled open the door while Thomas and I ran in. We expected one man but as figures rose from the floor, I saw that they had made changes since Louis had escaped. At least eight men rose to shout and grab their weapons. I cursed our luck. My brother needed silence to get into the hall where the majority of the men slept. The noise and the alarm meant that was impossible. I heard noises above us and knew that Charles of Dijon would not be taken in his sleep. He would be awake and armed. My brother had the majority of the men for we had thought we just had six men to deal with. That number was now doubled, at least.

Grandfather had taught us all well and told us that you never gave up, even when the odds seemed impossible. I shouted, "Ralph, take Edward and get to Sir Guillaume."

"Aye Sir Alfred! Out of my way you poxy bastard!" The veteran warrior slashed his sword diagonally across a sleepy mercenary and then punched another from his path as he headed for the cellar.

A spear was rammed from the gloomy dark and came towards my middle. I wore mail mittens and I used my left hand to deflect the head. I heard the steel rasp on my mail and my hand felt numb with the blow. I blindly swung my sword but had forgotten that the roof was low and my sword bit into a beam. The spearman swung the haft of his spear and it hit me in the side. I lurched and almost knocked into Thomas who was also busy fighting for his life. My first command since the walls of Bordeaux was not going well. I first freed and then brought my sword down and held it horizontally before the spearmen could stab again. I pushed forward. The spearman had chosen the wrong weapon and as I stepped forward, he could only whack me again with the haft. The edge of the sword struck his forehead and he reeled as blood began to flow. I pulled back and lowered the tip and I drove it into his throat. The sword that came from my left was not well struck but the tip broke some links and I felt it prick my side. I swung my sword around as I tried to face the new threat. The brigand brought his sword up to block it. The weaponsmith in Stockton had made a better job of forging my sword than the man I fought. My eyes had become accustomed to the gloom and as our blades collided with a shower of sparks and a shivering ring, I saw his blade buckle a little. The fear in his eyes told me that he knew his chances of surviving this encounter were now slimmer. We were close to the table, presumably where they ate, and it was on my right. I saw the chance to swing where he could not but the man was wily. He grabbed a beaker of something and hurled it at my face.

It was only a heartbeat but when I was showered by the ale he shouted, "Up to the first floor!" and hurling the broken sword at me he ran. He paused only to grab another sword from one of the dead and then ran up the stairs.

I looked around, Alan of Redmarshal lay bleeding and three of the brigands had been eliminated. I saw Edward and Ralph as they helped not only Sir Guillaume but two other, younger men, from the cellar. All looked in a bad way. I was not certain if we would manage to affect a rescue and so I shouted, "Take the three to my brother."

"Aye, my lord, you take care now, Sir Thomas!" Ralph was still concerned about his charge.

"Come, Thomas, it is time to seize the moment. Today we show that we have the blood of the Warlord."

Grinning he said, "Aye, cousin." We had lost Alan but there were still enough of us to do the job.

The stairs were wide enough for the two of us and we hurried after the fleeing men. One of them who was before us had a wound and he reached the door just a moment or two before we did. He tried to shut it but two mailed men proved too much and he was pushed against the wall behind the door. His body slumped to the ground and we found ourselves in a chamber that, compared with the one below seemed to be filled with people. There were at least nine warriors. I realised that Louis' escape had made Charles of Dijon change his plans. The man I took to be the leader was at the far side of the room, behind the bed, and had before him, three women. One was clearly Louis' mother and I took the other two to be his sisters. He held his sword across their throats. The threat was clear but as his men, the eight before him, outnumbered us, he did not need to carry out his threat.

"Kill these five and then find out where the rest of my men are!"

I did not look around but his words had told me that only three of my men had managed to reach the first floor. We could expect no help until my brother came and who knew if the new plans had meant he could not achieve that?

"Well cuz, let us see how many of these we can send to Hades!"

Thomas seemed happy as he almost shouted, "Aye! Grandfather, watch two of your grandsons try to emulate your deeds!"

Offence seemed preferable to waiting for the eight to attack us. We had the advantage that we were mailed and they were not. The exception was Charles of Dijon who had donned a hauberk and coif. We advanced rapidly and I thrust my sword up and under the swinging blade of the first warrior. I used my mailed mitten to grab the blade. My sword drove up into his ribs and I pushed his body from it as a sword was thrust at my chest. The tip, thankfully, was not like mine and sharpened, it hurt as it punched into my mail but did not break the links. I punched the crosspiece of my sword into the man's face and he was stunned. This was no time for mercy and I punched him hard in the side of the head with my mailed mitten. He dropped as though poleaxed.

Our sudden attack had divided the enemy and Thomas and I had driven a wedge between them. We had to stand back-to-back as the four who remained came at us. I saw that the three men who had come with us had been felled. I knew not if they were dead and this did not seem the right time to see. I reached behind me and pulled out my dagger.

"Kill the two and have done with it!" Charles of Dijon had yet to join the fray and seemed happy to shelter behind his hostages.

The four men who remained were the best for they were all veterans. It was like looking at a villainous version of Ralph and I knew this would be harder for us. I wondered where Henry Samuel was. We had saved the knight and his sons but the most precious of prizes, the three women were still in grave danger. I blocked the first blow with my dagger and then had to swing my sword to face the second. Had either man a second weapon then I would have been dead but they had risen and just grabbed their swords. I smiled as I realised the implication of that. They would not have had time to don their boots and as they both pulled back their weapons for a second strike I stepped forward and stamped hard upon the toes of one of them. His blow did not fall as he shouted and stepped back. I blocked the blow from the other and then used my sword to slide into his ribs and out of the other side. As I pulled the sword from him the one with the broken toes lunged at me and I had to pirouette to avoid being skewered. As he came next to me, I rammed my dagger into his skull but, as I did so I saw that Thomas, while he had managed to wound one man had been stabbed by the second. The man raised his sword to end the life of my cousin and I lunged with my sword. It went under his arm, through his body to emerge on the other side.

As much as I wanted to help Thomas, I had the brigand leader left. I decided to use words first, "Charles of Dijon, you have lost. Surrender and face trial."

He laughed, "Face trial? It is the hangman who awaits me and besides, you are the last one who is left. I will cut the throats of these three and then slay you."

It was then that the three women chose to act. I know not how they timed it so well but all three of them suddenly pushed back at the same time. The brigand overbalanced and his arms rose as he tried to regain his balance. While his sword nicked the flesh of the elder daughter the three were able to throw themselves onto the bed and roll across.

"Get downstairs. There is help coming."

The one who was bleeding said, "Not while this brave knight lies bleeding. Kill this man, sir, and we are eternally in your debt. He is the spawn of the devil. Make him suffer."

Charles of Dijon had leapt onto the bed. He held his sword and his dagger, "You shall not save them!"

He jumped down at me. The blows I had received earlier must have weakened me more than I expected for his sword struck my coif as he lunged at me. It was not a damaging blow but it made me reel and I had to take exaggerated steps to prevent myself from falling. He brought his sword up to strike at me and suffered the same problem I had; it stuck in the beam. I swept my sword around in an arc but he blocked it with his dagger. This mercenary had been trained well and it would take all my guile and skill to defeat him. He too had realised that I was a better warrior than my youth might have suggested. As we warily watched each other I was aware of the mother and her daughters pulling Thomas to safety. I think I must have been briefly distracted for the sword darted out like the snake of a tongue and although I pulled back it struck my cheek and I felt salty blood running down my face. The look he gave me was one that assumed the blood was a precursor to victory. My brother had endured wounds and survived. I ignored it and assessed my strengths and weaknesses. He was a better warrior and had more skill but I was younger and, as we circled each other looking for an opening I realised that while he had been able to don his hauberk, his legs were bare. Unlike me, he wore no chausse. Grandfather had taught us a move that hitherto I had not been able to use but I used it now. As my left hand darted out with my dagger, forcing him to block the strike with his sword, I swung my sword at his knee. In a perfect world, I would have aimed at his fleshy thigh but I could not take the risk that I might catch the hem of his hauberk. My hand jarred as the sword struck the bone of his kneecap. It began to bleed but I knew from the look on his face that I had hurt the kneecap and I pulled back to lunge again with my sword.

This time I struck his mail but my tip was sharpened and the blade made a hole and tore some of the links. I penetrated his gambeson and when I pulled back the sword, I saw blood.

"Hold on, brother! I am coming!"

It was Henry Samuel's voice but it seemed distant as though he was still outside. Help might be coming but not soon enough.

When the mercenary heard the shout, he knew I was not alone and his eyes went to the door. He did not panic and I saw him grit his teeth to ignore the pain from his knee. He came at me and rained blow after blow with sword and dagger as he tried to beat me to a pulp. I forced myself to think calmly and blocked each potentially fatal strike. They were so fast that I barely had time to think. His dagger scored a hit on my mail and the narrow blade ripped through it. All the time he was forcing me backwards. It suddenly became obvious what he was doing when he turned and headed for the door. The two girls and their mother were kneeling over my cousin. The mercenary did not even glance at them as he ran to escape. The girl who had been cut and had blood on her face threw out a leg and I watched as Charles of Dijon tumbled over her foot and through the door. I heard the crack as his head struck the stone wall and I hurried after him. By the time I reached him he was lying in a heap at the bottom of the stairs and my brother was standing over him. Henry Samuel knelt and then said, "He is dead. Where is Thomas?"

I had forgotten my cousin. Sheathing my sword I turned and shouted, "He is hurt! Find a healer." My brother nodded and headed back down the stairs. I dropped to my knees and said to the young woman, "Your face is cut too."

The mother seemed to see it for the first time, "Mary, what has that savage done to you?"

The girl she had called Mary almost absent-mindedly put her hand to her cheek and then looked at the blood. "He has paid for it with his life and it is a small price to pay."

Her mother tore a piece of sheet from the bed to make a bandage, "I will not sleep on those sheets again for they have been soiled by the animals!" She began to dab at the wound and I could see that it was the slightest of cuts and I doubted that it would leave much of a scar.

Mary looked at Thomas, "How is your friend?"

"He is my cousin and I know not." Rolling back my mittens I removed Thomas' coif and saw that he had been struck on the head. Was this a similar wound to my brother's? Was his life in danger? As I put my hand to his side it came away sticky with blood. Dick's head appeared around the door and he saw the carnage. "Dick, help me to take Thomas' mail from him, he is hurt." Turning to the other girl who looked in shock I said, "What is your name?"

"Eleanor."

"A pretty name. Tear some sheets for me, will you?" Between us, Dick and I managed to remove the mail. I suddenly realised Ralph was not there. As we pulled the mail over Thomas' head I said, "Where is Ralph?"

"He took a spear to his leg. He will live but I fear he will be a cripple. Thomas will need a new squire."

"And Edward?"

"Your squire lives and he is with Ralph."

I saw that Thomas' right side was caked in blood and it was still pouring from the wound. I ripped the gambeson apart and tore the vestment he wore beneath. The wound was a deep one. I took the bandage from the girl called Eleanor and pressed it tightly to the wound. Even though he was unconscious, there was a reaction. "I fear he has broken something."

The bleeding on Mary's face had stopped and she said, "Eleanor, go downstairs and find the honey for us. The healer may be some time."

The girl shook her head, "The evil men may be there!"

Her mother said, "Come, Eleanor, they are all dead and I will go with you."

Mary smiled and took the bandages from her sister's hand, "You must forgive her sir, this has been a trial for her."

"It is Alfred and you seem to have coped well. It took someone with a quick mind to trip him."

"I determined that I would not let them defeat us. Even when my brother escaped and we were whipped I remained strong."

"Whipped?" I could not believe my ears.

She smiled, "You have saved us, Alfred, from an evil creature. If the ill-treatment had gone on any longer then I would have tried to kill him, even though it would have meant my own death."

She handed me a fresh bandage for the one I used was sodden with blood. As she did our fingers touched. Hers were soft and when I looked up our eyes met, "And that death would have been a tragedy for I can see you have a strong spirit that needs to live."

She squeezed my fingers, "That is kind of you, Alfred, but I have little future. I fear that life as a nun is all that I can expect."

The new bandage helped me to see that I was slowing down the bleeding, "A nun? That would be a waste."

"I am soiled goods, sir. I was abused."

"Did he..."

I could not bring myself to say the words. She shook her head, "It was not for want of trying. Both my sister and I had to endure his roaming paws, stinking breath and slobbering lips. I knew that it was only a matter of time before we were both violated."

Dick shook his head, "Then his death was too swift."

"Do not worry, Dick. He will be punished for he will spend eternity in Hell!"

Mary's mother and the healer appeared. "We will take over, my lord."

Mary stood, "My lord?"

"I am, Sir Alfred."

"I am sorry for my familiarity, my lord."

I smiled, "I am not a very important knight and you may be as familiar as you wish."

The healer said, "If you could give me some space, my lord. Your brother waits below." He shook his head, "So many men died."

"Come, Mary, let us go outside. Dick, stay with the healer in case he needs any assistance."

Grinning Dick said, "Of course, cuz, and take your time. Sir Henry and the girl's father can deal with the other problems. It is you and Sir Thomas who are the heroes."

As we descended, I saw that not all of the men who had been with me were dead. The ones who had not ascended to the top floor were wounded and were being helped down the stairs.

"We had better wait here until they descend."

"You are thoughtful and so young to be a knight."

"And you are too beautiful to be a nun." I blurted the words out without thinking and she laughed. "I am sorry, I just think that it would be a waste when you have so much to give. There are many men who would give their right arm to have you as their wife."

Her eyes were mischievous as she said, jokingly, "And are you such a man?"

Perhaps it was the blood or the battle but all control of my mind had seemingly gone, I just said what was in my head, "Of course."

The mischief left her eyes and she took my hand, "Do not toy with a maid, my lord, for I am still a maiden and I do not like to be mocked."

"And I do not mock you."

Just then Edward appeared. He looked mightily relieved to see me, "My lord, your brother sent me to seek you. He thought that you were hurt like your cousin."

"We will go to him." I turned to Mary, "Mary we shall speak again but this charnel house is not the place nor the time." I turned to Edward, "Stay with Dick. My cousin may need you."

By the time we left the keep dawn had broken. We saw families reunited. Louis had told us that although the women and children saw their men each day, it was at a distance. They were making up for it. Mary spied her father and her brothers. Her sister Eleanor was with them. Mary ran to them and I watched her feeling strangely lost that she had left my side. Less than two hours earlier I had not even known what she looked like.

"Brother!" I turned and saw a very relieved Henry Samuel heading for me. "I feared you too had been hurt. How is Thomas?"

"It looks a bad wound. I think he was stunned by a blow to the head and then stabbed. There was a great deal of blood." I held up my hands and gestured to my tunic that was now carmine rather than blue.

He handed me an ale skin. I slaked my thirst and my bareheaded brother shook his head, "We might be of the blood of the Warlord but I fear the military genius of he and our grandfather was not passed on to me. My plan failed."

Shaking my head I pointed to Sir Guillaume and his reunited family, "We saved them."

"Yet we lost seven men and I almost had my cousin killed. Charles of Dijon hired more men after Louis escaped. We should have scouted out better. Grandfather would have." He was right, our grandfather always liked to know what he was walking into."

"Where is Geoffrey?"

"He suffered a slight blow but insisted on carrying on. I have sent him, along with Robert, Henry, and Jack to fetch the horses."

"How is Sir Guillaume?"

"He and his sons were treated badly and beaten."

"The women were whipped and their bodies sullied."

My brother's features hardened, "And all of this goes back to Simon de Montfort who set this series of crimes in place. There will be a reckoning."

"You think that King Henry will punish him?"

"The man is too powerful and King Henry is… well, King Henry. The reckoning will come from men like us and the Gascons who have seen what he is like. Come let us clean you up for you look as though you have been working in an abattoir."

We went to the well. I tore off the surcoat for it was too far gone to be cleaned. I had spare ones at the Seigneur's castle. "Help me, brother, to pull off the mail. When Edward returns, he can clean it."

I felt much cooler without the mail. My brother nodded at the rents and tears in my gambeson, "You were lucky, Alfred."

"I know. He was a fierce warrior and I will be black and blue for the next week."

Henry Samuel handed me a cloth and I dried myself. As I did, I looked around the village. It had potential but compared with Stockton it was primitive. Of course, here there was no river for protection but the castle was built on a higher piece of ground. I could see the remains of the motte upon which the first wooden castle had been built and the remains of the palisade destroyed by the mercenaries.

Henry Samuel said, "Aye, brother, I see what you see. A village that was ripe for plunder. It lacked protection."

"That protection should have come from the lord of this land. The Seigneur seems a well-meaning man but that is not enough in one who commands and The Lord Edward will have to do a great deal of work if he is to remedy the hurt done by his Seneschal."

"That will not be our problem, brother. When we are able, we shall return to Bordeaux. Robert seems to think that we shall have to go with the royal party to Castile. I do not want to go but it will be the price we pay for our passage back to England."

"You will have either a son or daughter now."

"Aye, and they will never have seen their father."

I looked at Mary now reunited with her family, "You were luckier than I. You knew our father. I can barely remember his face."

My brother smiled, "When you look in a pond then you shall see our father for you look more like him than either me or our sister Eleanor."

"No one said."

"The similarity is so obvious that we all take it for granted that you know it too. We forgot how young you were when our father was killed. That is why you are mother's favourite. She sees you and it is as though it is our father, young once more." He nodded, "It looks like Sir Guillaume and his family come to speak with us."

The two girls were helping their father who, it was clear to me, would take many weeks to heal. As they neared us, I saw the effects of his ill-treatment. He had lost teeth and his eyes were blackened. It looked like his nose had been broken. The two boys who had been beaten had fresher injuries and fewer of them. Louis, in contrast, seemed a perfect picture of health. His ordeal in escaping had been as nothing compared with the hardship of his brothers.

"Sir Alfred, Mary has told me of your courage and of your loss. I pray that your cousin lives for truly the two of you are heroes."

I shook my head, "We were rat catchers for the likes of Charles of Dijon and his men should not be called men. We rid the world of a pestilence and for that I am glad."

"And you are modest too. Both my son Louis and Mary cannot speak highly enough of you."

Although he was talking to me, I could not keep my eyes from Mary. It was as though her green eyes had bewitched me. I had seen her in the gloom of the bloody bedchamber and thought her pretty. Now I saw her bathed in the morning sunlight with her auburn hair glowing and shining and realised that she was beautiful. Her eyes were looking directly at me and a half-smile played upon her lips.

I was suddenly aware that my brother was speaking to me. "What, brother?"

He was smiling, "Sir Guillaume said he hoped that we could stay awhile. I pointed out that we are due back in Bordeaux."

We would be leaving Saint Severin and I would never see Mary again. My heart sank to my boots.

Chapter 18

Alfred

The bonds of blood

Edward and Dick came towards us and the attention was taken from me. "How is our cousin?"

Dick shook his head, "I fear, Sir Henry, that he will have to stay in the bloody bedchamber for a while."

Sir Guillaume said, "That is a small price to pay. Do not worry, Sir Henry, we will make other arrangements. We owe you all and had you not come then we might well be accommodated in the graveyard." He pointed to the small church that lay in the heart of the village.

My brother was more concerned with Thomas. He had been given the responsibility of looking after him and his life was in danger. "What does the healer say?"

"The blade broke a rib as well as causing a great loss of blood. He does not want Thomas moved. He says that he will regain consciousness but, at the moment, sleep is the best medicine. They have moved him into the bed and Lady Eleanor is having the chamber cleared."

Louis said, "I have done little yet and I will help."

Mary grabbed her sister Eleanor's hand, "Come we shall help for Sir Thomas almost died to save us." She turned and looked directly at me, "And thank you again, Sir Alfred, not only for your deeds but for your words. You are a most kind and thoughtful knight."

As she ran off, I was aware that all eyes were upon me and I began to colour. My brother grinned, "I see a new side to you, little brother, a knight errant!"

Sir Guillaume was also smiling, "And I am grateful to you, Sir Alfred, for you have brought the smile back to my eldest daughter and the sparkle that was gone. I feared, from what my sons told me when we were incarcerated, that the monster that held us captive had destroyed her soul and her heart. I can see now that both are whole." He turned to his sons, "Let us go into the castle. We are too weak to help clear it but our presence will show our people that we are not dead."

By the time it was getting on to dark the bodies of the dead brigands had been burned while the men we had lost were buried in the graveyard of the church in the village. Everyone attended their interment and it was a sombre end to a momentous day. Sir Guillaume, his wife and his two daughters had cleared the second bedchamber for them to use. They would attend Thomas who had been given a sleeping draught by the priest. He had woken and been told of the victory before slipping into the healing sleep. I envied him that Mary's gentle touch would soothe his fevered brow. The three sons shared our quarters in the hall. They ate with us. The survivors of the skirmish toasted the dead and then we devoured the much-needed food.

Ralph ate with us and was in great pain but being the stoic character he was he did not make much of it, "I am sorry, Sir Henry, that I was not able to protect my lord as I promised his father."

My brother shook his head, "You have nothing to be ashamed of. It was my brother who ordered you to take Sir Guillaume to safety."

"Aye, Ralph, it is my fault. I did my best to protect my cousin but Charles of Dijon was a dangerous man." I wanted to change the subject for I was beginning to see my own mistakes and how they had led us here. I looked at the three boys. "And you three, what are your hopes?"

Pierre, the eldest said, "I am my father's squire and we hoped that I would be knighted in a year or two." He shook his head, "I fear that I am not yet ready. I thought I was but now…"

I saw the same lack of confidence that Thomas had exhibited before we came to Gascony. I was about to offer sympathetic words of advice when Caspar, his second son, said, "I never wanted to be a knight and all of this has just convinced me that I am right. I am a farmer at heart. I love the land and I would be the steward for my father. I thank all of you for what you did but it has shown me that I could not do what you have done."

My brother turned to Louis, who was seated next to Robert, "And you, Louis? Has your adventure changed you?"

He was a thoughtful youth, "Not changed but confirmed how I would like my life to be. I admire all of you, Sir Henry. My father is a good knight and a man to admire but you are men who are warriors and I would be a warrior. My brother is my father's squire. I will visit the Seigneur and ask if he knows of a knight who needs a squire but while you are all here and before you head to Bordeaux, I would ask you to teach me to use a sword. I can see that the practice at the pel is one thing but you are warriors who know how to use a sword."

I smiled, "And we will happily do that."

Events, however, beyond the world of Saint Severin, came to dictate our future. My brother had sent a rider to the Seigneur to tell him of our success and the next day, at noon, a rider came to say that King Henry had finished his scouring of Gascony and we were ordered to Bordeaux to take a ship to Castile. It presented a dilemma. We could not disobey our king but Thomas, not to mention Ralph and another four of our men were in no condition to travel. It was when we sat in the now cleaned hall of the castle that my brother was the embodiment of our grandfather. He was calm and organised as he laid out his plans.

"We cannot leave our wounded here alone. I know that they would be cared for but Thomas is of our blood. Alfred, I would leave you and Edward here. When Thomas is ready to travel then head for Bordeaux. I will explain to the king and if there is any censure then I will bear it." He looked at Sir Guillaume, "Does that sit well with you, Sir Guillaume?"

He beamed, "I would be more than happy for all of you to stay as long as you wish."

"Then we will leave immediately. Prince Edward should be happy that we have saved part of his duchy and two of the valley knights will have to suffice."

The depleted conroi mounted. My brother leaned down and said, "Alfred I am more than proud of you. What you did to save Sir Guillaume's family is the stuff of songs sung by troubadours. I am happy for you to make the decision about when you leave." I saw him give a mischievous look in the direction of Mary and Eleanor. "And if you dally longer for your own reasons then we would all understand."

I found myself blushing, "I know not what you mean!"

He laughed as he wheeled his horse away, "Do not worry, little brother, everyone else does!"

I hated being the one that everyone was talking about and after the men had left, I became acutely aware of looks, glances and nudges whenever I passed. I was thankful when Sir Guillaume came to seek my advice about his defences.

"I know that you are young, Sir Alfred, but speaking to others it seems that you and your brother have a good knowledge of castles and how to defend the villages that they protect."

Sir Guillaume had a stick to help him to walk but we needed to cover a greater area. "Edward, find Pierre and saddle two horses so that Sir Guillaume and I may ride abroad."

The knight smiled, "That is considerate." We chatted about horses and the best for war as well as the ones for riding. As the saddled horses were brought, he said, "It is some time since I rode. I should do it more. Pierre helped him into the saddle and he said, "Perhaps I am more like Caspar now and a farmer."

Pierre laughed, "When the first raiders came then you fought like a lion. Do not let the last attack make you lose heart, father. I think that the coming of Sir Henry and his men has breathed new life into everyone." He threw me a sly look, "Some more than others, eh, Sir Alfred?"

I swung my leg over my saddle and spurred my horse. I was eager to concentrate on something with which I was more comfortable and that was the art of war. We rode across the bridge and I halted by the woods to view the whole village and castle. "You have a good castle. The entrance makes an attack hard but there is no palisade."

"We thought to make the old herisson a stone wall but stone is expensive and we delayed…"

"Your life and those of your family are more valuable but it need not be stone. In England, we use the men of the villages to be responsible for a perch of the wall. Why not do that? There is timber aplenty in the wood. If each family made a section of the palisade then it would go up in no time and if they kept it repaired then it would be good protection."

"It would be irregular."

"And that does not matter. It is to make a barrier. It does not even need a fighting platform. You do, however, need a good gatehouse. That too can be wood but you and your sons should build that. Edward and I will help. That way it could be a proper drawbridge." I wheeled my horse and headed around the ditch. "Let us view the village as though we were an attacker."

It was as we rode that he saw the blind spots where buildings, like the church, obscured the view from the top of the keep. He realised he either needed a new tower on the top of the keep or smaller wooden ones spread around the walls.

As we headed back to the bridge he said, "This is a great deal of work. What about the land?"

"It is almost November, my lord, make this the winter work. If the post holes are dug now while the ground is soft then if there is snow or a frost, it will not matter."

"I am inspired by your confidence but how long do you stay?"

"Until the healer says that Thomas is well enough. I cannot see that being any time soon. Let us work while we can for whatever we put in place it will be better than it is now and while the memory of the devils is fresh in their minds let us get the villagers to work."

And so began the hardest work I have ever had to do. Edward and I worked with Sir Guillaume and his sons. After we had dug the holes for the gatehouse posts we hewed and trimmed the wood and then laboured to build the towers. We packed the bases with stones and rammed in soil. It was not quick work but my days were lightened for Mary spent a great deal of time fetching us food and wine. Her sister and her mother were Thomas' nurses and I was grateful for the presence of the angel that was Mary. If her hand brushed mine I felt elated. When I smelled the rosemary in her hair my heart lightened and the work did not seem so hard. By the first of November, we had the gatehouse roughly in place. There was a fighting platform and there were two wooden towers. They could only accommodate two men but the space between could hold another four. Access was up a couple of ladders. It was crude, rough and ready but when it was finished, we celebrated with the new vintage of wine.

As we toasted each other Sir Guillaume said, "We should have a feast. What say that we take the day off tomorrow and the six of us go hunting. It has been some time since I have hunted deer."

That evening Thomas was deemed well enough to join us as we ate a simple meal of beans and trapped rabbits. He seemed almost apologetic as we ate and talked, "I am sorry that I have been such a trial cousin."

I leaned closer to him, "It has been no trial and I have felt guilty ever since I looked around and saw you laid low. My brother and I promised to keep you safe and we did not."

"No, Alfred, you promised to make me a knight and a warrior and for that, I am grateful for I believe you have succeeded."

"And when you are well and we return home we can find you a squire."

Sir Guillaume said, "Will not the wounded warrior return to his duties when he is well?"

Ralph had gone to Bordeaux with my brother. He and the other wounded men would take a ship and return to Stockton. Thomas shook his head, "He had one last adventure in him and his wound means he can never be the warrior he once was."

I nodded, "A man knows when it is time to hang up his sword."

Sir Guillaume nodded, "You are right, Sir Alfred and my time in the dark made me look inside myself. I failed to defend my family. Perhaps, when Pierre is ready, I shall knight him and then become a farmer."

Pierre shook his head, "And I am not ready yet. I thought I was but then we were fetched from the cellar and I saw ordinary men fighting with Sir Alfred and Sir Thomas I knew that I had much to learn. Keep teaching me, father. Since Louis and I have practised with Sir Alfred I feel I am a better swordsman but I have far to go."

"And you, Louis, do you still wish to be a warrior?"

"Yes, father."

"Then I will ask the Seigneur to take you on."

Louis shook his head, "Father I was the one who took the news and the Seigneur almost threw the task to Sir Henry. I would learn nothing from him." He looked pleadingly at Thomas, "Sir Thomas, you need a squire and I know that I am young but I am willing to learn."

Thomas said, "For my part I am happy but you know that Stockton is an ocean away and in a country far to the north?"

"If it makes men like you then that seems to me a good place to temper the steel of my body."

Thomas looked over to Sir Guillaume, "I am happy to do so but you, Sir Guillaume, what say you?"

"While I am loath to lose my son, I know that this is the right thing and that your coming has not only saved my family but changed it. You have my blessing."

I caught Mary's eye and saw joy there. My mind was too full of the implications of taking Louis back to England with us for me to grasp its significance.

Thomas stood at the new gatehouse to wave us off the next morning as we left for the hunt. Young Eleanor and Mary were close by for support but my cousin was anxious for us to return to England as soon as we could. December would soon be upon us and unless we sailed then we might not get a ship until February. We wore no mail as we rode towards the woods. Our swords hung from our belts but the weapons of choice were hunting spears. These were lighter than spears used for war as they could be thrown as well as thrust. We each carried two. Louis and Caspar each led a sumpter to carry any carcasses back to the castle. I wondered why we did not take a local to guide us to the trails but, as Sir Guillaume chattered away to his three sons it became clear that the purpose of the hunt was not to seek animals but for them to talk of their ordeal where the women of the hall could not hear them. The coming of Charles of Dijon had changed the family and Sir Guillaume used the ride for them to talk openly without women to overhear their words. Edward and I gave them space and rode ahead of them.

This was not our land but we had hunted many times before. The last time had been in Pickering with the king. We knew the signs we sought. This was a good time to hunt for the rut had just taken place and with the does now carrying the next generation of deer then any male was fair game. It was Edward's sharp eyes that spotted the stag with the broken antler. It was not moving well and I guessed that it had been hurt in combat with a more dominant male. I stopped and held up my hand. Sir Guillaume stopped speaking as I pointed to the clearing some one hundred paces from us. Even as he walked his horse to us, I could smell the deer and that meant he could not smell us as the breeze was bringing his smell to us. Louis and Caspar tethered the sumpters and his father signalled for them to join Edward and me. He mimed for us to head to the left while he and his two elder sons headed to the right.

I led and walked my horse between the trees trying to avoid any broken branches. The recent fall of leaves helped to deaden our horses' hooves. The closer we came the more obvious was the hurt to the animal. It was not moving well and it was not just antlers that had been damaged. We were less than forty paces from it when it smelled or heard us. Its instincts made it leap away and try to escape. It was clear to me that it would not manage to do so. A brave beast, it jinked and twisted but with three of us on each side, all it did was to tire itself out. With its injuries, we soon caught it and Sir Guillaume and I sent our spears at the same time. It died almost instantly.

While Louis and Caspar went for the sumpters we began to gut the animal. We would leave the stomach and bowels for the carrion. The liver, heart, kidneys and testicles would be removed. They were delicacies and the six of us would enjoy those at the feast. When the sumpters came we loaded the carcass and the offal on the back of one. It was still before noon and we might find another beast. Edward went into the woods to make water.

Sir Guillaume nodded towards the animal, "That is a lesson for me, Sir Alfred. The old deer has had a good life. See the antlers that remain show it to be a mighty one yet it was hurt by a younger stag and could not evade us. That is me. When we have finished our defences Caspar and I will make the manor rich again and use the profits to add more stone buildings. Your description of Stockton Castle has made me envious. We may never make a fortress as strong as yours but never again will my family endure brigands and bandits."

Edward rushed back, "Lord, there are men in the forest."

I looked at Sir Guillaume who shook his head, "The charcoal burners live to the west of these woods and Henri and his family if they were close, would have identified themselves. They would not risk being hurt by hunters. You say men, Edward?"

"I found the remains of a fire, my lord, and it was still warm. There were hovels and I saw where they had emptied their bowels. It was fresh dung."

This was Sir Guillaume's manor but he seemed to be confused. His time in the dark had sucked the life from him and it would take some time for the fighting spirit to return. "If these men are on your land when they should not be then their purposes cannot be good. We know that men came to join Charles of Dijon after Louis left and that King Henry has scoured the land of enemies. These may be some who have escaped. We could send to the Seigneur and ask him to find them…"

"Or we could hunt them." Sir Guillaume nodded, "Tie the sumpters. Sir Alfred, you are the warrior, you and your squire lead. Caspar, bring up the rear."

I did not mount but walked in the direction indicated by Edward. It was a camp but what I worked out was the number of men. I knew hovels and I had used them. These were small ones and the eight of them gave me the numbers. I kicked the ashes of the fire and saw the bones of both rabbits and a small deer. The men had blatantly ignored the rules of hunting. They had taken a doe. I saw the hunter's trail they had used and I mounted. The trail led down to, I presumed, a watercourse. I had secured one spear to the saddle and held the other. I did not hurry for that way I might miss something or alert the men.

Suddenly I heard from the woods ahead, the sound of a chase. I held up my hand and then waved my spear for the others to spread out as the chase was heading for us. "We will speak to them first. Their purpose may be innocent."

Sir Guillaume was to my right and he said, "But you think not."

"I think not but I do not want the blood of innocent men on my hands."

The stag hurtled from the woods and, seeing us, darted to our right. The men who followed were in a long line and I counted nine of them. They were soldiers. Two had mail hauberks and the rest wore leather brigandines and jacks. They all carried swords as well as holding spears.

Sir Guillaume said, "You are trespassing on my land. Explain yourselves and I may show leniency." Hunting without permission could result in death but more often than not either meant branding or the loss of fingers.

One of the men with a hauberk laughed, "We do not seek leniency but those horses you ride would allow us to find a better land in which to hunt. Give us your horses and swords and we shall allow you to live."

I was watching the man and I saw him make a sign with his left hand. Even before he had made the movement and he had raised his spear I spurred my horse. Edward was also as fast as I was and, surprisingly so was Louis. The three of us closed the gap to the warriors. The leader hurled his spear at Sir Guillaume who had not moved. My reflexes made me swing the haft of my spear and I deflected its trajectory. It was not aimed at me but those behind. I did not throw my spear but as the mailed man reached for his sword I leaned forward and rammed the spear into his chest. His falling body took it from my hand. Out of the corner of my eye, I saw Louis had thrown his spear and was now drawing his sword but three men, recognising his youth, were gathered around him. Drawing my sword I wheeled my horse which leapt over the dead man's body. Louis was giving a good account of himself but the odds were against him. I swung my sword to hack across the back of one of the men. His leather jack was tough but my blade was sharp and came away bloody. I saw Louis take advantage of the distraction as one man turned his head. Louis' sword split his skull but the last man pulled him from the saddle. Louis lay stunned as I tried to turn my horse. The warrior had one foot in the stirrup when Sir Guillaume's spear transfixed him. Louis rose and stared at the dead man.

I turned my horse and saw that the survivors were fleeing. There were four of them. Pierre and Edward were galloping after them. I said, over my shoulder, "See to your son and I will watch these two." We had no need to pursue the four men. They would leave the woods in any case. With their leader dead they were no longer a threat but Pierre and Edward were both young. It was Pierre who fell foul of them. Two of them had turned and as he had thrown his spear, they had run at his horse making it rear. The young Gascon fell from his horse and lay stunned. I hurried towards him as one man grabbed the reins of the horse and the other raised his sword to end Pierre's life. Edward hurled his spear. It was a prodigious throw for he was twenty paces away yet it struck the swordsman and knocked him to the ground. The second man dug in his heels and Pierre's horse took off.

"See to Pierre and watch for the other warriors!"

The man I chased was not a horseman. When my brother and I had taught the spearmen to ride we had learned that what came naturally to we two, having been trained on horses since an early age, was hard for older men to learn. The horse was taking the man rather than the man directing the horse. He had no control. He was not using his knees and the horse was too strong for him. It made the chase harder for me as I could not predict its movements. I did, however, gradually gain on him and that was his downfall, quite literally. As he turned to see where I was, Pierre's horse jerked to the right and a low branch smashed into the man's skull. The blow was so hard that I feared it had taken his head. As his body fell his boot in the stirrup acted as an anchor and made the horse stop. I slung the body on the back of the horse and, dismounted, walked back to the scene of the skirmish.

By the time I reached Pierre and Edward the Gascon had recovered although I could see that he had hurt his arm in the fall. I dismounted and manhandled the body of the man speared by Edward onto the saddle of my horse, "Come we will walk back to the others. We will have to dispose of the bodies and the camp seems the best place."

Edward nodded, "He has broken his arm, Sir Alfred."

"Then we will take you to the healer as soon as we can."

When we reached the camp I saw Sir Guillame, Caspar and Louis piling the bodies on the ashes of the fire. When they saw the injured Pierre, they ran to him, "I am only a little hurt, father. I have broken my arm but I would have been dead but for Edward and Sir Alfred."

The Gascon knight said, "And now I owe you for two sons' lives. This is a debt I can never repay. The others?"

"I believe there are two but finding them would be a waste of time. They will leave your woods. I fear that they will do others harm but we cannot rid the world of all the rats can we?"

The feast we had planned would have to be delayed. It was almost dark when we reached Saint Severin. We had waited long enough for the bodies to be burning before we headed back and we had gone slowly to avoid hurting Pierre any more than we had to. While the healer saw to Pierre, we told Sir Thomas and the three ladies of the adventure.

Thomas said, "I suppose it is good that we were here else…"

Sir Guillaume nodded, "You need not be polite for my sake, Sir Thomas, you are right. Today has shown me my inadequacies. I shall be sad when you leave."

I nodded, "And we must leave soon my lord. The seas between Bordeaux and England claim many lives, especially in winter. Unless we are to spend the winter here we must return as soon as we can."

Mary suddenly burst into tears and ran up the stairs to the bedchamber. We all looked at each other in shock but Lady Eleanor smiled, "I foresaw this coming. Guillaume, let us go and speak with Mary." He nodded. She smiled at me and took my hand, "You are a good man, Sir Alfred, and if I have not already thanked you for saving me, I now do so again for my eldest son and youngest son owe their lives to you."

I was confused at her words. Eleanor, her youngest daughter was grinning. Thomas frowned and said, "Eleanor, you have been my nurse and I believe we are friends. I pray you to stop grinning at my cousin's discomfort and tell us why your sister fled."

She nodded, "We all thought you knew, my lord. My sister loves you and has from the moment she laid eyes on you. You are both kind and gentle. The thought of you leaving is too much for her to bear."

"But what can I do? Stay here?"

Louis smiled, "No, my lord, wed her and take her to England. Since you came here my parents knew this day would come. They were just hoping that the inevitable might happen soon but Sir Thomas' recovery and your words mean that they will be losing a son and daughter before Christmas."

Thomas said, "And you, cousin, do you wish to marry her? Your brother and I saw that you were attracted to her but are you ready, yet, for marriage?"

It was a good question. Was I?

Epilogue

Henry Samuel
Bordeaux December 1254

The Lord Edward and Leonor of Castile had been wed in Castile at the Abbey of Santa María la Real de Las Huelgas. That they were made for each other was obvious to me. She and the future King of England needed little persuasion to become man and wife. For the King of Castile and the King of England, it was a political act that brought King Henry a fortune but for the couple, it was a happy event. As soon as they were wed, we were given permission to return, first to Bordeaux and thence to England. King Henry kept his word and both Robert and I were given manors. The men we had taken and Sir Geoffrey were also given Castilian crowns from the wedding settlement. The Lord Edward even insisted that Sir Thomas and my brother enjoy a reward and we had a chest of coins for each of them.

As our Castilian cog headed up the river to Bordeaux I turned to Geoffrey and Dick, "I suppose we will have to send a messenger to Saint Severin for our two knights."

Dick laughed, "I fear it will be a hard wrench for my cousin to be parted from the lovely Mary."

Sir Geoffrey said, "She is the first woman to come into his life. He will soon forget her."

I was not so sure, "We shall see."

Robert came to the prow to join us, "The captain says we will dock before sunset. I will go directly to the castle to get us a chamber." He smiled, "A royal warrant is a useful tool. I shall miss it when I am just a lord of the manor and have to pay for my bed."

"The king has done well, Robert. He has managed to rid himself of the thorn that was de Montfort without having to fight him and he has turned a potential enemy into an ally and has been paid for it into the bargain."

Robert laughed, "I knew, when I first met you, Henry Samuel, that you were a warrior and not a politician. King Henry has a cold and calculating mind. I do not think that the Castilian marriage was planned, for when I told him the news in London I could see that he was shocked but he quickly saw a way to use it to his advantage. We left almost as soon as his brother arrived."

"Aye, so the army was ready?"

Robert nodded, "Knowing that the bait was taken he was keen to spring the trap. It was why I was able to make such a speedy return."

"The gamble almost failed. The Seigneur of Périgueux almost succeeded."

"You do yourself an injustice; the king chose wisely. He knows the mettle of the men of the Tees."

Docking at Bordeaux was never easy and I was impatient to get ashore and arrange a passage back to England. I sent Geoffrey and our men directly to the castle while Robert, Dick and I sought a couple of vessels. One already had a couple of passengers booked but there would be enough room for us and our horses and we walked to the castle. It was good to stretch our legs and walk on solid ground. I was no sailor.

As we neared the castle, I saw that the damage from the siege was almost healed. New wood and mortar would soon blend in with the old and within a year none would know that there had been a battle here. We passed beneath the gate of the inner gatehouse and I saw my cousin, he was walking well and he strode towards us with outstretched arms. Embracing me he said, "We are reunited once more, cousin, and all will be well."

"Where is my brother?" I wondered why he had not greeted me and a chill of fear ran down my back. Had something untoward occurred? "Is he well?"

Laughing, the new Thomas shook his head, "He has never been better. You shall see."

I heard more laughter as we neared the hall and as we stepped in saw my brother and on his arm was the maid from Saint Severin, Mary. I suppose that was not really a surprise but the young Gascon, Louis, laughing with them was. They turned as I approached and I saw a grin on my brother's face as wide as the Garonne River.

"Brother, meet my wife, Lady Mary, for we were wed by the archbishop himself."

The young lady gave a slight bow and then stood on tiptoe to kiss me on both cheeks, "I am glad you are here, Sir Henry, for now, your brother will be content."

I put my arms around her and picked her up, "It is Henry and I am right glad that my brother has now found happiness. We all knew that you two were meant for each other." I turned to look at Louis, "And you, young Louis, what brings you here?"

"I am now the squire of Sir Thomas and I will travel to England to train to be a knight."

My brother retrieved his wife and said, "We have much to tell you, brother, and, no doubt you have much to tell us."

I nodded, "And the first news is this, the king gave me a new manor. It is a small one, Yarm, and there is no castle but I would give it to you as a wedding present. We cannot have Lady Mary living in someone else's home."

"But it is yours!"

"I have Elton and I am content."

Dick looked puzzled, "Yarm? Did that not belong to one of the knights who followed the Warlord?"

"Aye, Sir Richard. He was a fine knight but the plague took him and his family as well as decimating the hamlet. The manor needs work and that, I suspect, is why the king gave it to me. It is south of the river and has more associations with York than Durham. You will have the opportunity to make it your own. Dominican monks have just built a friarage there and I think the king wanted them protected. You shall do the job far better than I will." I put my arms around my brother and my cousin, "And now that I have an appetite, let us eat." A thought suddenly came to me, "You are the passengers who booked the passage on the same boat as we."

"We did not know when you would return or if you would sail directly to England."

"Do not apologise, brother. This is meant to be and we shall have a whole voyage to talk and to plan. And you, cousin, shall be the next to find a bride. We have a duty to grandfather and the Warlord to ensure that his blood passes to another generation for where would the kings of England be without it, eh?"

The End

Historical Note

There was a castle both at Bordeaux and Château de La Brède but both were rebuilt in the 1300s. That suited me as I was able to imagine the medieval castle that would have stood by the river.

I have portrayed Simon de Montfort as a villain. He was appointed by King Henry but I believe he regretted his decision as his Lord Lieutenant ran the duchy as though he was a tyrant. He was summoned to Westminster to account for his actions and then allowed to return to Gascony. This is a work of fiction and I have represented the tyranny through the use of brigands and mercenaries. There is no evidence that The Lord Edward travelled to Bordeaux in secret but then again there is none that he did not.

The Castilian threat was countered by the proposal of marriage. It turned out to be a good decision and the couple were devoted to each other.

I wrote about King Edward as a prince and a king in the Lord Edward's Archer series of books published by Lume.

Lord Edward's Archer
Lord Edward's Archer
King in Waiting
An Archer's Crusade
Targets of Treachery
The Great Cause (coming in 2022)

Canonical hours

There were, of course, few clocks at this time but the services used by the church were a means of measuring the progress of the day. Indeed until the coming of the railways, there was no need for clocks. Folk rose and slept with the rising and setting of the sun.

- Matins (nighttime)
- Lauds (early morning)
- Prime (first hour of daylight)

- Terce (third hour)
- Sext (noon)
- Nones (ninth hour)
- Vespers (sunset evening)
- Compline (end of the day)

All the maps used were made by me. Apologies, as usual, for any mistakes. They are honest ones!

Books used in the research:

- A Great and Terrible King-Edward 1- Marc Morris
- The Crusades-David Nicholle
- Norman Stone Castles- Gravett
- English Castles 1200-1300 -Gravett
- The Normans- David Nicolle
- Norman Knight AD 950-1204- Christopher Gravett
- The Norman Conquest of the North- William A Kappelle
- The Knight in History- Francis Gies
- The Norman Achievement- Richard F Cassady
- Knights- Constance Brittain Bouchard
- Knight Templar 1120-1312 -Helen Nicholson
- Feudal England: Historical Studies on the Eleventh and Twelfth Centuries- J. H. Round
- English Medieval Knight 1200-1300
- The Scottish and Welsh Wars 1250-1400- Rothero
- Chronicles of the age of chivalry ed Hallam
- Lewes and Evesham- 1264-65- Richard Brooks
- Ordnance Survey Kelso and Coldstream Landranger map #74
- The Tower of London-Lapper and Parnell
- Knight Hospitaller 1100-1306 Nicolle and Hook
- Old Series Ordnance Survey Maps 93 Middlesbrough
- Pickering Castle- English Heritage

Griff Hosker February 2022

Other books by Griff Hosker

If you enjoyed reading this book, then why not read another one by the author?

Ancient History

The Sword of Cartimandua Series
(Germania and Britannia 50 A.D. – 128 A.D.)
Ulpius Felix- Roman Warrior (prequel)
The Sword of Cartimandua
The Horse Warriors
Invasion Caledonia
Roman Retreat
Revolt of the Red Witch
Druid's Gold
Trajan's Hunters
The Last Frontier
Hero of Rome
Roman Hawk
Roman Treachery
Roman Wall
Roman Courage

The Wolf Warrior series
(Britain in the late 6th Century)
Saxon Dawn
Saxon Revenge
Saxon England
Saxon Blood
Saxon Slayer
Saxon Slaughter
Saxon Bane
Saxon Fall: Rise of the Warlord
Saxon Throne
Saxon Sword

Medieval History

The Dragon Heart Series
Viking Slave
Viking Warrior
Viking Jarl
Viking Kingdom
Viking Wolf
Viking War
Viking Sword
Viking Wrath
Viking Raid
Viking Legend
Viking Vengeance
Viking Dragon
Viking Treasure
Viking Enemy
Viking Witch
Viking Blood
Viking Weregeld
Viking Storm
Viking Warband
Viking Shadow
Viking Legacy
Viking Clan
Viking Bravery

The Norman Genesis Series
Hrolf the Viking
Horseman
The Battle for a Home
Revenge of the Franks
The Land of the Northmen
Ragnvald Hrolfsson
Brothers in Blood
Lord of Rouen
Drekar in the Seine
Duke of Normandy
The Duke and the King

Danelaw
(England and Denmark in the 11th Century)
Dragon Sword
Oathsword

New World Series
Blood on the Blade
Across the Seas
The Savage Wilderness
The Bear and the Wolf
Erik The Navigator

The Vengeance Trail

The Reconquista Chronicles
Castilian Knight
El Campeador
The Lord of Valencia

The Aelfraed Series
(Britain and Byzantium 1050 A.D. - 1085 A.D.)
Housecarl
Outlaw
Varangian

The Anarchy Series England 1120-1180
English Knight
Knight of the Empress
Northern Knight
Baron of the North
Earl
King Henry's Champion
The King is Dead
Warlord of the North
Enemy at the Gate
The Fallen Crown
Warlord's War

Kingmaker
Henry II
Crusader
The Welsh Marches
Irish War
Poisonous Plots
The Princes' Revolt
Earl Marshal
The Perfect Knight

Border Knight
1182-1300
Sword for Hire
Return of the Knight
Baron's War
Magna Carta
Welsh Wars
Henry III
The Bloody Border
Baron's Crusade
Sentinel of the North
War in the West
Debt of Honour
The Blood of the Warlord

Sir John Hawkwood Series
France and Italy 1339- 1387
Crécy: The Age of the Archer
Man At Arms
The White Company

Lord Edward's Archer
Lord Edward's Archer
King in Waiting
An Archer's Crusade
Targets of Treachery
The Great Cause (coming in 2022)

Struggle for a Crown

1360- 1485
Blood on the Crown
To Murder A King
The Throne
King Henry IV
The Road to Agincourt
St Crispin's Day
The Battle For France
The Last Knight

Tales from the Sword I
(Short stories from the Medieval period)

Tudor Warrior series
England and Scotland in the late 145th and early 15th century
Tudor Warrior

Conquistador
England and America in the 16th Century
Conquistador

Modern History

The Napoleonic Horseman Series
Chasseur à Cheval
Napoleon's Guard
British Light Dragoon
Soldier Spy
1808: The Road to Coruña
Talavera
The Lines of Torres Vedras
Bloody Badajoz
The Road to France
Waterloo

The Lucky Jack American Civil War series
Rebel Raiders
Confederate Rangers

The Road to Gettysburg

The British Ace Series
1914
1915 Fokker Scourge
1916 Angels over the Somme
1917 Eagles Fall
1918 We will remember them
From Arctic Snow to Desert Sand
Wings over Persia

Combined Operations series
1940-1945
Commando
Raider
Behind Enemy Lines
Dieppe
Toehold in Europe
Sword Beach
Breakout
The Battle for Antwerp
King Tiger
Beyond the Rhine
Korea
Korean Winter

Tales from the Sword II
(Short stories from the Modern period)

Other Books
Great Granny's Ghost (Aimed at 9-14-year-old young people)

For more information on all of the books then please visit the author's website at www.griffhosker.com where there is a link to contact him or visit his Facebook page: GriffHosker at Sword Books

Printed in Great Britain
by Amazon